Right Skills

jay gee heath

ISBN: 0989071200
ISBN-13: 9780989071208

Library of Congress Control Number: 2013904498
CreateSpace Independent Publishing Platform
North Charleston, South Carolina

Also by jay gee heath
Right Talents

Dedication

Sam, who probably won't read this:
who has always believed I can do anything I want.
And in this case, insisted I wanted to write a book.
Even though I was sure I didn't.
It's been great!

Acknowledgements

Thank you to my first readers, my proofers. It was scary sharing. I was afraid you would laugh. Or worse, not read my manuscript. Or wait to read it. Or spend days or even weeks reading it. But you read it all, right away. And you liked what you read. Thanks for all your help and support.

Vivian Horak
Janet Benjamins
Jo Anne Sullivan

Thursday

He watched her walking toward the house they had once lived in together. He had asked her to meet him. Here, in the park, across from the house. Anxious, he had arrived early. He wouldn't have recognized her. This wasn't the woman he had left ten months ago.

He would have walked right by this woman on the street. Well, no. No red-blooded American male would have walked right by her. They would take one look and go brain-dead, mouth hanging open. This woman walking toward him was a stunning, sensual woman. Like a living wet dream. No, this wasn't his wife.

He was glad he had come early. He really needed these extra few minutes to adjust to this new, sensual Cilla walking toward him.

If he hadn't seen the photos published in the online gossip blog, he wouldn't connect this beauty to Cilla. Not that he had been looking at the blog; it was Ron who found it. Ron was updating their file on Conrad on a daily basis, and he had found the pictures.

"Hey, is that your wife there with Conrad? That's her name with the photo, but it sure doesn't look like your Cilla. Wow, will you look at this," Ron had said, reading the caption, "Priscilla Jayden, socializing with Peter Conrad.

"You should see this picture, Jake. That's the woman you left last year. Look at her now. She's in the most-read gossip blog in the country. She looks more like Sheri than Cilla. She's pictured here with Conrad a couple of times. And John's in this blog too."

Jake read the blurb, "Peter Conrad with computer programmers Priscilla Jayden and John Browne." He just shook his head. Looked at the picture again. "That's Cilla alright. Though she sure looks different. And that's John. They're with Conrad. Cilla is arm in arm with Conrad," he had said, outraged and surprised by the stab of jealousy. He had looked at all the pictures and read the story again. The blurb wasn't a news story, just a comment: "Is this business or pleasure? Or maybe a little of both."

He had frowned and then he stood up. "That's our in. She can get us close to Conrad."

"How are you going to work that?" Ron had said it disapprovingly. "You haven't even talked to her in ten months. What makes you think she'll talk to you? Let alone get you a meet with Conrad."

"Ask her," he said easily. "I'll ask her. All I need is an in. And I think I know one. She was with Conrad. She's probably sleeping with Conrad. So she will want to protect Conrad. I'll use that if I need to." He had called her and asked her to meet him. That simple.

He was watching her now. Trying to see the old Cilla, his Cilla. His warm, happy Cilla. She seemed to just be out for a stroll. Though how she could stroll in those five-inch platforms, he didn't know. Red platforms with a lot of straps. Purse to match, large and hanging from her shoulder. He wondered if her laptop was in there. She never went anywhere without it. Or maybe it would be updated to an iPad by now. And her whole manner screamed sex. It hit him in the gut. Surprise, surprise. This was a new Cilla.

"Priscilla," she had said when he called. "I'm called Priscilla now."

This gorgeous woman was coming toward him. Hair sassy and spiked in all directions, frosted in many blond tones. Unrestrained, uninhibited. Made you wonder if the abandon carried over into the bedroom. Oops, how did he get there? He had moved out of her bedroom a long time ago. Back to his appraisal. She wore a bright blue suit with a short, very short, skirt. Fit every curve, emphasizing the small waist. She was small all over, boyish. She had a great body and muscle tone. From her Tai Chi and swimming.

She was wearing sunglasses. That was new too. She had never worn those. He couldn't see her eyes, couldn't tell what she was thinking.

She stopped, near enough to speak but not to touch. And were those multiple piercings in each ear? His sweet wife? Three on the left, four on the right? She looked too hot to touch. That suit, hair. He realized his mouth was open and shut it. He couldn't read anything on her face. Partly because of the sunglasses. Rose gold sunglasses. But mostly, he realized, because she had a purposely blank expression. Another new feature. Where had she learned that? Her face had always telegraphed her every thought and emotion. He had loved reading her. She had loved that he was able to.

She thought he looked good. Same dark, curly hair. Hers didn't curl but his did. How was that fair? But then there hadn't been much fairness with him. She'd loved to run her fingers through his hair; she'd loved the feel, soft and silky. His dark eyes looked the same. She still felt they could look right through her. He was a little thinner. A little older. They both were a little older, she thought. Just don't substitute mature for old.

She could tell he was surprised at how she was dressed, how she looked. A part of her thought, *Take that, you bastard, take that. Eat your heart out. This is what you left.* Almost made her smile, because this temptress she presented wasn't real. But it really made her sad. She had never seen that particular look on his face before. Not for her. And they had been married almost a year. But, that was the past, ten months since he had walked out. With Sheri. Left her without a word. And here he was now.

And now, today, she was Priscilla, the woman she had created and perfected.

"I'm here," she said simply, and waited.

"I wondered if you would meet me," he said.

"Me too," she said. "I have always avoided this street and the house. Such bad memories. Never occurred to me until just now that there were some good memories here too." She shrugged. "So, why am I here?" Maybe he would tell her. Because she sure didn't know. She didn't know why she had come. She'd been deep in computer code getting a loop just right when he had called. By the time she realized the phone was ringing, it had almost gone to voice mail, and she just grabbed it. Reflex maybe. She was so surprised to hear his voice, she didn't hear his words.

"What? What did you say? Repeat it, please." Gave her some time. She wasn't prepared to talk to him. She was confused? Hopeful? So when he asked her to meet, she had said yes. Her brain was still trying to deal with his reappearance and what it meant. She had been shocked to hear his voice out of the blue after all this time. She came because she had agreed to, before she came to her senses. She was curious.

And to tell the truth, she really wanted to see him. Look at him again. But this meeting would be hard. She wasn't over him, she never would be. She wanted to run to him, touch him, hold him. *Stop*, she told herself. *Get ahold of yourself. That's not why you're here. If he'd wanted you to hold him, he would have waylaid you on the street. He knew you would run to him like a lost puppy.*

"You look good, Cilla," he said. That was an understatement. She looked incredible. And he would have to find out what she meant by "avoiding this street" later.

"I told you on the phone, Priscilla. Not Cilla. Priscilla. I don't look like Cilla. Do I?" She had a suggestive tone that was also somehow condescending. Even her voice was different then he remembered.

"Seeing anyone?" he asked. Would she tell him about Conrad? They had found three pictures of her and Conrad. He was still surprised at how jealous the thought of her with another man had made him feel.

She just looked at him. And continued to look at him, but finally answered, "I didn't meet you to talk about my private life."

There was to be no small talk, he thought. But he tried anyway.

"You never filed for divorce." He made that a statement. He just couldn't seem to leave the past alone and get to the purpose of this meeting. But this was sort of his purpose too. It would help to know. He needed to know about her relationship with Conrad. Was she planning a divorce?

"Because you were the one who left. Not me. I assumed you would get around to it. I didn't need a divorce to get on with my life." More silence.

He didn't have a response for that. She was right. He was the one who had walked out of the marriage. But he hadn't been able to make himself end it legally.

"I need your help," he said simply.

"I'll sign papers. Just send them to me. We didn't have to meet for that."

He was puzzled and surprised at the momentary regret on her face. Then it dawned on him. "You think that's why I'm here? To get you to agree to a divorce?"

"Why else would you come back? Are you going to marry Sheri?"

Sheri? She thought he wanted to marry Sheri? Hadn't she seen the news? No. She never watched the news and he wasn't mentioned in any of the stories anyway. And Sheri had been using an alias.

"No. I don't want a divorce. But I do need your help."

She looked like she wanted to ask him why he didn't want a divorce but said, "I'm listening." She waited. She was good at waiting.

"I need to know your relationship with Conrad."

He saw puzzlement on her face. And confusion.

"Conrad? Peter Conrad?" She repeated the name. Not just stalling for time. She was confused.

"Yes," he said irritably. "Peter Conrad. How many Conrads do you know?"

"Only one, I guess. What part of, 'I didn't meet you to talk about my private life' don't you understand?"

He had known that this wouldn't be easy. But the fact that she had come gave him hope. He knew she could be stubborn. But she had always been honest. He remembered that. She wouldn't lie about her relationship; she just wouldn't say anything. He had hoped she would tell him, though the pictures left little doubt as to the relationship. He tried another tactic. "I need to know if you are involved. Going out with. Seeing Conrad. Romantically involved. Just say yes or no. Please?" he added politely.

"Yes or no? Let me repeat I am not going to discuss my personal life, my relationship with Peter." No, she was not romantically involved with Peter. But she wouldn't give him the satisfaction of an answer. How would he know about Peter and why would he care? Did he care? Then she had a new fear. Jake couldn't know, could he? No one but Peter and the gang knew. "He is a…let's call him an acquaintance. Beyond that it's none of your business."

He tried a new tactic. "What about the photos? You look involved with him."

"It is not any of your business what Peter and I are, have been, or will be. I am not going to discuss Peter with you. Are we done here?" What photos was he talking about?

"No. I want you to introduce me to Conrad."

She heard the words. But they made no sense. So she repeated them slowly, speaking the words one at a time. "You want …me…to introduce you…to Peter?"

"Yes," he replied.

"Well, that is certainly not anything I expected you to say. There are so many different levels here that won't work. What pictures? How could you even know about us?" How could he? Why would he even care if she were involved with Peter? He had left her.

Did he know it was the gang that was involved with Peter? The gang, as they called themselves, or the gang of five. Her friends from school. All computer geeks, her and John and their three best friends. Could he know what they were planning? He couldn't know, could he?

"I want an introduction to Conrad," he said.

"Yes. I heard you the first time. Why? And why would you ask me, your wife, whom you believe to be having an affair with Peter? Why would I bother to introduce you? How would that work? I just bring you to him and say, 'Sweetheart, meet my lover'? Or would that be, 'Sweetheart, meet my husband'?" She wondered which would be the lover and which the sweetheart. "And how is it important to me what you need?" She was curious both as to why he needed the introduction and why he thought she would help him. And she had to find out how much he knew about the gang's plan.

"That is, I need to know information."

"Oh, but yes, I would need to know." No surprise that he didn't want to tell her. There was so much he never told her. About Sheri. "I would need to know, because I would need a very good reason to take you with me to meet Peter." Take him anywhere, actually. Though she still wanted him. Wanted to take him home to bed. She wasn't surprised at the power of her need. God, she missed him still. Seeing him brought back all the feelings she thought she had buried. She shouldn't have come. It was a mistake.

"You can know after you agree to help me. That would be the only way for you to find out. And if you want to help Conrad, you do need to know."

What she needed was to sit down. But that would show weakness.

"Let's walk," she said to give herself a little time. She had come here today because he had asked. At first, when she heard him on the phone, she had hoped he wanted to come back. That he still loved her. *He wants me back*, was her first thought. But immediately she realized that if he had wanted to get back together, he would have contacted her in person. Not by phone. He knew she could just hang up the phone.

She wanted to touch him. So she did touch him. She took his arm and started into the park. Walking beside him. Feeling him. It felt good, but at the same time it hurt. Because he was the one who had left. Without a word. Without an explanation. Now he was proposing (and wasn't that a stupid play on words?) some clandestine arrangement with a man he thought was her lover?

"OK, give me a minute here. Let me summarize." Because she was a computer geek, she wanted things precise. "You need to meet Peter. Somehow you know about a connection between Peter and me. And you need to meet him. And, for some reason, you have decided I will introduce you?"

"Yes."

"OK, now I have to sit down." It was sit down and show weakness or fall down. Her mind was in a fog, and her knees were weak. She had to find out how he knew about Peter. If he knew about the gang. About their plan.

She tried to find some connection, maybe his work. "Are you with the same firm now? Rescuing start-up businesses?"

"Yes, the same firm."

"Are you looking for a new client? I don't understand. Why Peter? He's not a start-up. Why do you need to meet him?" She kept finding more questions, but maybe she should let him answer a few.

"Well, it is the same business, but we never rescued start-ups."

"Oh." What did that mean? Not a rescue business? "What then? Explain."

"That is still need-to-know," he said.

"Fine, I don't need to know. I'm not introducing you." He still had not answered any of her questions. And she needed answers. If there was a leak in the plans, the gang had to know. She couldn't leave yet.

"What's wrong?" he asked with a sneer. "Afraid he might not like you being with your husband? Afraid he might think you're doing both of us? You can't keep your hands off me even now." Looking at her hand, still on his arm. That was low. He saw the hurt flash across her face. He hadn't meant to hurt her. He shouldn't care that she was with Conrad.

She looked at her hand. Yes, it was truly a problem for her. She really couldn't trust herself when Jake was near. It had always been that way. She lost all her reason. One look from him and she would melt. That hadn't changed.

Angered, she chided, "Well, why don't you just tell me what you think of me, Jake? And what you say might almost be true. Never was anything wrong with your ego, Jake. You know, I always did need to touch you."

"Yeah, John too," he said.

"Didn't take you long to go there, Jake. But John wasn't the problem between us. That's just a convenient fantasy of yours. One I don't think you even believe. Which is it, Peter or John? Or maybe you think I'm doing both."

She was close to John; they were family. Or what passed for family in her world. And he was her business partner now. Never a lover. Besides, John was gay. And in the closet. And she wouldn't out him as gay, even to Jake. Now Jake had invented some sort of liaison between her and John? An excuse for him to have left her?

"I shouldn't have said that. I was wrong."

"About what, Jake?"

He looked puzzled.

"What were you wrong about, Jake?" she said louder and watched him calm himself.

"I got off track here. I'm sorry. I didn't mean that about John. I don't think you would be with two men at one time. This isn't supposed to be personal. This is business. Life and death business."

"Let's get back on track. I need an introduction to Conrad. You can do that. I'm still your husband. Everyone knows that."

"Everyone knows you disappeared without a word. No one will believe that I have gone back to you."

"Yes, they will. They know you love me." He wasn't so sure that was true. It was hard talking to her when he couldn't see her eyes. Her face gave nothing away.

"OK, they might believe I would go back to you. But none of them would believe that you would come back to me. You were the one who walked out. Left."

Ouch. He had done that.

"Never mind," she said, fuming. "Even if we were back together, I certainly wouldn't introduce you to Peter, my lover. The whole idea is ridiculous."

"You have every reason to be angry. Angry with me. But you came here today. To meet me," he reasoned. "Conrad is in trouble. You could help him. If you want to help him. I need your word not to repeat anything I say. To anyone. Not even John. Do you promise?"

"You'll just accept my word?"

"Yes. Your word has always been good. You have always been honorable."

She was a little surprised to hear him say that. So why did he think she was sleeping with two different men? She knew if she agreed, she would be bound by her word. But she would also find out how much Jake knew or thought he knew.

"OK then, I will not repeat what you tell me. Not even to John. Now, convince me to help you."

"Let's go to the coffee shop." He led her down the street to the shop, guided her to a back booth, and went to the counter to order the coffees. She watched him. He had done the same thing so many times before. She had thought they were happy. Stupid. Now he was back because he wanted an introduction to a wealthy man? He had changed. He was harder now. Or had he always been that way and she'd been too much in love to notice? He had a limp. Slight, but there. When had that happened? He handed her a coffee, startling her.

"Heavy on the cream and sugar, along with your favorite, a sticky bun."

Another surprise for her that he remembered. Maybe he was trying to bribe her with his attention to detail, along with that earlier bit about her being an honorable person.

"Here is what I can tell you. We are a security firm. We design the physical security for a plant or business; we provide threat assessment, employee background checks, and protection and bodyguard service. We specialize in firms with government contracts. Right now it looks like Conrad is involved in some very high-level corporate espionage." He stopped.

She waited for more. No way. She'd know it if Peter had done that. The gang had investigated him thoroughly before they had approached him. She waited for Jake to substantiate his accusation.

"We have reason to believe that Conrad is involved in industrial espionage, hijacking research in weapons and drone technology from two different companies under contract to the military. If we can get an introduction, we might be able to find something conclusive. Maybe clear him. We thought that you and I could appear to get back together, or maybe say we're working out a separation agreement."

When she didn't reply, he added, "You can help us, if you will. And at the same time help Conrad, because it looks very bad for him now. I could move back in with you for a few days while we work out the details. Or you could move into my place." He snuck that last sentence in for her reaction. Then he waited.

She was quiet for a long time, thinking. Wow. Huh. It was a lot to grasp. This is why he contacted her? Because he believed that Peter was involved in industrial espionage? And Jake wasn't an investment consultant, as he'd told her. If it were true about Peter, would that have an effect on the gang's plan? She didn't believe it was true, couldn't be true. The gang had researched Peter thoroughly. They knew him now. No way was he into espionage.

She was still wondering how Jake could be so wrong when the last sentences got through to her. He thought she would just move in with him? Had that all planned out, did he? And she had thought she was the planner. *In his dreams*, she thought.

"Move in together? When hell freezes over. How do you know about Peter and me?"

"Ron saw pictures online, in a gossip blog."

With relief, she thought, *we don't have a leak. And neither does Peter. But we did screw up there.* How had pictures ended up online in a blog? Did it matter? Probably not. She would have to think about that, look at those pictures and see what was actually published.

"I know Peter," she said. "He didn't do what you're saying. I'll think about what I want to do."

"You need to give me an answer now." He was trying to push her.

"There is still a little of Cilla left in me. You remember the part where I have to think on things a long time before I make a decision? Give me your cell number and I'll call you later today."

"Cilla…Priscilla," he corrected before she could. "You need to decide now."

She cut him off. "If you want an answer now, the answer is no. I will not introduce you. If you continue to badger me, the answer will be no. If you just get up and walk away, I'll think about it and get back to you." She said it firmly. She had to be alone now. Not looking at this man who looked so much like the man she loved. So much like the man who had loved her.

She had to organize and arrange everything she'd just heard. Lay it out and examine it. She couldn't do that here. Or with him nearby. She had to be at home in her nest.

He looked at her, trying to read her. But she had become adept at masking her intentions, as well as her feelings. He couldn't tell what she was thinking.

"OK," he finally agreed, "I'll wait to hear from you."

She sat awhile after he left, then she headed home. She could think better there. She couldn't do it as Priscilla. Priscilla was a sham that she had designed. She was an empty shell. An imitation of a real, sensual woman. Cilla was the planner, the coder, the geek. 'The mousy, helpless geek' Sheri had called her. Cilla knew Sheri didn't understand. Sheri thought beauty was power. Didn't know that power and strength came from within. Coding was simply a gift. An ability. A skill that gave Cilla an identity.

Cilla needed to make a list of each fact she had to consider, and to look at all the ramifications and possible consequences and outcomes of any decision she made. She would deal with each point the same way she dealt with her work. Empirically and systematically, both singly and in combination. None of the combinations would include any possibility of Jake and her back together. Didn't look like he wanted that. Not today. Not ever. He had said nothing to imply that he might. Had said no kind words. Hadn't talked about his feelings for her. Hadn't touched her. Could barely stand that she had touched him. She stood and walked home to think about her choices and their consequences.

Home was no longer the house she had lived in with Jake. Now home was a warm comfortable condo with a cat, Tiff. Tiff was the only one she'd lived with since Jake left. She had found Tiff on her deck. A lost kitten. She had no idea how he got up on the penthouse roof. But it was love at first sight for both of them. Her friend, her confidant. They slept together. He was never far away when she was home. Tiff had a cat door, so he could come and go into the penthouse garden and a self-filling food dish for those times she became lost in code. Tiff would comfort her while she deliberated.

Jake wasn't sure if she would call. Did she love Conrad enough? He hated that she might love Conrad. He worried when an hour turned into two and then three and he hadn't heard from her. He was just thinking of calling her when his cell rang. It was her.

"Jake," he answered.

Without preamble she said, "OK, I'll introduce you. I'm not doing it for you, though. I don't owe you anything. I don't owe us anything. I'll do it because I want answers, and I want to prove Peter is not a thief or spy. So I'll be helping him, not you. But I have conditions and you have to answer my questions."

"OK. The reason you help doesn't matter. You agree to do it my way?" Why did he want them both under the same roof?

"No way. But we can talk through my conditions and your demands and work out the problems, compromise. Remember, I'm a detail person."

He had been pretty sure she would balk at moving in together, but it was one of his stipulations. And he had some items he could sacrifice, making it look like he was compromising.

"OK. You want to come over here? Or should I come to the house?"

"Why would you want to go to the house?"

"Well, you live there, don't you?"

She looked at her cell, puzzled. He cared so little, he didn't even know where she lived now? He thought he knew secrets about Peter, but he didn't even know where his own wife lived? How good could he actually be at security if he didn't check the details? He didn't know that she'd moved out of their house, one month after she realized he was not coming back. She had loved that house, their life together. But couldn't survive there alone. So she'd moved. More accurately, the gang had done an intervention and moved her out.

The move had been the first step in leaving her married life behind. She had wallowed in pain and loss for that month. With the move, she had found her backbone and determined to move forward. She had been OK before Jake; she would be OK after Jake. Lonely and abandoned maybe, but she could deal with lonely. And had already survived being abandoned a long time before.

"I don't live in the house. Come to my condo. Take down my address: Eight Hundred Bartholomew. Park in the garage, Three A. Take the elevator to the first floor and tell security that you're visiting Priscilla. He'll show you up. You can answer my questions when you get here."

"I'll be over within an hour," Jake said.

"Be prepared to explain or any deal is off." She hung up before he could reply. It was time for her to get some answers. She had moved on without him, had no choice, but there were still a few things she wanted to know.

She would have to go across the entryway to the other condo, Priscilla's condo. She had bought both penthouse condos. She lived in one with Tiff. This one she had redecorated to her own comfortable taste. The other had been designed for someone like Priscilla. She used that condo when she needed to visualize or reason out the Priscilla persona. How Priscilla, the sensual temptress, might act or react. It was the perfect backdrop for a woman like Priscilla. It allowed Cilla to reach accurate assumptions on behavior.

She would probably have to answer some of Jake's questions. About her and Peter. How much to tell him before the premiere on Friday was the question, though. Would she tell him about the two condos? About what the gang of five was doing? No. She wasn't going to tell him anything. Let him find out what the five were doing. He was the big detective.

She wouldn't tell him about the gang's company. It had started before Jake left, when the five had been sitting around kibitzing at the gatehouse. Before Jake left physically, he had already been gone emotionally for some weeks. Sarah mentioned it would only take her ten years to get enough capital together to open her safe haven for children, Sarah's Child. She said it somewhat regretfully, because it would take so long, and somewhat enthusiastically, since it would happen in the foreseeable future. Sarah, a child psychologist, was small, petite, looked fragile and delicate. But she was tough as nails. Had to be, to have survived her childhood.

The gang decided right then that if Sarah wanted Sarah's Child, she would have it.

The five were too smart to fit in. Too poor. Mistreated and neglected at home, if they even had a home. Ostracized from the popular groups, didn't fit into the Goth or fat groups. They had formed their own group, their own gang. The Gang of Five, they called themselves. All geeks, all expert computer programmers, all skillful hackers. It was the five against the world. They weren't out to save the world; they had to save themselves first. Later they wanted to help the weak and underprivileged, the outcasts, like themselves.

That's why Sarah, the computer hacker who could track anyone anywhere online, became a child psychologist. And John Browne, who could break into any online site, no matter how secure, was a child advocate attorney. They each excelled in different professions. Cilla's strength was pure code. She lived it, breathed it. She designed business software for clients. Penney, the geek with the flaming red hair, was a finance investment guru. Kevin was born rich, a difference that made him an outcast too. Tough, gruff Kevin was an attorney who specialized in business and real estate. They were all cyber-nerds. Any of them could hack into locked websites, though John was the best.

The gatehouse where the gang met originally was his parents' gatekeeper's quarters. It had been their hideout when they were in school. Later the gatehouse became the place they got together to kibitz.

Both Penney, the freaking financial wizard, and Kevin thought the gang could form a partnership or corporation to raise funds for Sarah. They threw around names for the company, settled on SC Digital, SC for Sarah's Child.

"You know, Sarah, I've been playing with some applications I created," Cilla said. "They are great apps. I never expected to sell them or make money from them, I wrote them just for fun, to see if they would work. And they're good. One of them, for videos, we could sell it to the right buyer. I'm guessing for something around a million dollars. That would help Sarah's Child. And I have three or four others we could sell as a package. I'm working on a cool one for gardening. We could use the money from the sales for Sarah's Child."

Kevin chimed in with a nearly completed app for locating real estate in default. With a concomitant app for location, location, location. He was making the application for himself, but it would be marketable. There was a great demand right now for an easy way to match default properties with good location.

Penney had a couple of apps she'd designed for investment. She had designed them for herself. They would sell.

And John had a game. He was a little embarrassed when he admitted that. They all looked at him, because he was a serious geek. He wouldn't be caught dead writing a game. He wrote serious code, like Cilla.

"Well, I had an idea. I sat down to see if it could work, and I just kept going, and it turned into a game. What can I say?" He was a little defensive. He shrugged his shoulders. "I'm a geek. The game works and has spectacular action scenes. But it needs more. I don't know about blood and guts. It has a little, but it needs more, even though it's an intellectual game of buying, selling, and investing. So we would need to add some blood and guts to make it a real world game. And my female lead character, Malissa, I have to tell you, she's boring as hell and very one-dimensional. Which is bad, since the game is 3D. I don't know anything about women, especially sexy women. Someone would have to develop and expand her."

And that's how Cilla's Priscilla was born. Priscilla became the female lead.

They made a couple of lists, a want list and a don't-want list. At the top of the want list, each of them wanted to be able to continue doing the work he was already engaged in. That matched the top of the don't-want list, which was that no one wanted to run or manage a company. So their company, partnership, foundation, would have to be small and short-lived. They decided on a duration of one year. At the end of the year, they would reexamine their goals and achievements. Also on the want list was the need for Sarah's Child to have start-up funds and income, forever. And the don't-want list, Sarah's Child should never need to raise money again. So the S. C. digital needed to raise a lot of money for the foundation.

Sarah insisted that everyone should get an equal share of the income, since they would all contribute to the overall success. And Sarah's Child would have an equal share.

Cilla suggested money be set aside for a trust for The Boys and Becca and the other rescues. Penney ran several alternatives through her iPad and determined, tax-wise, that the trust should be a seventh share. That money would be deposited directly into trusts for the rescues. Rescue might not be a politically correct term, but it was what they all were. Rescued. The funds would be tax free, available immediately.

Penney calculated that they would need to raise $300 million. That would be a huge amount for one year. Their time line would cover two calendar years, making the taxes a little less.

At the end of the year, the five would reassess the plan. See if anyone wanted to continue. The feeling right now was no, they were each happy with their own lives, doing what they wanted, but they would leave all their options open. Money wouldn't hurt, and a little extra would be nice, but none of them needed money or wealth or power. They had learned the hard way that you needed love and fulfillment to survive. The gang provided love and family; their work provided their fulfillment. So, make that $300 million split seven ways, the five of them, the trusts, and Sarah's Child. That should be the right amount for the endowment to Sarah's Child to be self-perpetuating and able to pay top dollar for doctors, nutritionists, and advisors. Sarah would make that list. All their projects would be sold. The proceeds would go into the SC account. The funds would be immediately divided into seven parts and paid out after taxes. No one would have to worry about making estimated tax payments. The company would not retain rights to anything, though some of the software would retain royalties, which would go directly to Sarah's Child.

No one wanted any outsiders, so no employees, no hiring or firing or payroll, with its tax problems.

Penney said they would need start-up capital; they needed to rent an office, buy the computers, and load them with the hardware and software they would need. Cell phones, tablets. All the digital equipment would have to be secured both physically and electronically. They could each make a list of what they needed, and then they would compile their lists into one master list. Well maybe not compile, that was a pure programming term, combine might be a better word. Penney and Kevin would buy all the equipment and supplies. Only encrypted cells (well, duh!) for texting and e-mails. Lots of state-of-the-art anti spyware. Cool fun stuff! No office phone.

That's when Kevin offered his gatehouse for an office. The gatehouse itself would need some security. They could work together on that.

Each application would be reviewed and evaluated for sale. They would do serious research into potential buyers, especially for the game. That buyer would need to be very wealthy.

And a doctor. They would need a doctor for Sarah's Child. A person who put children first. One with their own ideals.

They would start with Cilla's apps. Since she already had them up and running, all they had to do was test them to ensure they ran smoothly. Another duh. If they were Cilla's, they were perfect.

Penney and Kevin would decide on a fair selling price and then research and select the appropriate buyers.

Penney would handle all the finances and advise the company on everything financial. She would help the members invest their proceeds. Kevin would help with real estate.

As they talked and made their lists, Cilla said she had three additional business-specific software applications they could sell. The software just needed a little more polishing and testing.

The game would need the additional work John mentioned, but should be ready in a few months. They would design advertising and posters to sell it online only. SC would keep the game for twelve hours, then turn it over to a buyer, who would buy the game outright and develop DVDs and any associated gear. SC might retain royalties during the first year. The new partner might want a sequel, but John felt that writing a sequel would be boring. He wasn't sure yet if he had more to say. They could make that decision later.

Cilla knew she would be putting a large percent of her share back into Sarah's Child. She would have to tell Penney so they could avoid the taxation caused by disbursing the funds to her first. She hoped she would never feel comfortable with whatever number millions of dollars she would keep. One million even made her queasy. She wondered what the magic number would be for her comfort. Money wouldn't buy happiness. Happiness was sharing success. Life should be lived and enjoyed, not dependent on how many dollars you had.

The gang had pretty quickly decided on Peter Conrad as a buyer for the game. He was a self-made multimillionaire. They researched him online and slyly talked to a few of his acquaintances and to some employees of the companies he had purchased. He seemed to prefer buying failing businesses and turning them around. He always paid a fair, if low, price. He kept most employees on, giving them the option to buy into the company. With the employees working for themselves, they worked harder and better. They became motivated. It was generally easier to turn the companies around and make them profitable if the employees were motivated, so they became voting shareholders.

The gang hacked into Peter's e-mail accounts and studied his business procedures and bank accounts. His family and his family history.

They found a few secrets. Peter was a geek, sort of. And he sometimes hacked companies before he purchased them. The five certainly identified with that and didn't consider it a negative factor. Nor did they consider it dishonest. Other than that, they found nothing unscrupulous. Everything they found on Peter was a plus for the gang.

They did find one secret. Peter was gay. In the closet. John told them that. Well, so was John. No big deal there either.

They had decided to approach Peter with an option to buy when the game was within two or three months of sale.

SC Digital made $20 million in the first month of sales by selling one app, her app, and three more small software apps. Kevin's foreclosure mapping app, Sarah's security app, and Penney's investment app sold for more than $15 million each. In the following four months, they made another $45 million. And now the five were ready to unveil John's new game on Friday. They expected the game to raise over $100 million.

Cilla wasn't the only one to turn back some of her share. They all did. The children needed a safe place. Just as Sarah had needed a safe place. Sarah's safe place and Becca's safe place had been Kevin's gatehouse. Penney set up trusts for each of them. She also opened an investment account in Jake's name. For Jake. Because Cilla said it seemed like the right thing to do. Penney didn't like the idea—by then Jake had left—but she did it. Cilla still had their joint account from which she paid all the bills for the house electronically, automatically. Had Jake ever wondered how she paid the bills? Electric, water, insurance? Did he ever think about her?

Cilla had purchased the two condominium penthouses in a complex of small buildings the same day she had received her first big check, using her maiden name, Cilla West, and dropping the Jayden. Penney had recommended the condos as a good investment, and Kevin had agreed. One of Penney's clients had originally purchased them for rental income, but he didn't like being a landlord. He had a new venture lined up but was strapped for cash when the economy turned down.

Cilla decided to live in one, and rent the other. The move would be a major step back to her independence. She had known by then that Jake was not coming back. She had loved the house they lived in together, but she couldn't return there without him. She couldn't live in the gatehouse forever. Buying the condos made good business sense. She set up her condo, with her work as a focal point.

She had two more software applications under contract with a client for more income too. Funny, she thought, there wasn't much she felt she needed to buy. She loved her work; money didn't change that. The five were all like that, all the members of the gang. Money just gave them more freedom to do what they loved. And to still write code. They were happy with their work, their lifestyles. She wondered if the money would change any of them over time. It hadn't yet. They all still had their same goals.

She roused herself from her memories. She'd better walk over to Priscilla's so she would be there when Jake arrived. It wouldn't do for him to find her in her sanctuary with her cat.

Jake was surprised. *She doesn't live in the house? When did she move out? Why? Why didn't he know? Why hadn't he ever wondered? Didn't they run a search on her?*

"Ron," he yelled as he walked toward his office. "Get in here."

"Yes, boss, what's up?" Ron was the second in command, the business organizer. He planned all the strategy, protection, and training. Ron had run the business while Jake was gone. They had stayed in communication, but day-to-day management had fallen on Ron. Their computer specialist was out of the country, and their backup computer guy was sick, so Ron was running the searches and background checks.

"Did you research my wife?"

"No, boss, we know your wife," he said, puzzled. He looked like an accountant. Medium size, average height, black-rimmed glasses.

"Do we know where she lives? Where does she live?"

"Your house, doesn't she? The bills are paid electronically from your checking account. I know that."

"Well, she tells me she's living at Eight Hundred Bartholomew. Maybe you ought to try to find out what you missed. Like when she moved. And how she can afford to live in that neighborhood? That's a pretty upscale community. Who's paying for it? Conrad? Get current information on her. We should have done that before I contacted her." *And while you're at it*, he thought, *find out when she changed too. When my wife became a slut.*

That wasn't fair. He knew it, but he was angry. He guessed he knew the answer to her move too, right after he left ten months ago, when he ripped her life apart. Disgusted with himself, he threw the address at Ron.

"My fault. My fault. Just assumed that nothing would change with her when I left. That everything would remain the same. Research her now."

Ron was back in twenty minutes. "We might have a problem here, boss." He stopped, as if he didn't know what to say next.

"I'm waiting, Ron. Just tell me." This wasn't going to be good. Ron never got flustered.

"We did the original search on your wife, Priscilla Jayden, and found just what we already knew. I just ran a search on Cilla West, her maiden name." He took a breath. "Cilla is a partner in a very up-and-coming software firm named SC Digital, incorporated nine months ago. That would have been right after you, um…left. Um…had to leave," he said when Jake just glared at him. "She and John and three others are partners in the company, along with a trust."

"Shit. That means that I just told secrets to someone I don't even know."

"Yup," Ron said with a grin.

"What are you smiling about?" he said angrily.

"Well, this is some smart lady, boss. You always said she was a smart geek and she is. SC Digital developed apps that they sold for millions. SC has made around one hundred million since inception."

"You're crazy. No one can do that." He stood up, couldn't sit, needed to move.

"She did it, or maybe they did it. And there's more, if you'll be quiet and sit down." He waited and then continued. "There is a new game, which is due out Friday, tomorrow. I've been reading about it and watching. It's bleeding edge. All the gamers are waiting. That includes me, man. It's pretty secret. There are only tweets, posts, rumors, and these little teaser tidbits feeding the frenzy. The game doesn't have any advertising. But some clips have leaked. On purpose, probably."

He paused for effect. "And some rumors say SC Digital is producing it. No one really knows." He paused again. "And the rumors are saying this game will probably gross between $150 and $200 million the first day."

"Who even thinks in these numbers?" Jake asked. "You think Cilla's company is making that game? Seriously?"

"That's what some of the leaks are suggesting."

"If the game isn't theirs, they still have hit the big-time," Jake said. *No wonder she changed*, he thought. All that money would change anyone. His sweet geek. Millions of dollars. Not a word of that to him today. He had a new thought.

"Anyone managing the money coming in? Or are they just spending it? Do you know? Where is the money going?" he asked while still trying to assimilate the magnitude. Millions!

"Whoever is managing the money, I don't know yet. But she, Cilla, owns that condo she lives in. Owns both penthouses, one under her maiden name, one under Priscilla Jayden. After she bought both penthouses, she opened an investment and checking account in her maiden name. Has the utilities for both condos paid electronically from that checking account. I've found about half of what she received; I'm still looking for the rest. I don't know how she spent it yet."

"Well, keep looking," he said furiously. "It would be nice to know how and where she spent all that money. I have to go. She expects me at Eight Hundred Bartholomew. Call me when you get some answers."

All the way over, he got angrier and angrier. She knew before he left. She knew, had to know that the gang of five would incorporate. Were about to make millions. Why had she never told him? Given him a heads-up?

He parked in A, noticed that B was empty. That was curious. She should have a car there. And he wondered what kind of car she bought with her new funds. There were some pretty hot vehicles in the garage. He looked around and saw her old Mustang—Blue, she'd named it— near the back stairs. She had always been attached to that car. Had it before they got married and wouldn't let him buy her a new one. He took the elevator to the first floor as directed. All the other floors were locked and required a special key. That made him angrier.

The front-desk security man looked at him when he got off the elevator and said politely, "Can I help you, sir?"

"Jake Jayden to see Priscilla."

"Yes, sir, she called. Step in the elevator; I'll code it for her floor. It will take you right up. Miss Priscilla is in A."

"Thanks," he ground out and did as he was told. The ride was quick and silent. But it was long enough to get his temper under control. The doors opened to a hallway that was plush, colorful, and looked comfortable. Somehow that made him think of Cilla.

She was waiting for him in the doorway, motioning him in, closing the door behind him. "Security notified me that you were on the way up."

God, she was beautiful, he thought, but he took his eyes off her and looked around. The entranceway was formal and cold. The living room beyond was huge. All glass, metal, and modern. The paintings were modern, loud splotches of color. Looked like the new favorite artists. He would check when he could get closer.

"Do you want to see the rest, make sure it meets with your approval?" she asked indifferently.

"Yeah, sure." He really was just curious. Was it all this modern and contemporary? Had she changed that much? Or would maybe the bedrooms reflect his Cilla's warm, comfortable style?

"Help yourself. I think you can find your way around. Want me to get you something to drink? I have only the best bourbons. Your favorite brand included." She said it in her new, cold, couldn't-care-less tone.

"OK. I'll do a quick walk-through." He really needed a drink, but it could wait. The place looked like a spread out of a magazine featuring homes for the rich and famous. Every room outdid the last. He counted four bedrooms, all plush, with their own baths, also plush. Ultra-modern, full room showers with multiple source sprays. He wondered what had happened to Cilla, the dreamer. Cilla, who put the green in conservation. Cilla, who was going to save the world, protect the children. The Cilla he had known and loved. Money, he guessed. Money changed people. Huh. Just look at Priscilla.

The master bedroom was the most luxurious. Red and even colder than the rest of the condo. The walk-in closet, when he opened the door, was almost empty. That was strange. Half a dozen outfits with matching shoes and purses. All designer-name clothes. The drawers were also mostly empty. The master bath had a built-in whirlpool, and was that a steam shower? One huge wall was solid mirror. Impressive. Looked like a presidential suite in an upscale hotel. The medicine cabinet was empty. Did she even live here? Yep. Her makeup covered the vanity. That was new too, she never used to wear makeup.

He walked back into the bedroom and over to the window which was covered with dark drapes. This also was not the Cilla he had known. That Cilla loved light, sunlight. She hadn't even put curtains on some of the windows in their house. And the first thing she did every morning was open the few curtains she had hung. She only closed them for privacy.

There was a continuation of the balcony outside the window. He opened the slider and saw that it was a wraparound deck, with nothing on it. No furniture, no plants. Again, the Cilla he had known would have covered the deck with flowers the same as she had the porch and the backyard at home. She had planted flowers everywhere. She had never had flowers growing up, and she delighted in the vast variety of colors and shapes with or without fragrance. She had run to get him when she saw the first butterfly. He remembered the joy and wonder in her face. How happy she had been, how happy that had made him. He turned away from the bare deck, saddened. He closed the door and drapes. Shut out the memories.

The kitchen was all stainless steel and granite and had every modern appliance. Looked like they had never been used. He opened the refrigerator. Empty except for one lonely bottle of water. The cabinets, empty too. Curious. His Cilla had loved to cook. Apparently Priscilla didn't. A back door led to the back entranceway, quaint, with stairs and a garbage chute. Both penthouses opened onto it.

He came back to the living room. She pointed to his drink on a table by the couch. She was sitting in a chair in the corner. Not drinking. He remembered she didn't drink much. A fire was burning in the fireplace. That was the only warm, comfortable spot in the condo.

He had gotten back some control, again, while walking through the apartment. He sat on the couch, which was just as uncomfortable as it looked. Where to start?

"You own this condo. Did you decorate it yourself?"

"The hallway outside. This condo, I kept it the way it was when I bought it. Matches my new self. Suits Priscilla perfectly, I think, don't you?"

That explained why the hallway reminded him of his Cilla. And this apartment did look like the residence of the woman sitting across from him. Severe, austere, cold. Where was the Cilla he had known, the one of color, warmth, softness?

"So when did this all happen? When did you become a businessperson, incorporate? Was it while we were still living together? It must have been, for the timing to work. How come I didn't know? How come you didn't tell me?" It all came out angrily in one breath. So much for being under control.

Seems he had done some research, Cilla thought. Finally. She wondered how much he had found. "To answer your first few questions, yes, we, the gang of five, incorporated while you were still living with me, before you left, before you moved out. Why didn't you know? I think I'll let you figure that one out for yourself. You're a smart man."

She remembered she'd told him, and she had asked him for help with the incorporation. After all, that was his field, rescuing start-ups. She had wanted to talk it over with him. But he was gone by then. Oh, not physically gone, but gone just the same. One day, when they were sitting at the counter, just talking, he had turned on the radio for the news. She had been in the middle of a sentence. She had stopped talking, shocked, her mouth open.

"Are we through talking?" she'd asked. And waited.

Finally, he had looked at her and, distracted by the news, said, "What?"

"Are we through talking? You turned on the radio when I was telling you a story."

"Oh, I thought you were done." Still distracted.

"Yes, I am done," she'd said and left the room, her feelings hurt, while he continued listening to nothing on the radio. He had stopped listening to her. About the same time, he had stopped noticing her. She had never talked geek to him, so it wasn't that. She tried not to talk geek to anyone but the gang. She had just seemed to stop existing for him She wasn't there anymore. He would look at her and not see her. Like she was invisible. He didn't smile at her anymore either. He had loved her once. Loved her mind. Loved "his geek."

During that month she had felt more and more invisible. He wasn't interested in anything she said. He would turn on the radio or open the newspaper in the middle of a sentence. He didn't hear her anymore. He didn't see her. And about the same time, didn't want her. And then he left. She was actually surprised that it took as long as it had.

She shook herself and brought herself back to the present.

"Yeah, you figure that one out. Why don't you get your questions out of the way before I start mine," she suggested.

"Where is the rest of your money? We can only find half."

"You don't know? You really don't know, do you?" She said that with some disbelief. "I thought you knew when you said I was an honorable person. But you really don't know." She said it wonderingly, and almost to herself, and OK, there was a little smugness in there too. Gave a little laugh. She really wanted to see his face when he found out. She wasn't telling him.

"Did you spend it all then? Throw it away? Did you even see a financial advisor?" This last was said critically.

She couldn't help herself. She laughed out loud.

"What kind of research department do you have at your firm anyway? First you don't know I moved. Now you can't find my money. Maybe you guys are not as smart as you think. And you should know who my financial advisor is." She paused and then added, "You know my financial advisor."

"Where did you spend the money, Cilla?"

"Priscilla, Jake, Priscilla."

"OK. How did you spend the money, *Priscilla?*" he repeated with the emphasis on her name.

"Let your research department find it, Jake. I don't think I'm telling."

That was two questions she hadn't answered. But let him do the research.

"You did blow it, didn't you? Probably used it to try to convince yourself that you're part of the social set. Part of Conrad's elite jet set. Buy your way in," he sneered.

"Don't be insulting. You know I don't care about social prestige. Except maybe for the gang, I don't fit in anywhere. Be careful you don't say too much you may have to apologize for, Jake," she said warningly, disgusted.

"Did you buy jewelry? Or was it a gift for services? That necklace you have on? The one you keep touching, caressing almost. You keep touching it and smiling."

"This? I love it. Isn't it great!" she said with pleasure. "I got it from Bob—" She stopped short. She'd almost said Bob's Resale Treasures. But Priscilla wouldn't buy there. Only Cilla. And it was a great find. Not an expensive piece, but one both Priscilla and Cilla could wear. She kept touching it for comfort. Because it was Cilla's necklace. Not Priscilla's. It grounded her. She loved the smoothness and the colors. What would he think, the millionaire buying her jewelry in a consignment shop? She smiled to herself again.

The smile must have shown, though, because his attitude went from disgusted interrogation to angry accusation.

"Bob, who's Bob? You are still a married woman, you know."

"I know. I'm surprised that you remember." She really hadn't meant to imply a man. But it might be good for him to think there was a man, or men, in her life.

She went on the offensive. He wasn't going to walk into her apartment and accuse her of infidelity when he had walked out. Left her for another woman! She remembered the last time she'd talked to him. She had waited and waited for him for dinner and finally called when he hadn't come home. It took a long time for him to answer the phone.

"Are you OK?" she'd asked. "Where are you?"

"I'm fine," he'd said shortly.

"Is something wrong? When are you coming home?"

"I'm not. Don't call. I won't answer the phone. I'm not coming back."

"I don't understand, what do you mean? Not coming back?" But she'd asked those questions to a dead phone. He had hung up. And just like that, her world had dissolved. He wouldn't answer his phone when she called him. Wouldn't talk to her.

She remembered that like it was just moments ago.

"I know I'm a married woman," she repeated. "Do you? Do you still think of me as a wife? You left. Remember? With another woman. Why should what I do matter to you? You were the one who walked out. After…you stopped looking at me."

"Well, I'm looking at you now, and I'm not much liking what I am seeing." Sickened at the thought of her with another man. Men. There was a lot he wanted to know. What had she done when he left? Were there other men? How many? Why didn't she ask him why he left? Why didn't she ask him about the women in his life? She had asked about Sheri.

"No?" said a haughty Priscilla. "You don't like what you're seeing? That's funny; I got a very different impression." Priscilla slowly, seductively, looked him up and down.

He went cold. Hot. He didn't know. Stood up and walked to the window. His back turned to her. Trying to get control, again. And aroused. How did she do that? And he was enraged. He wanted to slap some sense into her for acting like a slut. Where had that come from? He didn't hit women. How had she changed that much in those few short months? From sweet geek to cold seductress. Was it the money?

He suddenly realized who the financial advisor was. "Penney. Your financial advisor must be Penney. Penney, from your gang."

"Right in one, boyo." Boyo? She didn't say boyo, did she?

"Penney who made you a little nervous because she looked like a freak. Oh, that must be why you wouldn't talk finance with Penney. Because you weren't in finance. Not because she was a freak. Your best friend, Lenny, called her an ugly freak. I was looking right at Penney when she overheard that. Saw her run to the restroom, found her in there crying. Not crying because her feelings were hurt. She was crying because she thought you were the world and she was scared for you. Scared that you might be falling under Lenny's spell. And Sheri's."

Cilla took a breath and continued, "But that was a long time ago. And Penney the Freak—that's her nom de plume now, she's proud of that title—well, Penney the Freak helped us make a lot of money. And has even increased our investments in a down market.

"Yes, Penney is my financial advisor. She is advisor for us and for SC Digital. She's a freaking financial geek genius. She found this condo for me."

"She was right about Lenny," he said miserably. "He was vicious, verbally and physically. Evil." He stopped himself. He didn't want her to know how bad it had been. Couldn't talk about it.

"How long before you figured that out?" Cilla asked. "We all knew it the first time we met him. But geeks know about people and body language. We have to be able to recognize someone who is off, to survive.

"Lenny was slick on the outside, slimy all over. Gruesome filth on the inside. Hope you didn't find out the hard way." She had wondered about that. Was it coincidence that Jake stopped "seeing" her about the same time he began hanging with Lenny? Lenny and Sheri?

"And how is Sheri?" she asked, as if she didn't really care, an innocent inquiry.

He wasn't going to talk about Sheri. "So where is the rest of the money, Cilla?" he asked again, ignoring her question as his cell rang. Ron's ringtone. He pulled it out. "You find it?" he snarled.

"Yes, all but about a half million. And you're not going to believe it. Are you sitting down? You better be sitting down."

"I'm sitting, just spit it out."

"I couldn't find anything in either of her names, so I checked movements of large sums of money. You said she's an honest person. I think that I can put your mind at rest about the honest part." He paused and then said, "The other half of her share was deposited into a second investment account. The day she got the money, she opened an account in your name. Half of the money is there, at the bank where your shared checking account is."

Ron sounded vindicated. He'd always liked Cilla and was probably thrilled to see her come out on top.

Jake's reaction was all Ron could have hoped for. He turned pale as he listened. Choked. Incredulous. Looked directly into Priscilla's eyes. Frozen, he put the phone away.

"You gave it to me?" he asked, his voice hoarse. "You put it in an investment account for me?" He couldn't speak. She gave it to him? Why would she give it to him?

She laughed. She threw her head back and laughed. Holding her stomach. The truly happy belly laugh that he remembered. "If you could see your face now." She bent over double. Laughed for a long time. Wiping her eyes, she said, "I wish I could have seen inside your brain. That's worth every single penny. All that money? I blew it just for that reaction. That makes my day." She finally wound down. "I put it in an account for you because it was the right thing to do. Not you, really—the old you, before Sheri.

"Don't worry about my money, honey," she continued, placing insulting emphasis on *honey*. It was a word she never used. "I'm set for life. The gang is set for life. We have a business plan, a financial plan, and a game plan. It was all written out before we incorporated. We don't need any other financial advisor to help us. Penney takes care of it. A lot more money will be coming in, and it's all scheduled to go directly into selected investments. What you found so far, well, that was just the beginning. So don't worry your pretty little mind over the money or us."

She thought she carried that off pretty well. And she breathed a sigh of relief. It didn't appear Jake had found out about Midnight +1 yet.

He looked at her with amazement. And admiration? Wonder? The way he used to look at her when he still saw her, loved her. Was that what was in his face?

She didn't like seeing him look at her fake Priscilla that way. "Don't start thinking you like the new me, honey. Because if you get involved with Priscilla, you are going to get hurt. Get hurt very badly. I guarantee it. That's a warning. You can take that to the bank."

She gave him a minute. "And now it's my turn. Now is probably a good time, while you are confused. And I have nothing more to say about the gang or SC Digital." She had her questions and her facts organized in her mind. The order might change, and the questions might change depending on how he answered, and how she judged his veracity.

"First a statement. I am not going to lie to my friends. I will tell them that we are considering divorce. Trying it out. Have an arrangement. No way could I fake being in love with you." She wouldn't have to fake that. She was still in love with him. Or rather, she was in love with the Jake who had loved her. Not this cold, overbearing bully. *What kind of idiot did that make her*, she wondered.

"I'm not going to play touchy-feely and dopey lovey-dovey with you."

OK, that would work for him. "Works for me," he said easily.

"Now my questions. What is your real name?"

"Jake Jayden, you know that."

"No. I don't. I don't know anything. Does this Jake Jayden have any family?"

"No. Everything you know about me, Jake, is real." He was angry now.

"Does that include your work as an investment counselor rescuing fledgling businesses?"

"Christ!" he spit out.

"You need to remember that I'm a geek. I need to know what is fact. I can't write good code on top of bad code. I have to know where the bugs are before I can make the program run. I have let you control both these meetings so far, and now it's my turn. I warned you that I would be asking questions. If you don't want to answer, then you can leave."

She said it calmly. Being prepared always helped. This loop could only end one of two ways: he would leave, or he would stay and answer. She was betting on stay. Everything pointed to that. He needed her. She waited.

He walked to the window again. And just stood. And started speaking slowly.

"The fledgling business story is our cover story. It's part of our mission plan even. We get our customers by word of mouth. Anyone who comes to us needing assistance with investment counseling is told we have all the work we can handle right now and are sent off to a reputable firm. The story helps us be invisible, maintain a low profile. And it's not really that far off from what we do. So it's just easier, safer, to always say investment counseling. We need the anonymity." He wiped his hands through his hair.

"Do any of your employees' spouses know your real business?"

"Ron's wife knows," he admitted calmly. "But she was in the same field. That's how they met. I don't know about the others. I don't know what they tell in bed." He was under control again.

Apparently she didn't warrant any truths in bed. He hadn't told her. Didn't trust her? Or just didn't intend to stay, so he didn't need to share? Back to now.

"Do you have actual proof against Peter? Or just suggestions that seem to point to him?"

"Depends on what you call proof. Two different companies have been hacked and both trails point toward Conrad. That's a lot of coincidence."

She breathed a sigh of relief. No real proof. Just indications. "I still have questions, but I can't help injecting here that you're not giving Peter much credit. Your firm did a piss-poor job of investigating me. So you've messed up, missed something. You're wrong about Peter."

"Is this your brain talking or your heart? If it is your brain, if you are right, it could mean we are on the wrong trail. Being purposely misled."

"Both. And I'm not the only one who will stand up for Peter." All the gang would. Especially John. John had fallen hard for Peter. They had fallen for each other. John would help clear him. The gang would help. Peter, himself, would help. When she could tell them.

"I want to see what you've found that seems to point to Peter. And I also want to see how and where you found it. I want the gang to look at it too. Later. You need to let me help you find the real culprit. That is one of my conditions."

While she had his attention, she continued, "We need to set up some ground rules. The first is that my business and my personal life are not your business. You're going to have to accept that."

He stared at her for a while. As if trying to read her.

"OK, for now," he said. "Unless something happens that might make it important."

"Makes sense. The next rule: you will need to sign a non-disclosure agreement before we go any further."

"Don't trust my word?" He said that with a sneer. "I took yours." Hostile.

"No, I don't trust your word," she said quietly. She didn't embroider that. They both knew she couldn't trust his word. "And there are other people involved."

"Do I have a choice?"

"Not if you want to continue." She handed him the form. She'd printed it earlier.

"I don't expect to learn anything about the gang to disclose." He signed it angrily.

"I'll make you a copy tomorrow at the office." She paused. "That's it. You have anything else?"

"I need to be with you. You can move in with me. I have a spare room."

"Why?" She was puzzled. "We don't need to live together for this to work."

"You know too much now. For a few days, until we get this settled, I want to be where I can watch you."

"You said I was honorable. You have my word."

"I could stay here. You have room for an army. We can explain it to Conrad. Tell him I insisted while we work out the separation. That we have to make it look like we tried to get together for a separation agreement to work."

She thought again, biting her lip. "OK, you can stay here. Pick your bedroom. Whatever. Stay out of my way. Stay out of my bedroom."

"OK, there's no problem with that one."

"You need a special key for the elevator," Cilla continued. "I am not going to give you one. That means you only use the elevator when you're with me."

"No, that won't work. I need to be able to come in and out at will. I can't wait for you to be fixing your face or straightening your stockings." He meant that to be insulting, but she surprised him with her belly laugh. Her pure delight again.

"OK, I'll get you a key; I'll change the code after we clear Peter." She went to her bedroom and came back with a spare keycard.

"What about the security code?" he asked. "I noticed the panel and the cameras."

"Those came with the condo. I don't use them." Well, she didn't live here, so why would she use them? And Joey, one of The Boys, had upgraded them when he was home on leave. "There is enough security on the first floor and with the elevator key as well as cameras in the elevator and in the main entranceway outside."

"I don't think those are good excuses," he complained. "I am in security after all. The equipment is here; it is functional, and it should be used."

"Will you bring the file on Peter?" she asked him ignoring his authoritative attitude.

"Maybe. There are still things you aren't telling me. Tit for tat. I'm going to my truck for my duffle. I want to go with you to your office tomorrow, and after I look around, I'll decide if you get the file."

"Clearing Peter is the deal breaker. You have to decide now if I can have the file. The whole file. And I want to look at the original data too."

He considered, thinking, and finally said, "OK. Deal."

"And it will be a superficial look around our office. There is a lot of proprietary information on the computers and in the files. You won't be able to sit in on meetings, even though you signed the non-disclo-sure. And I will have to give my partners a heads-up tonight. I can text them while you're out getting supper. There's no food here. No coffee. I don't cook. I don't eat here. So you might want to get groceries when you go for your duffle."

As soon as he left, she texted her partners. "Jake is back. He'll be coming into the office with me tomorrow." So she used complete words and sentences. Sue her. She signed it Priscilla. Not Cilla. Nothing wrong with that and not breaking her promise, but it would be a heads-up for them. Of course, mentioning Jake would be a heads-up.

She sat and tried to analyze how this new development, Jake's arrival, would or could change their plan. But each time she tried an

If-THEN-ELSE loop, she couldn't get it to execute. *Give it up. Go feed Tiff now, he didn't like the automatic refill dish. Do it before Jake comes back.* She would probably spend the night here in Priscilla's bedroom, and she didn't want Tiff hungry as well as lonely.

Tomorrow would be OK, she assured herself. The gang could have a meeting to decide how much to tell Jake. All the work was done for the game's premiere. The game, Midnight +1, would be available at multiple download sites at midnight plus one minute. They would make a few more careful leaks. Anonymous tweets and posts to preselected blogs about the Midnight +1 release. Peter would be there. At the office. He was as involved as the gang. Maybe an introduction tomorrow would be enough for Jake, and he would be gone by the time the game premiered. Maybe he wouldn't notice that Peter and John were silly in love with each other. Hopefully Peter and John would be wearing their professional faces.

She gave up after she had looped back three times to where she had started. There was not going to be any simple IF-THEN code for this. She decided to feed her cat and get ready for dinner. She put out two place settings at the counter and turned the TV to news. Maybe she wouldn't have to carry on a conversation.

Jake came in with his duffle over his shoulder, a shopping bag from the market in one hand and, oh good, Chinese takeout from their favorite restaurant. What used to be their favorite restaurant. She relieved him of the bags and told him to go freshen up while she put out dinner.

He had bought coffee for the drip machine, milk, bread, eggs, sliced cheese, bologna (for his favorite sandwich), mustard, and butter.

Her ruse worked with the TV. Or maybe he didn't want to talk either.

They ate in silence. She cleaned up as he watched the TV, and then she said she was tired and going to bed and he could make himself comfortable.

He wouldn't know about Cilla's condo. She would have to be Priscilla again in the morning; she hadn't planned on that. Being Priscilla again. She better get some rest tonight, because tomorrow would be a very long day. Maybe she could sneak next door to her own bed after he was asleep.

He couldn't sleep. Took one of the leather and metal chairs out to the deck. Sat and watched the skyline. He had really screwed up. He had screwed up his life with Cilla, screwed up Cilla too, if you could judge by Priscilla and this condo. Screwed up at work by not investigating Cilla. Screwed up if Peter wasn't their hacker. He had made nothing but mistakes since he had screwed up with Sheri.

He thought of Cilla in that cold, dark bedroom. Couldn't get his mind off her in bed. In bunny jammies? Probably not Priscilla's style, and he hadn't noticed any in the drawers. He could just peek in. The more he thought about it, the better he liked the idea. He wouldn't actually go into her room. Just look in. He got as far as her door before he stopped. *Fuck it*, he thought. Turned and went to bed.

Friday

She smelled coffee and was confused for a minute. Jake. Jake was making coffee. She was still in Priscilla's condo. She must have fallen asleep. It was a quarter after nine, she saw. Late. Better get up; she had a long day ahead. Made longer by the fact that Jake was there. She showered and put on Priscilla's green dress and went to the kitchen. He was sitting shirtless at the counter eating eggs and toast.

"I made coffee. Doesn't look like you ever used that machine."

"Umph," was all she said. She hadn't ever touched that machine. She got herself a cup and leaned against the stove, watching him eat.

"Kind of late for you to be going to work, isn't it? Sleep in? Rich-girl hours?" He was angry and annoyed.

"Yeah, rich-girl hours," she agreed. Guess she was going to just go along with his insults today. And she hadn't slept. Tossed and turned. Remembering. Reminding herself to stay strong. This wasn't the Jake she'd married. He was gone. Finally, she did fall asleep. The game debuted today, tonight really, and they had a lot riding on it. She was revved, and she expected to be up for the next thirty-six hours straight.

The game would debut at midnight plus one minute. SC owned it for the first twelve hours. The sales contract for the game was signed, but the actual price would be calculated based on the first twelve hours of sales. No one really knew how the leak advertising would work or what the first twelve hours of sales would look like. So the contract had a sliding scale Penney had created. It was an esoteric function that examined the sales from midnight plus one minute to noon plus one minute, the frequency of sales, and the rate of sales. That was one of Penney's apps, the sliding scale. Penney and Peter understood it. Kevin claimed to.

So SC grossed, and in this case the net was the same, all the sales for the first twelve hours. Then they acquired an amount from Peter based on the sliding scale, and royalties for the first year. The royalties were based on another of Penney's formulas. Everyone expected the sales for the first twelve hours to be around 100 million with a higher rate for the next six hours. Peter expected to pay them over $100 million for the game. It was weird talking in hundreds of millions. And it was kind of fun, the uncertainty, and the risk. It made the release even more exciting. The gang had side bets on the actual amount.

"I'm going to the deli for breakfast and then to work," she announced. "You want to meet me there?" She hoped.

"No, it would be better if we go in together. I'll cook breakfast here for you and then drive you to work." He got up and went to the stove, which he thought didn't look used either.

The eggs smelled wonderful, and she was starving, but after that comment about rich girls, she wasn't going to let him know she appreciated him cooking. So she reluctantly agreed and just let him make breakfast without any comment.

"I usually walk to work when the weather is nice." Guess she wasn't going to go along easy after all.

"Today you ride with me. I may need wheels."

They ate in silence. They had said everything last night.

An hour later, in the garage, "You're going to have to give me directions," he snarled. "To where you work," he added defeated.

She just looked at him. She didn't really feel like she had to point out that neither he nor his research division had done their homework. She just shook her head and directed him to the gatehouse. It was less than a mile. They had to stop at the gate so she could hit the numbers in the panel. She wouldn't give him her password. They continued on down the drive to the square one-story bungalow. It had a wraparound porch bordered by bright flowers. The wood and glass manor where Kevin lived was farther along the lane.

She had him park by the main entrance, a white door with an etched oval glass center. They climbed the three steps to the covered deck. White wicker chairs and tables were spread randomly around. An array of white hanging baskets with blossoms cascading down the sides hung from white hooks. She led him across the porch and through the main entrance. They walked into the great room.

It was a large comfortable room. About forty feet square. Cathedral ceiling, white, with dark wood beams. Skylights. The walls were white too. Wood floor. Fireplace. The eclectic furniture was mostly comfortable. Low bookcases and shelving ran along the perimeter of the room below the windows. There was an oversize monitor hung below the ceiling on each wall.

Tablets, cells, laptops, computers, both PCs and Macs, were scattered everywhere. About what you might expect from a bunch of geeks. Posters of something called Midnight +1 covered the wall areas, with what almost looked like pictures of Priscilla. There, that was her blue suit from yesterday in that poster. The green dress she was wearing today in another.

Cilla didn't explain the layout, but each of the gang had her own area. Clockwise from where they were in the doorway, to their right, was Sarah's, a pleasant work area, oak desk and chair facing the center of the room, plus a rose-colored loveseat and recliner.

A fireplace with a giant screen centered above the mantel was on the wall between Sarah's corner and Cilla's. And a seating area was in the center of the room, with two couches, three recliners, and tables scattered around. For those lazy times when they worked together.

Her own area had another oak desk and chair, facing out toward the double doors opening into the morning sun and the garden. A small, low, floral couch separated her area from Penney's in the next corner with another giant screen monitor was on the wall.

Penney's corner vibrated with bright, loud, screaming colors. Penney said she found the colors restful. Which was strange. Cilla sometimes felt that all the color froze her brain; maybe that's what Penney meant by restful.

John's area was across from Penney's and to Jake's and Cilla's left as they stood inside the door. No color here. His was glass and dark wood with two black beanbag chairs. Cilla smiled whenever she looked at them.

A third monitor hung on this wall between John and Sarah's spaces.

A long oak dining room table with a dozen chairs was positioned between Penney and John's areas, for when the gang did serious work together. And for meals. Not that they ever had twelve people in the room. The table was covered with coffee, muffins, and rolls. Annie's work, Cilla was sure.

A long counter at right angles to the dining room table ran across the back of the room, with six high stools. This was where Kevin preferred to work. He could sit there and work for hours, without moving, like a statue.

Behind that was an open kitchen, the back wall of which had cabinets, up and down, with a functional counter. A Jenn Air stove with two ovens, a microwave, a refrigerator, and a freezer, fully stocked for the geeks, filled the space. They could cook or have food delivered, and Annie, Kevin's cook and the gang's mentor, frequently brought over tasty snacks and meals.

A corridor on either side of the kitchen, on the outside walls, led to four bedrooms separated by two full baths. They provided a refuge from any commotion in the great room. They each had their own room. Every one of them had spent more than a few nights here when the group had become lost in code and didn't want to go home. It was convenient and comfortable. Each room reflected the owner, and each room had a computer station.

The gang was waiting. The security would have chimed to notify them of Cilla's arrival. They would have watched Cilla and Jake approach the front door.

John stepped forward as they walked in. Spokesman.

"Cilla, we need to talk. Privately," he said with an angry look at Jake.

"First let me speak." She had already thought this out. She knew how her friends felt about Jake. About how he had deserted her. "Jake and I have an arrangement. Temporary. Business. Personal. It should lead to finalizing our relationship." So far, the truth. "Possibly a separation agreement and then a divorce." Not a lie. She could divorce this Jake; she didn't like him. She wanted the one who had loved her. "I am not going to do anything crazy." Thank goodness she didn't have to make gooey faces at Jake.

"Are you back with him?" John demanded.

"No. But he will be hanging around with me for the next few days while we work things out. And he is staying with Priscilla." Code for staying in the empty condo.

"Since he's here, can I tear his effing heart out?" John growled, looking Jake in the eye.

"No. Not today, maybe later," she said with the smile Jake remembered.

Jake just stood. He had expected the gang to be angry. Protective. He could take his lumps. He deserved them.

"Are you really bringing him in?" Penney asked. "How much does he know?" She had been so happy when Cilla had found Jake. And devastated when he had left.

"Nothing. He knows nothing. We need to decide what he can know. I have a signed non-disclosure."

She stopped, because the security chimed and the monitors showed Peter driving in. She could see Jake looking with interest at the monitors. The system was state of the art. As good as what his company installed she bet, even better. She hadn't mentioned that Conrad would be here this morning. They watched him get out of his Mercedes and walk toward the door.

Conrad calmly walked inside. Cilla knew John would have given him a heads-up. Peter knew all the sad details of Jake's abandonment.

"Peter, I want you to meet my husband, Jake. Jake, meet Peter Conrad." This was one of those "WHEN" loops that she tried to run. It always failed. She had no idea what would happen now.

Jake reached out his hand to shake, saying, but not meaning, "Pleasure to meet you, Conrad."

And Peter hit Jake in the face with a powerful left, knocking him down.

Surprise kept Jake on the floor.

"That's for Cilla," Conrad said. The gang was surprised but looked delighted, standing behind Conrad.

"OK, you get that one free," Jake said as he picked himself up. "But maybe you should be thanking me for leaving, 'cause that left the door open for you with Cilla."

Conrad looked at him, surprised. "Why, you no-good scum. You think me and Cilla…me and Cilla…You're crazy."

Cilla walked over and gave Peter a hug and a kiss on the cheek. "It's OK, Peter. He's a jerk. Remember? Leave it. Let's just get back to work."

"OK." But he looked at Jake smugly and said, "Cilla and me? We would have gotten together whether you left or not." They would have, because of Midnight. "I've heard a lot about you, Jayden." He was changing the subject.

"Imagine you have, being around this gang. Nothing good, I'm sure."

"No, I meant in security circles. Watermark's Johnson is a good friend." While Jake was trying to think of something to say, Peter continued, "I had you investigated then, when you helped Johnson, and again when I decided to join the gang." Peter noted Jake's surprise. "Didn't know we were in business together, huh? Cilla can keep a secret. I know she had you sign a non-disclosure for SC. That will cover this meeting. But we go no further until you also sign mine."

Jake felt a little like he might be in an alternate universe. Conrad in business with Cilla and the gang? How come he didn't know? And how come everyone called Priscilla, Cilla? Johnson had never mentioned he knew Conrad; that's the sort of thing some people brag about, knowing celebrities. Jake's company had done good work for Johnson. Thank goodness. He noticed Conrad had the agreement on the desk and was holding out a pen. Jake read the document, making them wait.

He read it through twice, partly because he needed time to get his head together, partly to irritate them. Then he signed both copies, folding one up and putting it in his pocket.

Conrad took his copy and pocketed it.

"Oooh-Kay, let's see where we are," John said. "With the non-disclosures, Jake can be here. But he doesn't get to talk. And I don't want him to talk. Especially if he's going to say more stupid things."

John waited for agreement and then continued, "Michael called, and he can't make it now, maybe later. We can fill him in. All the time-delay leaks went out, and the posts and blogs were made. There is a lot of static and talk about Midnight Plus One. More than we expected. And most of it is positive. I'll drop some favorable posts about our earlier 'accidental' leaks. So that plan is all looking good. We just wait, let the posts do their work, and see what happens. Meantime I have news." He paused and looked around. "I want to make the sequel. I have a lot more to say. I didn't get it all out yet."

Sarah went over and knelt in front of him, touching his knee, looking into his eyes. "Are you sure, John? You want to? You want to do it for you? You're not doing it for me, are you? Because I don't want that."

"Yeah, I'm sure. I have a few ideas that didn't fit in Midnight, a couple of things I already programmed. I know how they'll work, and I want to see this sequel. I've got to do something with those ideas. So if it's OK with you guys, I want to continue." He was really eager.

"Oh, I am so glad, because I have an experiment I want Malissa to try too," Penney said. "It's a whole new personality. I can make it work with whatever you're planning."

"Oh man, you won't believe what I have, and it all began with my gardening," Cilla said. "I was working with my flowers and I saw it. I wrote it out, because, well, you know how it is, when you see it, you have to write it. And it works. It will be great. I'm so excited, I can hardly wait to see if my episode will fit in. But I would never have said anything, if we didn't make a sequel. Writing it will get it out of my system. And I will use it myself. It will be a cool app. Thank you, John, thank you. Three cheers for John."

Jake watched, tearing his eyes from the posters, as they actually cheered John, who seemed a little embarrassed. He saw Conrad nod, so

Conrad already knew. Something going on there. So was Priscilla with John? Or Conrad? Both? He couldn't let his mind go there.

Kevin said he had two more posts he would slip into game blogs, in addition to the timed-release ones. Then he mentioned that his app was ready for testing and he would send it to them.

Another cheer went up.

Jake was glad they all knew what they were talking about, obviously something to do with a game. The game had to be the one Ron had mentioned. He would make Priscilla explain later. He was rubbing his sore chin. Conrad could hit.

The gang each took a turn updating their projects. They broke up to fine-tune today's premiere, still sending angry glances his way.

Jake followed Cilla. "Want to tell me what's happening? What's the premiere? What's Midnight Plus One? And who is Michael?"

"We are releasing a game tonight. Midnight Plus One, or sometimes referred to as M Plus One, or just Midnight. We are releasing it exactly at midnight plus one minute. In a nutshell the plan is to sell the game online. No advertising. No advertising, partly because none of us do advertising. John suggested that we write some well-placed comments on blogs, some tweets, and a few controlled leaks to stimulate interest and, we hope, incite a buying frenzy. So we dropped hints on selected blogs, did some tweeting. Asked if anyone knows what Midnight Plus One is? That sort of thing. We won't know how it all works out until noon tomorrow, so we are all a little on edge right now. Bear with us."

"How much money are you talking about anyhow?" he asked, though he remembered what Ron had said. Same game? Fit the parameters.

"We think, our best estimates are, over one hundred million dollars the first twelve hours."

"One hundred million dollars?" he gasped. "You're crazy, you are all crazy. You can't do this. This can't work. It's impractical, unrealistic, and impossible. You're not talking play money here. This isn't a game," he thundered. "Do you guys have any idea what you're doing? How could you take this on without professional management? Are you serious? No one sells a product like that."

He was flabbergasted at what they were doing. "You're like children playing at grown-up." And it was probably too late to help them with marketing and sales. Maybe he could slow them down.

"Oh, Jake. Don't worry. Calm down, take it easy. We might be geeks, but none of us is stupid. We have it under control. Do you remember the money SC has already made? Shouldn't that show you we have some business acumen? This might be a different method of promotion, but all our research shows it should work." She said it like she might be talking to a simpleton.

But he wasn't going to calm down. They couldn't be doing this. "You have no experience."

She laughed at him. Actually laughed. That belly laugh of hers again. "That's so sweet that you are worried about us. But you're wrong. This *is* a game. We *are* playing a game. It's only money, after all. We have nothing invested but a little time. Fun time. We're geeks, remember. We did all this, the game, the release plans. It's all a game. A digital game within a reality game. Penney did the sales plan. That was her game, her design. And we are going to make a bucket load of money. You have no trouble believing we have a game worth one hundred million, but you can't believe we know how to market it? Give us a break." She took a deep breath and went for it.

"And I guess, while you are acting so angry and loud, you should know that we are selling the game to Peter tomorrow at noon plus one."

He tried to control himself and calm down. They were going to sell what they thought would be a hundred-million-dollar game to Conrad? How did that happen? Where? In bed? Instead of just asking, he said dangerously, "Is that smart? Can you trust Conrad? Are you making decisions in the bedroom that should be made in the office?"

"You are such a jerk, Jake. None of this is your problem. You left, remember. Just be quiet, sit back, and watch. And shut up. Not another word. Just stop. If you can't watch quietly, leave. Now. Stop criticizing us and criticizing me. Stop insulting me. Go. Or be quiet. Those are your only two options. Decide now."

He took a deep breath, grit his teeth, pursed his lips. "Lips sealed," he growled.

"Good. Now I'm going to work with the geek stuff. You can stay if you keep quiet and you can get comfortable. This should take about an hour."

"One more question. Who's Michael?"

And now he did see that smile. That smile that warmed a room. The "I am happy" smile that made everyone grin.

"Sarah's fiancé." She almost said more about Michael and Sarah and how in love they were, how perfectly matched. How the gang had found Michael, a doctor and nutritionist, the same way they had found Peter. Michael was already in the trenches working in a children's clinic. But then Cilla remembered to whom she was speaking. The man who tossed her over for a tramp and never looked back. He wouldn't understand.

"Help yourself to coffee, snacks," she said as she got her mug and poured her own. "Kevin brings food from the main house. His housekeeper, Annie, keeps us fed. You'll probably meet her later."

He was suddenly hungry, so he got coffee and a plate of snacks, and followed her to the front area overlooking the garden. Of course. All Cilla here. Warm and comfortable. A Mac and a PC, two tablets and a couple of cells. One wall had preliminary sketches alongside photos showing the progression from a plain woman—Cilla?—to the beguiling seductress of M +1. Malissa?

She saw him looking at the series. Had forgotten they were there. But she was proud of them and explained. "I designed her. I made Malissa, one line of code at a time. Then I tested her out in the real world and incorporated reactions back into the test model. She is the perfect seductress. The love-to-hate heroine. If you ever play the game, you will love her. And hate her. She's a temptress."

And, Cilla didn't add, modeled after Sheri and created in Priscilla's condo. "She is fake. The perfect woman. Malissa. I designed her piece by piece for the game. And I became her and tried her out to see how she worked. How she related to the world. How she was viewed and accepted. Perfected her, so the game would be real."

She decided to tell him. "I probably knew before you did that there was trouble in paradise. I watched you during those last few weeks we were still together. I saw how you looked at Sheri. I saw the desire on your face when she walked by. I saw the bland looks I got. Priscilla is all those things you seemed to want in a woman. I could almost give you credit for creating her, because she was modeled after what you seemed to desire, which was everything I wasn't. At first I thought that if I could be what you were looking for, if I could be Priscilla, then I could get you back. Why shouldn't you have the perfect woman? I had the perfect man. Malissa is just the personification of that perfect woman.

But then I realized that I didn't like Malissa. I didn't want the man who would want Priscilla. If I had to be Priscilla to have you, I didn't want you."

Cilla knew she was not Priscilla. And never would be. Once the game went to market, Priscilla would go away forever and Cilla would come back. Geek Cilla. She liked Cilla, liked herself, and felt comfortable in her skin. Always had. She had lost her sense of self for a while when Jake left, but with the help of her friends, she had fought her way back. Priscilla's last day was supposed to be yesterday. She'd be put away today. Didn't need her for the sequel.

Jake studied the series and saw the change from a plain two-dimensional image to an enticing three dimensions. He watched Cilla while she worked, totally immersed in what she was doing. So lost in her work at her desk with her toys. So focused, so intense. His Cilla. The strong, self-confident geek.

Her eyes focused as she reverted to now and realized that she had lost an hour. She noticed him and her face went blank, as she became Priscilla again. "Oh, forgot you were here. Why are you still here? You met Peter. I don't think he is going to be your best friend forever." A small smile there. "And why would you even expect a man, whom you seem to know is your wife's lover, why would you expect him to be friendly?" This really puzzled her.

"Don't need him to be friendly, just approachable. What exactly is your relationship with him?"

"Remember our deal? My personal life is personal. You just keep on drawing your own conclusions. I am pretty sure you're going to think whatever you want to think anyhow."

"You decorate all the rooms or just this area?" because he didn't want to think of her with Peter and this corner had that Cilla comfort.

"I did it all. That was my assignment. Each section is set up to reflect each one of us. Just my bedroom back there and this corner are me." The decorating project had given her an objective beyond coding. Kept her mind off Jake. She had lived here for a month before the condo was ready. After Jake had left, when she realized he wasn't coming back, she couldn't live in that house alone. Hated it. She had lost so much there. When the gang had moved her here, they had instructed her to decorate. "Everyone designed her own individual space."

Then she stood. "I'm going to the gym and then home to work. I'm sure the rest of the gang will be moving out also, if they haven't already." She looked around and noticed they had left. "The limo will pick me up at home at ten thirty to take me to Peter's. Travel in style. We're all meeting there for the premiere. We expect to spend the first twelve hours together, sign the contract, and celebrate a little. And then have the limos carry us home. I can't say you'll be welcome, but you can ride with me."

"I'll go with you."

"OK. Now I'm off to the gym."

"I'll take you. I could work out too."

"No." Thank goodness, that wasn't going to happen. "All-girl gym," she lied.

"I'll drop you off and I'll wait back at the apartment."

"You could get me the data I need to review and your evidence on Peter. Bring that back to the condo with you." Maybe that would keep him busy.

"I said I'd consider turning that over to you. I'm still thinking."

"You cheat in business too, then. Not just marriage. You said we had a deal. How long are you 'going to be thinking'?"

"Till tomorrow." He ground out the words.

She just looked at him. Nodded. "I'm out of here."

"Wait, I'll drive you."

"No thanks, I can walk. Prefer to walk. Alone. You just finish your thinking. I kept my side of the bargain. I introduced you to Peter." And with that she walked out.

Jake drove to the office. He'd sat and watched Cilla work and wondered. What had she done when he left? Why had he never checked on her? When had she left their house? Why? When he walked in, Ron took one look at him and said, "What happened to you?"

"I met Conrad." Rubbing his chin.

"Doesn't look like a friendly meeting. What happened?"

"He said he didn't like the way I treated Cilla. Said it with his fist."

"He should have had to get in line then. Behind the gang of five. Even behind me. I told you to talk to her."

"Too late now," Jake said. "You should see her. Hot as those pictures. Cold as a glacier. A lot like Sheri. Hard."

"You should have talked to her. Explained. Not leave her like that, with no explanation. That was just wrong. She had a right to know."

"Yeah, probably. Couldn't. Can't. Let it be." Then he added, "The plan worked. Not only did I meet Conrad but I go to his place tonight with Priscilla. I should be able to do some spying of my own."

"How did you work that?"

"Played on her feelings for fairness and for Conrad. She'd do anything to clear his name. Wants access to what we have on him. Not just printouts. Wants to go into the actual coding. And I'm almost convinced to let her. I'll make a decision tonight. Well, not tonight. Tomorrow. You were right about that game. It's theirs. Debuting tonight and the gang is going to watch the first twelve hours of sales online. Watch and track the downloads and sales, and then they're selling the game to Conrad."

"Wow," was all Ron could come up with. "Well, I'll have everything together if you decide to let her look."

"It might be the whole gang that looks. They're all hackers to some degree, as I recall. They may find something we're overlooking. Let me see how it plays out tonight." He was tired and still felt a need to hit something. "I'm going to the gym and then back to her place. I'll call when I know something."

The walk to the gym calmed Cilla. The weather, a perfect spring day. Maybe she would sit on the deck when she got home. She worked out some of her anger on the punching bag, and then completed her Tai Chi form, emptying her mind. And then, because she felt like it, swam laps. She was pretty sure she wouldn't be able to do them at home. She was exhausted when she finally stopped, a good physical exhaustion that left her mind clear. She was wondering about the garden scenario when she entered the lobby. Paul signaled her over.

"Your guest, Mr. Jayden, has tipped me to call him when you came in."

"How much?" she asked, curious to know what prior knowledge of her arrival was worth to him.

"Forty bucks. He tried twenty, but I held out." He was enjoying himself.

"Cool. Buy Mary something pretty. And thanks." She didn't offer to tip him. She knew he'd be insulted.

She got off the elevator and opened the door to bright sunlight. Priscilla generally kept the drapes drawn tight.

"Hard to believe you don't have a computer here, where you live," Jake said suspiciously.

Oops. "Use my tablet and cell at home." It wasn't a complete lie. She always had her tablet and cell. The computers were next door where she, Cilla, lived. Not here, where Priscilla lived.

"No food, no coffee, no play clothes, no jammies."

"I can get food and coffee out. And do I look like I wear jammies?" With the seductive voice. "You going through my drawers?"

"I'll bet you do still live in the house after all. There's no trash. No laundry. This is like a model home. You don't live here. Where do you live? With Peter? Or John. Or is there another man besides the two of them? Bob?" He'd been pacing. Steaming. Imagining.

"Finally acting like a detective, Jake? Ask your research department. I'm not answering any questions. Where I spend my nights, how many men I'm sleeping with, is really none of your business anymore. You threw away the privilege to know."

She started to walk past him, but he reached out and grabbed her arm and pulled her around to face him. "Tell me," he snarled.

"You're hurting me," she said softly, calmly. "Let go."

"I'm sorry, I didn't mean that. I'm your husband. Tell me where you're living."

She shook her arm. "You don't have the right to run the husband line. It won't compile. The Jake that Cilla married was a kind, loving, compassionate man. One who laughed. And he left a long time before you left physically. Before the cold, hard, calculating Jake you became left. This Jake, you, now, would be this Priscilla's husband. You both are a perfect match. Priscilla is fashioned on Sheri, the woman you preferred over your own wife. But you're not getting this Priscilla. So don't use the husband line on me. You have no rights."

She watched him. Watched that register. Actually saw a reaction. So he had some feeling still.

She decided she wouldn't explain where she lived. She turned again to leave. "I'll be back to pick you up."

She went out and closed the door behind her. Waited a few minutes, but he didn't follow. Then she went into her own apartment, breathing a sigh of relief at the view of the garden, the soft sunlight. She sank into the comfy rocking recliner. Tiff jumped up and curled around in her lap. Purring. Nothing as comforting as a cat purring. She rocked and thought. She wasn't going to cry.

After a while she told herself, *I really need to get out of these clothes. Now.* Stripping on her way to the shower, she turned the water hot and stepped in. Washed Priscilla off. Priscilla was being deep sixed today. She was done with Priscilla. She loved Priscilla's easy hairdo, though. And the earrings. They made her happy. So she would keep those when she shed Priscilla forever.

Cilla's shower stall was the normal shower stall, not a room-sized shower. No overhead rainfall showers with surrounding light. No steam generator, no hydrotherapy massage jets. Just the one spray nozzle with a simple, easy-to-use three-way setting. But she did indulge in long hot showers.

She hung the hated green dress and folded the rest of the outfit for cleaning and storage. Pulled on her comfy jammies. Set out a meal for Tiff. Relaxed with a late lunch on the deck in the sun amid her flowers. She owed this time to herself. And she sat and thought code. Walked through the code for the garden app. It really could work.

She thought about making her famous stuffed potato snacks, but Peter would have a grand buffet. She would just sit and enjoy her flower garden with Tiff in her lap.

She was ready when security called about the limo, right on time. She was revved. Excited. Would their plans work as projected? The sales be as good?

She knocked on his door. Laughed at herself. His door. He should fit right into the décor there. Priscilla was so much Sheri that he should be comfortable there. Cilla probably should hope he didn't invite Sheri over. Come to think of it, he never had told her what became of Sheri. Or if another woman—women?—had taken her place.

Oops, he would wonder why she was knocking on the door instead of calling from the limo. She'd go inside and get a thumb drive. Didn't have to explain.

He was ready. The door opened before she finished knocking. Ready, but not rested, he looked tired. He started to say something and just stopped. And stared at her. A full range of emotions passed over his face. She couldn't read them. What were they all about? But his face quickly settled on blank. He must be tired to slip like that. Then she realized she had not put on Priscilla's costume; she was Cilla again. Wearing the universal geek outfit of T-shirt, jeans, and sandals. Not hot Priscilla, Sheri's emulation. Not his type. She went in and got the thumb drive, not waiting for him to ask where she kept her change of clothes.

They didn't say anything on the way down. Jake probably because he was practicing not saying anything stupid, and he was thinking the only way to do that was to keep his mouth shut. *What a difference a day makes,* he thought. Yesterday the cold, impersonal seductress. Beautiful, yes. Hot, yes. Did he want that woman? No way. Not ever. Today, though, his warm, strong Cilla was back. The one he wanted. Needed. Loved. Lost. She didn't want him. He had made her hate him. He had lost so much. Destroyed it. Thrown it away.

Cilla said good night to Jameson, the night security guard, and told him they would be back tomorrow afternoon.

They arrived to a party atmosphere. The gang was high on anticipation, nibbling on snacks and watching the three giant screens Peter had set up. He proudly explained, "Each download site is shown on this main screen. Each site will register the sales as they happen. Total sales here," he pointed, "and the 'esoteric formula' will run at the bottom and keep a real time tally of my cost."

He took a breath and continued, "The second screen has the blogs where we have made posts already. It will show any M Plus One communications as they are generated. We can see response to sales and the game on the last screen." They settled in to wait for midnight.

Saturday

Exactly one minute after midnight, the downloads began. They appeared to be the same across the country. The formula was already displaying Peter's cost.

When twenty minutes elapsed and nothing appeared on the other two screens, Jake suggested, "Couldn't you salt the mine, so to speak, and post great reviews on the blogs?" He trailed off because they all looked at him as if he had suggested murder. "What? It would be just like you posted the original comments." He said this defensively. He felt very much the outsider here.

"The original posts are marketing promotion," Penney explained as if to a poor student. "What you are suggesting is illegal. As you should know, judging by the con term you used. We don't do illegal. Besides, we don't need to. The game is good and will sell itself." She had barely finished speaking when the other two screens activated at the same time.

"Look," she said. "The posts are coming now." And they were good. "Amazing graphics! Unique challenges! Great action!" And the tributes kept coming.

Jake was saved from further embarrassment as the gang tried to keep up with all the comments. Numbers flashed by on the first screen as downloads increased. At the end of the first hour, they took time for snacks, still watching.

For the next few hours, they snacked, wandering around the room, watching the screens, talking desultorily. Pointing out some extreme comment or post. They would wander off to sit and play with their own computers, calling one another over to look at some code in progress. Cilla was working on something she said was her garden app. John was busy inputting the code for the new chapters of the sequel, and they all wandered over to advise and offer input.

All except Sarah and Michael, who stayed by the screens. Jake had finally met Michael. And it did appear that he and Sarah would be doing more than work together.

Jake observed the close camaraderie of the gang and saw Cilla wander outside. Then he saw Conrad follow her. When he decided to tag along, he saw Conrad with his arms around Cilla, his chin on her head, rubbing her back. Comforting her softly. "It's all right honey. It's all right. What can I do to make it better?"

Jake saw red. "Yes, what can you do to make it better for my wife, Conrad?" he growled.

They both stiffened. "Dry your eyes, honey, go on in. I'll talk to Jake," Conrad said to her calmly, comforting.

Cilla backed away, one hand wiping her eyes. "Don't hit him again, Peter, please? Just talk. OK? Promise me?"

"Just talk, Cilla."

They both watched her go inside, head down. She never looked at Jake.

Peter took out a cigarette. Offered one to Jake, who shook his head.

"Dirty habit, I know, but sometimes circumstances call for one." He lit up, giving himself time to decide where to start.

"The gang came to me about three months ago. They found me at my morning coffee with this wild tale about a new, bleeding-edge game they wanted to sell me. Sounds crazy. But I listened because they shouldn't have been able to track me down there or get to me, and I wanted to know how they did it.

"That Penney, she knows how to present an investment," he continued. "The plan actually made sense. And they're cute kids, you know? Smart. Sharp. They understand how the world works and want to make it better. They showed me the game. Let me play for a while. Awhile? They stopped me after an hour. That's all the time they gave me. And it was all I needed to make a decision. I was hooked in the first few minutes. We went back to my office and signed papers. Right then. Crazy. Didn't even do due diligence. Did it later, though." He shook his head, remembering.

"Over the last couple of months, I have spent a vast amount of time with that gang, working with them. They are amazing, but then I imagine you know that. They make me feel alive. Their enthusiasm for life is contagious. And Cilla? I love Cilla. I will tell you, I love Cilla like a sister. I can see you don't believe that, but it's the truth. You are so wrong about so much that you might never get straight. If I had known you when you hurt her so bad, I like to think you would not be walking around now. That's neither here nor there, though. Stick around until we finish the sale. I have a couple of announcements that might make things a little clearer to you." Then he walked inside.

Jake felt exhausted. He just kept on saying stupid things. And regretting them. His leg hurt. He laughed at that. Big surprise. His leg always hurt. Another way he had managed to screw up. He decided to stay where he was for the rest of the evening. He couldn't say anything stupid to anyone if he was out here by himself. When the sun came up, he went back in for the breakfast buffet.

The numbers on the board showed that the gang's estimates had been low. They watched the numbers march past the fifty-million dollar mark and then up to and past the ninety-million mark. And it looked like 90 percent of the online posts were positive.

The morning continued much the same as the night before. The gang working on tablets, eating, napping, cheering the board if an especially good post came through. Even Conrad seemed happy to see the numbers go up. The morning dragged for Jake.

They were down to the last half hour when Peter asked for their attention. The gang had already cleared an easy $105.2 million, probably would end near $110 million. Penney's esoteric formula had been flattening for the last hour, and Peter's price tag could be determined.

"I would like to suggest two changes in our contract," he said to them.

Here it comes, thought Jake. He wants to change the formula and pay less. Jake looked around, but the gang just waited until Peter continued.

"Royalties for Sarah's Child should be double what we decided in the contract and they should last indefinitely. That will be my contribution to Sarah's Child. Sarah's Child will be guaranteed that income. The royalties should not be subtracted from my cost. They will be in addition to my payment." That Bronx cheer the gang did so well went up again.

"Thank you," said Michael, who was holding Sarah as she cried.

"And," Peter added after a pause, when he was sure he had their attention. He went to John and took his hand. "John has agreed to marry me. We will make a formal announcement soon. It means we are both out of the closet, and I hope it doesn't cost any of you any distress." Now there was a real Bronx cheer. "There is champagne to celebrate," he finished, slightly self-conscious.

They laughed and hugged each other. Apparently it was no surprise to the gang. They appeared to be thrilled for the two of them.

Not the announcement Jake had expected. He really was a fool. Accusing Cilla of sleeping with either man. Both of them. Even when he knew it wasn't true, that she wouldn't have. But he was so jealous. And how could he not have seen John and Peter? He should have known.

They celebrated for another hour and then broke up to go home and take the rest of the day off. They would meet back in the office tomorrow. Jake rode back with Cilla.

"You can look at what we have on Conrad in the morning," he said.

She looked over at him. "Thank you. I appreciate it. At the risk of alienating you, would you tell me why?"

"I like him."

"Because he's not sleeping with me?"

"No, because he protected you. Leave it there. OK? Go home, wherever that is, get some rest. Tomorrow you can go with me to my office and look at what we have. Call me when you're ready." With that he put his head back and closed his eyes. He would call Ron and have him available in the morning.

Sunday

She knocked on his door at seven thirty the following morning and found him ready to take her to the office. They picked up breakfast on the way.

Ron greeted her with a hug. He had always liked her, and he had everything ready for her, their findings and the web addresses, so she could look at the original evidence. She sat down and got started, sipping on her coffee. Food could wait.

Jake watched her as she worked. His geek. He remembered her. He had loved to watch her get lost in the code in her head. He would get lost himself, watching her work through a routine, or module, she called them. She'd described them as a group of lines of code that did a single separate task. A task that the computer program might call upon multiple times. She compared her code to a remote control and the modules to the buttons. You didn't have to walk over to the TV each time you wanted to control it. You reached for the remote control and selected a button. The code would be the remote, the modules would be the buttons. A sort of short cut.

He could almost see the steps on her face as she shut out the world and worked the code line by line. Sometimes with her eyes shut, sometimes gazing into the ether. He could even tell when she made a mistake and went back to fix it. He could tell. So he watched her now. This time he was watching her going over someone else's code. Savoring what he once had. What he had lost.

He watched her work her way through, picking her way. Fascinated. Saw when she found the weak spot and slowly followed it. She was puzzled, he could tell. And she slowed down, moving carefully. Saw her eyes widen and the small, "Oh" as she found something. She was moving almost furtively now. And stopped abruptly, looking up. Shocked. He stood, worried.

"What happened?" he asked.

She saw him and shook her head, still thinking. Her head was tilted sideways as she considered, only her eyes moving.

He saw her eyes widen as she reached a conclusion. She viewed the monitor. Not quite believing. Her eyes scanning the code. Nodding once. Making a decision. She slowly picked out more lines. Finally, she said to herself, "That should do it. We should be OK now." Double-checked herself, nodded again. "Yes, we're OK."

"What?" he demanded. "What?"

"Give me a minute," she said. "To translate out of geek speak." She took five minutes; he could see her working it out.

"OK. Going in it looked like really bad hacking. Someone who only thinks he knows what he is doing. Amateurish. Not Peter's type of work at all."

"'Oh yeah," Jake said. "Of course you would say that."

"No, it's not Peter's. Ask anyone. Coding is like handwriting; everyone has his own style. This isn't Peter's."

"Maybe he's disguising it."

"It's possible, this code is so bad. There really is no signature. This code is stuffed with unnecessary and useless lines that go nowhere. It's sloppy and unprofessional." She stopped, held up her hand.

"Wait. I'm not finished. Bad code. That's what I thought at first. But there's more. That bad code is a cover for more advanced code underneath. Not Peter's again. I found where the coder laid down the fake trail for you to follow. But that's not the worst of it. There is a trap. He, the hacker, left a trap to spring whenever anyone found and followed the fake trail. And then the trap leads him back to the investigating source. You sprang that trap. You might have led him right back here.

"Right back here," she repeated. "They know you found the trail to Peter. And they know who you are. You've been compromised. Most likely. And they may even be in your system. Depends on your security." She held up her hand again.

"Wait, it's even worse. There was another trap. I was looking for it. Found it. I think it leads to a backdoor into your client company's network. A backdoor created and left open by your hacker. I don't think the guy hacked in. He didn't get by the security. I think a door was left partially open for him. A backdoor. Only someone who helped write the original code could do that. Or someone who was around when the code was updated, if it was updated.

"This guy is good—not as good as me, though," she said with the smile he loved. "And he didn't try to hide his tracks. Felt safe. Didn't think anyone would follow him this far without getting caught. And even though he didn't hack in, the traps should lead back to him as a coder. And I'm betting the other company was hacked the same way. You probably have one person who was involved with both client companies. You can check their IT, technology, payrolls. You should be able to find him that way. Although, there are only so many coders, and you might find an overlap of people."

Ron spoke up then. "You're saying that one person worked on the original code for both companies. Or helped update the code. That person left, what, a hole? A hole he could climb through whenever he wanted and get inside the secure areas? And his code also let him know if anyone came looking for him? And he set up a false trail of little bread crumbs to Conrad? Why Conrad?"

"Yes. All of that. You need to examine all of that, but you need to go outside to a clean secure unit and check your own security and see if there has been a breach, if you have been hacked. Then you can work your way through the code. You need my gang for that. My gang and Peter, maybe. He's not an expert, but he is capable. And you probably need some of our new security software. It will protect us as we follow his tracks and stalk him. We have some great camouflage and masking code. No one knows about it because it's not on the open market. Yet. We haven't decided if, when, or how we want to sell it. And any code we don't have, we can write if we need it." They would deal with that if the problem came up.

"But that's off track. Nobody can catch a thief like a thief. And Sarah is the person you need here. She might be able to recognize this guy's code signature. It has a vague feeling. Like I have seen it some-where before. And John. Both of them. I don't know why they picked Peter. Might have just picked a name out of a hat.

"Also, we can scrub your system. After we catch the guy. If it's infected, we might want to leave it as is until we catch him, might need it to catch him. So meanwhile you will need a secure location. That's us again. No one does secure like we do," she bragged.

"Both Sarah and John should look at this program. They're experts. And, it just occurs to me, we did research on Peter. We need to go back and see if we tripped anything. But we would have noticed, I'm sure. Wonder how long this trap has been out there," she said almost to herself.

Ron and Jake looked at each other. "Can you show me?" Ron asked.

"I don't think we should chance it again on your system. I laid down a false trail for them just now. They'll think you were just going back for a second look. Let's go to the gatehouse. It's secure there. I don't want them to see us going in again from here. They might get suspicious. There's no reason for you to keep going back if you believe Peter did it. And I don't want to make copies. I don't know how far they might be into your system."

There was silence while Jake thought about her conclusions. Finally, he looked up at Cilla. "OK, the three of us can take a break. Go out for a late lunch and then wander over to the gatehouse. No calls to any-one, yet. Both hacked companies have top-level government security contracts. God, this is a mess. We don't know who they are or if they're actually watching us. We need to have some ideas before we notify the FBI. Let's go."

They ate a quick lunch at the café. Ron and Cilla talked about the game. Jake worried about all the consequences. He would have to notify Munson, their man in the FBI. Later. When they knew if, and how badly, they might have been infiltrated. And when they had some ideas for fixing the problems. Then it would be time to call counter terrorism.

While Cilla walked ahead, crossing the street, the two men lagged behind, discussing how to handle the possible consequences. Jake looked up at the screech of tires and a revving engine and saw a car heading directly for Cilla. Saw her stumble when she turned to look.

He jumped forward, grabbing her by the arm, twisting and dragging her back. He lost his balance as the car narrowly missed them, and they both tumbled into the gutter.

"Goddamn, goddamn. Are you alright? Cilla? Cilla. Answer me." Jake sounded panic-stricken, turning her over and checking her.

She stared at him a second, dazed. "Just got the breath knocked out of me when we fell. I'm OK. Let me up."

He helped her up and held her until he was sure she was steady. Or maybe until he was steady.

"Did you see that?" Ron was yelling. "Did you see that? That crazy idiot almost ran her down. I can't believe it. Is she OK? Are you both OK?"

"Yeah, we are. Did anyone get a tag number?" he asked, looking at Ron, who shook his head, and then around at the crowd that had rushed over.

"It didn't have a tag," one young kid said. He was excited. "I was looking for it. I thought I was going to be the hero, but it didn't have a tag."

Jake shrugged when Cilla said, "I'm OK, no harm done. Just another careless idiot. Let's go." But he wasn't happy. The car had accelerated as it headed toward Cilla. It hadn't veered away but aimed for her. Accident? Or something more?

Jake stayed nearby the rest of the way to the gatehouse. He would be keeping a close eye on her. That meant he would have to find out where she was living. And then he realized he probably knew.

Cilla had texted Sarah, who was waiting for them. Cilla explained what she had discovered, and then they waited while Sarah took a look. She sent them away. Couldn't work with them all breathing down her neck and asking questions.

"Go to the other side of the room, or leave," Sarah said. "Out of my office. It looks like you're right. This will take a while. Probably a long while. Hours. As I see it, there are a number of things we need to know. Probably, in order of priority, the list would be..."

She counted the items off on her fingers.

"One, clear Peter. Why or how does the supposed trail lead back to him? We all know he's not involved, but we have to prove it to Jake."

She said this with obvious distaste. She didn't like Jake. "Two, do I need to cloak or mask my approaches? Three, how many traps and where are they? Four, unravel the traps. Five, can their system be hacked?

"Six, is there a backdoor built into both networks, and can I find it? I don't know how you found that first one, Cilla. Seven, who built it? And is that the same person who set the traps? We might be able to tell that from the coding.

"Eight, Jake needs to match IT employee lists from both client firms and see if he gets a hit. Though I agree with Cilla. I would expect to find three or four names the same on both lists. If the firms went for the best, I would expect some overlap. Nine, if two systems are compromised, are there more systems compromised? Ten, is the system compromised at your office, Jake? And finally, I repeat, clear Peter."

She looked at them. "Anything else anyone can think of? No? OK. Get out. Go away. I can't concentrate with a bunch of people breathing down my neck."

"Can I stay?" Ron asked.

"If you can be quiet. And sneak out when you get bored watching me. First I need to give myself a cloak and then find the traps. That alone will take a few hours. I need to be sure I find all the traps. I'm sure there are more than one. Then I will try hacking into the system to see how difficult that might be for a normal hacker. I'll be at least all night."

"Can do," Ron agreed. "I want to see, learn."

"I'll call your wife and tell her I have you on an overnight assignment," Jake told Ron. He turned to Cilla, "I have some errands to run. I'll come back and take you home in about three hours."

"I can get home by myself," she protested.

"No. I'll be back. Wait for me." It sounded like an order.

"I. Can. Get. Home. By. Myself," she repeated slowly. "I have been walking to work and back by myself for eight months now. And I intend to continue doing so. You will be wasting your time if you come back. I am going home when I get ready, when I catch up on my coding here. I am not waiting for you." She was unyielding. "Besides, you don't even know where I live. Or whom I'm living with. Just how do you propose to take me home?

He gave up and stalked out. She was right, and he supposed he would keep hearing variations of the theme. Besides, he wanted to check out their house to eliminate it as her address. He wanted to verify she wasn't living there.

He had been by their house earlier, outside, when he had first waited for her. Now he used his key and went inside. He had expected to have to break in, but she hadn't changed the lock. So he could get in when he came back? *If he came back?* he wondered. The house looked as if it had just been scrubbed, and he remembered there was an invoice for weekly cleaning. No food in the kitchen. Even emptier then Priscilla's condo. The house felt cold, empty. It had always been a warm, happy refuge when they'd lived here together. No one was living here now. He understood why she had left. There was no warmth here. No love. It was a cold, stark shell. A sad, empty place. They had been so happy there, until he had ruined it.

He walked into the dining room. Touched the table, remembering he had taken her there. She'd worked him up and then run away, laughing, "Catch me." They had just had breakfast and were doing dishes. She washing, he drying.

She had passed him the wet plate from the sink, licking her lip, smiling at him. Daring him. At first just the tip of her tongue, just barely poking it out, on her upper lip. Then she licked across her upper lip to the corner of her smug smile. She could make him hard in a heartbeat, and she knew it. His eyes were riveted on her mouth and unconsciously he licked his upper lip, copying her. When her tongue reached the corner of her mouth, he reached out with his free hand and grabbed her, pulling her close to him, the plate wedged between them. He licked her lips. And when she opened, he invaded her mouth.

Their tongues battled for a moment; she tasted so sweet, of maple syrup, because she had made pancakes for breakfast. She rubbed her hips against that part of him that was sticking out. They kissed for a long time, letting the passion take over. Breathing heavy. Trying different angles, their tongues performing different dances. She finally pushed him away, and that was when she had run off. Not far. She'd only made it to the dining room.

He grabbed her and lifted her onto the table as she kissed him hungrily.

"Hurry," she said. He pulled off her T-shirt. That was all she had on. He looked at her. God, he never got tired of just looking at her. Slowly his gaze came back to her face. She had started it; he was going to finish it on his own schedule. He smiled into her eyes and leaned down to her breast, first licking lightly. His tongue twirling around her nipple as it hardened. Then sucking. When he had her moaning, he went to work on the other breast, rubbing the first with his thumb. Thanking God for two. He didn't stop until he had her thrashing.

When she reached for his pajama bottoms, he caught her hands and leaned her back on the table, holding both hands above her head. Now it was his turn to laugh at her. He held her with one hand and reached down with the other to stroke her between her thighs. She was wet. Ready for him.

"Now," she pleaded. "Now, please."

"Oh no. Not yet. My turn to tease." He stroked her slowly, back and forth, watching her eyes heat with passion. Stuck two fingers in her wetness and saw those eyes go blank as her hips came off the table, arching into his hand. She was panting.

"Please, please."

He smiled and freed himself, questioned her with his eyes, and at her nod, guided himself and pressed slowly into her. Now her eyes rolled up.

She felt so good around him as he worked his way in slowly. Just stopped to enjoy her warmth, and tightness. She squeezed him tighter, making him move, sucking him in further. All the way.

"OK, OK, this won't take long," he'd promised her. But it did. It took a long time. He was having such fun that he brought her to a peak and stopped. And waited. Then set a rhythm, slowly pushed in and out, while sucking her breast. Bringing her to a peak again.

"Jake, stop playing, you're killing me. Finish," she panted the order. He knew she was close because she was barely breathing, he worked her hard. She tried to hurry him. Grabbing his butt, pulling him deeper. That just made her more distressed. She wiggled her hips. Breathed into his ear. Bit his earlobe. Those generally worked for her.

And maybe they did, because this time he took pity on her, and when he thrust again, he sent her rolling over the cliff into free fall, into an orgasm that rippled and rolled through her. And almost finished him off. But he waited through it, straining not to lose control as the spasms swept through her. She smiled as she clung to him through it and finally fell back, weak from the exertion. When she caught her breath, he started all over again, pumping slowly in and out till he brought her to the edge again, and this time he let himself go over the cliff with her, holding her tight.

They lay across the table for a long, long time, both of them sated and smiling. She'd laughed at him when she could.

"You always come through for me. I love you. You always know what I need. On the dining room table? You just did me on the dining room table? I'll never be able to eat here again."

"You never have eaten here," he had said. "I don't know why we had to buy it. We always eat in the kitchen. Even when we have company, we eat in the kitchen." He smiled. "I finally found a use for the dining room table."

And she just looked at him self-contentedly, waiting.

"Oh, OK, I get it. Works for me. The real purpose of a dining room table." And he had picked her up and taken her to the bedroom, because he wasn't done with her yet.

He had been her first. He was both surprised and pleased somehow. He had expected her to be experienced. When he asked her why, how had she not ever had sex, she had said that she always knew there was only one man for her. She hadn't saved herself for him; she just hadn't been interested in anyone else. She didn't want to play the dating game, kiss men she didn't really like. Didn't want to waste her time. She was busy anyhow. Maybe if she got to be fifty without her one man, maybe then she would settle. Well, maybe forty. She had thought she would enjoy sex. She had plenty of time.

She knew he was the one the first time she met him. He was the one she was waiting for.

"So why did you make it so difficult for me?" he'd asked.

"Well, you had to know I was the only one for you," she said simply. Her logic. She saw things so clearly. Surely she would have listened to him. If he could have explained back then. If he could have talked about it.

He was hard just remembering her here. He touched the table again. That spot was always special. She gave so much of herself to him. All of herself. They were so in tune. Every time. How could it be so good every time? He didn't have to see her to get hard. Just thinking about her could do it. How could he have just walked away from that?

He went upstairs. Looked through the rooms. She wasn't living here. He didn't want to go into their bedroom, but forced himself. Empty and cold. He wasn't going to think of the times they had spent themselves in the bed. He didn't look at it. He saw her engagement ring on the dresser. At first he felt anger that she had left it behind, but then he remembered it was he who had left the marriage behind. His fault the ring was here and not on her finger. She must have a top-notch maid service for it to be just lying out like that.

He drove back to the condo. Used his key on the elevator and walked over to the other apartment. The door was locked, of course, but he picked the lock. Took a while; it was a good lock. He opened the door and walked in. Recognized Cilla's familiar fragrance. Fresh and clean. And the rooms were bright, cheerful, comfortable. The curtains open, the sun shining in. He walked through, breathing in her scent. Admiring the furniture. Sure this was Cilla. This was the Cilla he had married. Eclectic was the only word he could use. Old mixed with new. Dark wood mixed with light wood. And everywhere, color and flowers. Soft color, happy. Not loud like Penney. A little more subdued, pastels maybe.

He looked out through the glass doors at the rooftop. A colorful garden. Of course she would have a garden. And what looked to be a lap pool beyond the garden.

He was just reaching for the door to go out and look closer when he saw movement from the corner of his eye. He twisted, crouched down behind the chair, and pulled his gun from his back all in one smooth motion. Didn't see anyone. But he knew something had moved. He looked lower.

A cat. An angry orange cat snarled at him. And jumped up on an armoire. He laughed at himself. Put his gun away. A cat. He shook his head. She had always wanted a cat. He had been reluctant. Same as he had been about a pool. He was happy she had been able to finally get them for herself. Walked over to pat the cat.

"Hi, kitty," he said as he reached a hand up to rub the cat's head. The cat snarled at him again and brought blood with a swift swipe of his claws.

"Shit, cat." He looked at the blood welling and pulled out his handkerchief and wrapped it around his hand. The cat just smiled at him. "Figures she would have an attack cat."

He shook his head and went back to the slider. Opened it and walked into Cilla's lush garden. It smelled sweet out here, flowery. He saw some tomatoes and peppers growing. More, but those were all he recognized.

He walked to the lap pool. She had asked for a pool when they were married. He had meant to get around to it. Seemed she had managed it by herself. He went back in and sat down in the living room, looking out over the flower garden. It was peaceful. Restful. Of course it was Cilla's. It would be.

The next thing he knew, he heard the door opening and her voice calling, "Hey, Tiff. I'm home."

She walked in and saw him sitting there. After a startled moment, a look of disgust on her face. Like she smelled something rotten.

"So you finally figured it out," she said. "And you couldn't ask, or tell me you figured it out. You had to invade my privacy. Just felt like you would be welcome in my home?" She reproved him and then she noticed the handkerchief around his hand.

"Good. Tiff had a go at you. Too bad he's not an attack dog. I could have found you in pieces then. You are so arrogant. So sure of yourself. Tell me how you feel. To force your way into my home. Wander around. Touch my things. Were you in my panty drawer? Do you feel like a peeping tom? A voyeur? A rapist? Because that's what you being here feels like to me. Makes me feel dirty to see you in here. Sitting in my chair. You make me feel violated. Filthy."

"No," he said. "I never intended that. I never meant for you to feel that way. I just had to know if I was right about where you live."

"It is always you. What you want. What you feel. What you need to know. You never considered how I might feel to find you in my home." She was so angry, she didn't dare yell. Because it was more than anger. New disappointment in him. She spoke softly, the venom just beneath the surface. Softly, angry.

"Get out. Now. Take your superior, satisfied self and leave. And now that you know Peter didn't do any hacking, and you have an expert hacker helping you, it might be time for you to move out of my condo and drop me out of the loop. I'll tell Sarah to deal directly with you. There is no more reason for you to need to speak to me. Get out."

She stepped away from the door, leaving it open for him.

"I'm sorry," he said. He reached out to touch her, but she stepped back.

"Don't touch me. Just leave."

Admitting defeat, he left and went back to Priscilla's cold, empty condo.

Cilla stooped and picked up Tiff and sat in her rocking chair. Not the chair he had been in.

"What a good cat. You are such a good cat. You get tuna as a reward for scratching that mean old man." She gave the cat a hug and went to get him the tuna. She wasn't going to cry over this. She really wasn't surprised that Jake had let himself in. Just offended and hurt. And she was sure it would wear off.

She really missed the Jake she had married. The kind man who loved her. Maybe now that this Jake was back, they could get divorced. She had not considered divorce before. Well, he hadn't been around and she had expected that he would file. Maybe being married gave him more freedom to play the field. She would miss the Jake she loved, but he was gone anyway. Losing this Jake would be no loss. It hurt to see the man she loved as this rigid, hard-hearted person. One who seemed happy to cut her to the bone whenever he got the chance.

She loved him, still expected to see him transform into her warm, caring Jake. Silly girl. She would have to talk to him about divorce.

Tomorrow. There was a goal for her. To be single. To move into her cottage by the beach with Tiff.

Tiff ate his tuna. Big surprise. Purring all the while. So she would do the garden and swim in the lap pool. A long swim. Work on that code in her head. And plug it into the computer later. Those things always settled her.

She spent an hour in the garden. It was a peaceful, calm place. She loved the feel of the soil under her fingernails. She sat back and looked and was pleased with the arrangement and added another subroutine to the app in her head. She made a mental note to be sure to include shape, size, and color of blooms and plants when first set in the ground and then again during growth, and again when full grown.

She swam a long time. Wore out her body. Was surprised to see that another hour had passed. Fixed herself dinner, a fried egg sandwich with lots of mayonnaise, some spinach, and cheese. Tiff got a quarter of it. His without the spinach. She sat and ate at the small oval oak table she had found at a garage sale. It fit here perfectly.

Her mind went back to her code as she looked at the Mac alongside a printer on the counter and the iPad beside it. The pretty vases in soft colors in the window. And the clutter of mail, notes, and bills. *Home*, she thought. *My home, my sanctuary.* Tiff purred as he tore his sandwich apart. Didn't seem to remember he had eaten most of a can of tuna earlier. *I really like it here*, she thought. *Why do I want that cottage on the beach? I might have to rethink that.*

Jake was right, of course. This is what she needed to survive. A refuge. Peace and comfort. Not the pristine, perfectly arranged, very proper magazine spread next door. She wondered how he had known that. He must still have some understanding of her. Was that a good thing? And what was she doing thinking about him again? She would ask him about a divorce tomorrow.

"Come on, Tiff, let's go to the playroom and get some of this code typed out."

Her playroom, two of the bedrooms combined with the adjoining wall removed. Another spot, with a view of the garden that made her happy. Lots of counter space for individual projects. She had the counters made special so she could leave her projects out and open.

She could just pick out the one she wanted and work on it. Two more computers and a laptop. And two printers and a top-of-the-line scanner. Maybe all the equipment was overkill. Not overkill. Just enough. Why did she buy that scanner? Oh, yes, it was a special project that required her to scan in some large diagrams.

And she had a second project in mind, if she could just get around to it. A map, one street in a small town. With each house located on it drawn to size. Each house with a story. A story told by an audio track with closed captioning. Printable. Who built it, who lived there, who were their families, their descendants, how they lived. She pulled out a new legal pad and wrote "Scan in the maps," and "Insert the interactive buttons on the houses." Can I find pictures of the houses, then and now? Pictures of the builders and their families? The current occupants? Talk to some of the families living there now. People told everything online. In e-mails and blogs, Twitter, Tumblr. Should be easy enough to get current stuff. Look in the library. Maybe the historical society. Where had she stopped in the project? She had it partially done, both the research and the programming. Better check that out. Later. Right now, she went over to work on the gardening app.

The next time she looked up, it was midnight. Tiff was curled up by her mouse. She stretched and patted herself on the back. *Good work, girl,* she told herself. This might be another moneymaking app as well as a scene for the game sequel.

She went to bed and slept with the cat.

Monday

Sarah called at nine. She had some of what they needed. Which meant Cilla had to call Jake.

When he answered, she told him to meet at the gatehouse when he was ready. She was leaving in ten minutes. And hung up. Didn't give him a chance to insist that he drive. She expected he would call back and was surprised that he didn't. It had been raining, so she was taking her car. She expected he would be in the entranceway or the garage. She was actually singing a little tune as she drove out of the garage without seeing him.

Sarah must have been successful on all fronts. Cilla hoped there was good evidence clearing Peter because that would mean that this Jake, whom she didn't like, would be gone. No longer reminding her every time she saw him of the Jake she had loved. Then she mentally kicked herself. It was the old Jake she loved who had left her. She didn't like either Jake. *Note to self, meet with Jake, and move forward with divorce.*

Her rear tires skidded as she left the garage. There had been just enough rain to make the roads slick. She tried to pay more attention to her driving. As she turned into the drive to the gatehouse, she heard a snap, and the steering wheel lost all resistance and spun in her hand. It was no longer steering the car. She was heading right for the solid brick buttress at the gated entrance. She tried again to steer into the turn, but the wheel just spun around uselessly in her hands.

"No, no," she said hopelessly. "Stop. Stop." *As if that will work,* a part of her thought. She knew her words wouldn't help. She was standing on the brake, but still going much too fast as the piling seemed to grow and then smashed into the front of the car. She was aware of a loud sound of tearing metal and shattering glass and then felt the shoulder strap tighten like a vise. The airbag smashed into her face.

"Cilla? Cilla? Are you OK? God. Are you OK?" She heard Jake's voice as if from a distance.

Jake couldn't get the driver's door open; it was wedged. He ran around the passenger side, pulling out his cell and hitting 911.

"Cilla?" he said gently. "You OK? Please be OK, please." He prayed under his breath. He got in and reached across to her wrist. To feel for a pulse.

Her hand moved. She opened her eyes with horror.

"Ooh, that was scary. Am I OK?" she asked groggily.

"Don't move. Let me see." Then, into the phone, he said. "I have a single-car accident at Bayside. One person, I'm checking for injuries. But you should send an ambulance."

He reached for her wrist again to check her pulse. "Just sit still, kitten. Give me a minute to see how you are. Do you hurt anywhere?"

"Yeah, I hurt all over." She took a deep breath. Not smart. "No. I think I'm OK. Just achy from the airbag and the scare. I'm OK."

Her pulse was fast, as you would expect. He checked her eyes. And felt her all over gently.

"The ambulance is coming. Just sit there. I think you're OK, though." He hugged her and kissed her forehead.

The ambulance was quick and the paramedics took over, agreeing with his assessment but wanting to have her checked out at the hospital. Sometimes the airbags caused damage. They helped her out of the car.

"How could you have missed that turn? What were you doing? Texting?" Jake demanded furiously.

Wow, she thought. Her head was clear now. She had liked the gentle, caring Jake. But now that other one was back. She looked at him with distaste.

"Oh, go away."

But at that point, a cop said, "You were texting, lady?"

Cilla had not even been aware that the police had arrived, she jumped.

"No," Cilla said patiently. "I was not texting. That was just another thoughtless assumption from the jerk who will soon be my ex-husband. The steering wheel broke just as I made the turn. There was no resistance, and the wheel just spun. So I couldn't straighten the car. I stood on the brake as hard as I could. I wasn't even going that fast. Thank goodness." She was back to clear thinking and enunciation. She could tell the cop, a sergeant, was doubtful but impressed.

"What? Why didn't you tell me?" Jake demanded.

"Well, when did you give me a chance? You were just sure that I had been careless. I am not a careless driver and you know it. Go away," she told him again.

The sergeant turned to his partner and said. "Go look at the car." And then to both of them, "Can I see some ID here, please? Both of you."

"Mine is in my purse in the car," Cilla said. "And the registration is in the glove compartment."

The sergeant yelled at his partner to get those too. And took Jake's license. He was copying down information when the second cop came back and said, "Um, Sarge?" He moved his head to the side to indicate that the sergeant should come with him. He handed over the purse and registration.

"The purse was on the floor, passenger side, and the cell phone was down there too, in the bottom of it. Sarge, it sure looks like that steering column cable has been cut, not broken. You want to take a look?"

"What?" Jake bellowed. "She crashed because someone tampered with her steering?" He had followed the sergeant and overheard. "Someone tried to run her down yesterday," he said it again, out loud, with incredulity. "Someone tried to run her down yesterday."

"Did you report it?"

"No. We thought it was an accident. Just some crazy driver. But if someone tampered with her car today, it probably isn't a coincidence."

The sergeant considered that and put in a call to the sheriff.

"Who would want to hurt her?" the sergeant asked. "I mean besides you, her soon-to-be ex-husband? The one who immediately accused her of being careless. Don't answer that. Just wait over there for the sheriff to get here."

"I want to go to the hospital with her."

"No. Wait here. No one is going anywhere for a while." Then he went back to talk to Cilla again, passing her the purse. "Can you get your license, please, ma'am? I have the registration."

She pulled it out and handed it over. "Here, take my cell too. Check when it was last used. I don't want anyone thinking I was driving and texting. I want you to check it and write it down. Sometimes Jake can be an ass."

"OK." He copied the information from her license and registration and handed those back. Then checked her phone and wrote that down also.

He had Cilla run through her story again about the near miss the day before. When the sheriff arrived he told her to wait and walked over, motioning his partner with him.

Cilla watched them talking. The sheriff could be the model for small-town sheriffs. Tall, broad shoulders, handsome, probably had a nice smile. Though he wasn't smiling now.

"Hey, Cav, this is a strange one." The sergeant ran through the story.

"Well, I sure can't identify a cut steering cable," the sheriff said. "Probably can't even tell a steering cable." He looked at the officer and asked, "How sure are you, Jones?"

"I work on old cars. This Mustang is a classic. The cable is cut. Not broken or worn. The car is in great shape. Or was." He looked at the wreck sadly.

"OK, let's get it towed to the cop shop. I'll talk to the driver first." He looked at the notes. "Priscilla Jayden, first, and then the spouse." He looked at the husband's license. "Jake? This is Jake Jayden?" He looked around and saw Jake over by the ambulance trying to talk to the patient, who had her back to him and was obviously ignoring him.

"And it just got a little bit messier." Both officers looked at him questioningly.

"This is the guy who busted the Webbs." They all looked at Jake. The young officer looked impressed and said, "Wow."

"I'm still going to talk to the wife first. Especially if there is some friction there. And then we can send her to the hospital. Stay with Jake and the tow truck when it comes.

She watched him walk over to her.

"Mrs. Jayden? I'm Sheriff Cavanaugh. Could you please repeat your story for me?"

Patiently she complied. "I was turning in here when I heard a snap, and the steering wheel wouldn't respond."

"Why were you turning in here?"

"I work here. I need my phone to call and tell them I'm out here."

"In a few minutes. Let's finish this first. What type of work do you do here? Secretary? Housekeeper?"

"We run a technology business out of the gatehouse."

A little shamefaced at assuming she was household help, he asked, "Who is we?"

"Do you really have to know this? How is it relevant? My car broke and smashed into a wall."

"Humor me. Who is we and what technology business?"

"We are SC Digital, a business incorporated by me and my four friends to raise money for a children's charity. Do you need my friends' names?"

"Maybe later. Why is your office in a private residence?"

"One of the five—the gang of five, we call ourselves—owns this house, and we use the gatehouse for free."

Then he asked her to go over the near-miss accident the day before.

She lost her patience. "Look. No one is trying to kill me. Everyone likes me. Well, everyone but my husband, and he already has proven that he will just simply walk away and disappear for ten months. That's the only way he hurts me." She paused and then said, "I'm sorry, that was petty and rude. And I am not generally petty or rude. But really, no one is trying to hurt me, no one is angry at me. These are just accidents. I am due one more if three is the rule," she said with a laugh.

"The near miss? Tell me about it please," he repeated.

"All I remember is hearing the squeal of tires and stumbling when I turned to look. And Jake grabbed me and pulled me out of the street. We fell in the gutter. That's all."

"Jake grabbed you? And pulled you out of the way? I thought he didn't like you."

"Well, he wouldn't let me be run down. You don't need to like someone to drag her out of harm's way." Exasperated now.

"OK, call your friend, and I want to talk to him when he gets here."

"Her."

"What?"

"Her, the person I'm calling is a her."

"I want to talk to her when she gets here."

He listened while she spoke.

"Sarah, don't worry. Everything is OK, but I just wrecked Blue on the front gate. The EMTs are getting ready to take me to the hospital." She paused, and he could hear yelling in the background. "No, I'm fine; they just want to make sure. I'll need a ride back; maybe Annie could meet me at the hospital. And Jake is here at the gate and needs to get in." More yelling in the background. "No, he was in his truck behind me. Just Blue and me, um, I wrecked Blue, did I say that already?" More talking. "Sarah! Stop. Just because he's an idiot doesn't mean he should be hurt. Look, the cops are here too, and the sheriff wants to talk to you. Make sure to look him up."

Cavanaugh looked enquiring, so Cilla said, "Sarah doesn't much like my husband. She'll find you."

Then the sheriff went over to Jake, who turned and said, "Cav, how's it hanging?"

"OK, how are you doing, Jake? How's the leg?"

"Still got it, for a while anyhow. Time will tell. You going to be handling this? I don't like the idea of some crazy after my wife."

"You want to tell me what happened here?"

"I didn't see it. I was a few seconds behind her. I saw her make the turn and then heard the crash." A chill went through him when he said that.

Cavanaugh noticed, took a few more notes, and said, "Tell me about yesterday." And listened to the same story but from a different perspective. Jake added that the vehicle didn't have a tag.

"Who would want to hurt her?" Cav asked.

"God, I don't know. She never had an enemy. Never met a person who didn't like her. Well, except for the Webbs. No surprise there. And the feeling was mutual. But I don't know Cilla's current status. Except for the last week, I've been out of the picture for ten months."

"Yes, I wanted to ask you about that. Is there a problem there? Between the two of you? We both know the spouse is always the first suspect, so I have to ask," he explained apologetically.

"We're talking. Separation. But it's amicable. Strained."

"We'll come back to that. If you've been gone, is there a current boyfriend?"

"I don't know, she's not telling."

"Her friends? Any friction, competition, jealousy?"

"That group? No. It wouldn't occur to any of them. They've been friends since grammar school, most of them. Each of them was always the odd man out. Geeks. So they formed their own gang. They defend one another, protect one another. They're each successful in their own area of expertise, and they respect one another. They're tight. I know it sounds hokey, but they're family. Good family." He paused. "Me, they might hurt. Her, never."

"How's that?"

"I left her. Back before we busted Webb. They hate me for that. They think I left her for another woman. They think I left her for Sheri."

The sheriff choked.

"Tell me about it. But it's easier for me to let them think that, for now anyway," Jake said.

"What do you know about her work here? Anything dangerous?"

Jake laughed, shaking his head. "No. The gang set up a business. Man, you aren't going to believe this. Right now they're all pretty jubilant. High fiving each other." He shook his head, still incredulous. He looked at Cav with a funny grin.

"How so?" Cavanaugh inquired as Jake hesitated.

"This is going to sound, well, kind of weird, I guess from your viewpoint." He stopped.

Cavanaugh waited.

"It's complicated."

"I can do complicated. How so?"

"Simply put, their business has made a lot of money. But no one gains if she's hurt. Her money will go to a children's charity. The gang went into business together ten months ago to raise the money to get the charity started and keep it running. They're making a lot of money right now. They each take a share, and the charity gets an equal share. No one is jealous or angry. On the contrary, they're all excited and thrilled by their success and the money they're making for their charity. Not even considering the money they're making for themselves. Money has never been high on their list of important things."

"It does sound complicated, and I might need to talk to the business partners. How much money?"

"To date, around two hundred or two hundred and fifty million dollars. Give or take."

Cavanaugh was afraid his mouth was hanging open. "Millions? In ten months? For charity?"

"Yeah. That's just the way the partners feel. Just kind of shocked. They really don't care about the money. They're having fun. They're setting up a charity."

Cavanaugh let that sit for a minute, thinking, watching Cilla talking to the EMTs. "So about thirty million each? Before taxes?"

"The corporation paid the taxes before they distributed the funds. About half that, I would guess."

"Still a lot of money. Well, what about you? The spouse. You going to get any of that money? Is that part of the separation talk?"

Jake was shaking his head again. "The woman I left ten months ago? She gave me half of her share as soon as she got it. Had it all deposited into an account for me. Waiting. Even though I was gone. 'It's the right thing to do,' is all she said. Just plunked millions of dollars into an account she had set up for the man who deserted her. You're talking to a multimillionaire. I didn't do a thing. And not a one of them begrudges me the money. If that's what Cilla wants, it's what they want. But they still don't like me. If they were behind these accidents, it would be me having problems. Actually, from what I know of this gang, if they were behind this, no one would even suspect anything. I'd be dead and gone, and no one would question the circumstances."

"Hmm."

Jake was waiting for her when they released her from the hospital. Annie had texted to warn her.

"I can't believe how angry I am. First, because you accused me of texting while driving, and second, because you insisted someone was out to hurt me, thus necessitating all the interest from the police. The trip to the hospital." She told him as he led her to his truck and opened the door for her to slide in. He went around and got in himself.

He didn't know what he could say. Felt like she had a solid wall of ice completely surrounding her. His heart had stopped when he saw her miss the turn and head for the buttress. He should have been with her, not right behind her. His fault again. When she had called this morning, he was fiddling with the security system in Priscilla's condo. He had found the code inside the panel. It always amazed him how people would leave the code right where the burglar would look for it. How helpful was that? He had gone to the control box and turned on the cameras, which he now could access with his cell. And he had input a second code, which he could use if anyone—Cilla?—changed the original.

He had needed something to take his mind off what a jerk he had been. It had never occurred to him that she would object to him entering her home. He was an ass. She was right. Why was he always doing the wrong thing with her? Was he destined to make her unhappy whenever he came near her? What would it take for him to just do the right thing when he was with her? Could telling her, explaining what had happened and why, help? Was that the answer? It couldn't possibly make it worse. Could it? Maybe he should have listened to Ron, way back when. Maybe he should do it now. But he couldn't. He still hadn't come to grips with it himself. Until he did, he couldn't talk about it.

And then there he was, making a bigger ass of himself. Again, invading her privacy. He wasn't sure why he'd been fiddling with her security. Just because he could? He would tell her. Be up front about it.

Show her. And then if she wanted, he would undo it all. Meanwhile, he felt a little better, playing with the remote control with his cell. He was just finishing up when she'd called, and he was concentrating on ensuring it worked. So he didn't ask her to wait or argue about her leaving without him. He was only a minute behind her.

He should have argued. He shouldn't have let her go alone. How could he have been so careless?

Calmly—well, if talking through gritted teeth counts as calmly—she continued, "We need to talk about divorce. Now that you're back. Now that Peter has been cleared. We need to get on with our separate lives. You have made it more than clear that you can't bear to be around me. And to tell you the truth, I find it distressing to always be on guard against your accusations and insults. I've done nothing to deserve your cruelty. I have told the gang we're discussing separation arrangements, and it's now time for us to do that. You can keep the money, if that's your problem. I don't want it back."

"No."

"What do you mean, no? What does that mean?"

"I don't need your damn money. The money isn't my problem." His turn to talk through gritted teeth. "Now is not the time." He wasn't ready. He didn't want to be divorced from her. How did he tell her that? *Just spit it out*, he told himself. But instead he said, "Peter is not cleared."

"Near enough. We don't have to be together for you to finish the process. You can work with Peter and John and Sarah. I prefer to be out of the loop."

"No. I'm staying close to you. Someone is after you, trying to hurt you."

"That's ridiculous. No one wants to hurt me. Those accidents were just that, accidents. And I don't need a bodyguard. If I do, Peter will find me one. I don't want to be around you."

"That's too bad. I'm sticking."

"Why? What possible reason could you have to want to protect me? You left me. Remember? You walked out. I saw you that day. That next day after you didn't come home? I saw you help your girlfriend into your car, smile at me, and get in with her and drive off. With her. And not come back. Not call. Not write. Not a word. Not an explanation.

Just…gone. How do you think anyone could possibly hurt me worse than that?"

He was stunned. He hadn't seen her that day. "That's not what you saw."

"Now you're telling me what I saw? What did I see then? Tell me that."

He couldn't tell her. Couldn't explain that he was undercover. That he was on assignment. That he was doing the job. For some reason he couldn't say the words to her. They locked in his throat.

She waited. Then said, "Yes, that's what I've been hearing from you for ten months. Silence." She took a breath.

"Jake," she said gently. "It's time to cut our losses. If you loved me, it would be different. We might be able to salvage something. But you don't. You need to let me go. You don't love me, do you?"

But still he didn't speak. She couldn't stop the tears but she looked away from him, out the window.

He entered the code when they got to the gate, Sarah had shared it. As soon as he stopped the truck, she got out and went inside, shook her head at the gang gathered there, and went into her bedroom, shutting the door behind her. For all the good it did. Peter walked right in behind her.

"I want to be alone." She didn't want him to see her crying either.

"No, you don't. Come over here," he said, pulling her toward him, wrapping his arms around her, holding her. She cried into his shoulder. He held her close, comforting.

She finally stopped crying. Sniffling, she asked, "Didn't I just do this a couple of nights ago? What am I going to do? It hurts so bad to be around him. He looks so much like my Jake, but he treats me like garbage. He won't say he loves me. Won't say he doesn't. What am I supposed to do? What am I supposed to think?"

He let her cry some more, soaking his shirt, just holding her. Had no words of comfort for her. When she finally stopped, he handed her his handkerchief.

"He won't go away. He won't talk divorce. He says I'm in danger and he needs to protect me. I told him you could get me a bodyguard, but he won't listen. I'm whining. Stop me." She moved back and blew her nose. Looked at the handkerchief. "This is mine now. Why do you even carry these? No one carries handkerchiefs anymore." She said this more to distract herself than anything else.

He laughed. "Love is tough. You got to be tough to love. I know. You know too. Sometimes you win, if only for a little while. You won for a while. As long as he doesn't say he hates you, there might be hope. Keep your head up and keep fighting. Maybe it would help to think of this man as Jake's evil twin."

"I guess. I can't let him keep upsetting me this way. I need some way to distance myself from this person who looks so much like the man I loved. Your idea might actually work. Jake is dead. This is his evil twin. Yeah. That's what I'll say to myself next time he messes me up." She sniffled some more and wiped her eyes. "Now tell me why he's saying you're not cleared yet."

"He wants us to find out more for him, I think. We discovered more in one night than he's been able to in weeks. So he knows we can find more and find it quicker. He doesn't realize that everyone is pretty much hooked on this project now anyway and wouldn't stop even if he told us to. He thinks he has to threaten us to keep us going. Doesn't realize the challenge. John loves a digital challenge. All you guys do.

"Jake found a lot of matches," he continued. "The IT lists? A lot of the same people worked at both firms, as you suspected might be the case. And none of you have been able to put a name on the person writing that code." He paused. "So I'm cleared in his mind. Don't worry about that. He's just playing us for more help. Can we talk about the accidents?"

"They were accidents," she said angrily.

"Well, I'm not so sure. One, maybe. Two? No. I think Jake is right about this. I think it would be better to have him with you. I'd feel better anyhow."

"Argghhh," she snarled. "They were accidents. No one wants to hurt me."

"I think that maybe someone does." He put up his hand. "I think that—bear with me here, this is just a feeling—but I wonder if this might be spun off from Jake. From his work."

She started to tell him again that the accidents were coincidences, but stopped as the idea registered.

"Oh, I think I understand what you're saying. Someone who Jake has caught or captured. Someone who lost money or position. They want to hurt me? To hurt Jake? All the more reason to announce that we're separated." And then, "Do you think Jake believes that's what is happening?"

"No. Not in his brain yet. But I do think he senses it in his gut. Probably going to check into all your boyfriends and eliminate them first, though."

"Ha. That will take him a long time, since there weren't any," she said, and they both laughed. "And he might get hurt himself if he goes after Tiff again." She took a deep breath. "OK, I feel better. Let me go wash my face and then look at what you all came up with on this security hacking. Sarah texted it was pretty much as I thought."

She washed her face and they went back out into the great room. The gang was on one side staring daggers at Jake. He was talking with an animated Ron. Or listening. Ron was excitedly telling him that Sarah was amazing. The things she could do, the things she knew. He needed to spend time with her to learn more.

When Cilla came out, she went over to the gang to help plan their strategy. John hugged her and Sarah patted her shoulder. Showing support and comforting her. Glaring at Jake.

They let Jake and Ron sit in on their planning session, but ignored them and didn't explain any of the techno geek speak.

John still thought the code had a familiar feel to it. He just couldn't place where or when he had seen it before. Cilla agreed. She had the same impression, and she was just going to let it sit and see if it would come to her.

They all agreed the hacking was faked. The perps, Penney's word. She giggled because she had always wanted to use that term. Said it twice. "The perps used a backdoor at both firms. They didn't hack in. There is no sign of serious hacking. They didn't have to be hackers."

But the trail to Peter, that was a different matter and might have been designed by a professional. The perps had been unable to hack into any part of Peter's system, so they had mirrored his website and uploaded data. Then they had partially erased it, but left enough of it to be identified. There was just enough information to cause Peter trouble but not anything of value. The perps left footprints from the hacked firms to the website that anyone could follow, as Ron had. Leaving the trail wouldn't have required an expert programmer either.

And the traps, those were professional at both the client firms and at the fake website. Though some of that code could have been downloaded from the web.

"So they know that Jake's people have followed the tracks to the fake website. And they can be pretty sure that Jake has been looking at Peter," John continued. He normally took charge of their meetings. Kept them on track. "But Jake's computer system is clean. So are his cells. His security worked as it was designed."

"What do we do now?" John asked. "Suggestions?"

"I'd like to put more security on Jake's system and on his cells," Kevin said, and Ron agreed he could go along with that. It was a good idea.

"And we should look at our own security again and Peter's." This from Sarah. "Though I think we're good. And we can set up an auto check every few hours to be on the safe side." They all agreed they would take extra precautions.

John wanted to put some of their own traps on the fake website. He felt confident that "the perps"—he nodded at Penney with a smile— would go back there. Both to check on Jake's progress and to add more incriminating evidence. They would track those hackers back home.

He looked at Jake and asked, "How about it, Jake? Can you guess where they might strike next, based on where they've been and what they have taken? Is there a next logical step for them where we can set up our own trap and wait? Be preemptive?"

Jake looked around the group, seeing where this was going. Good idea. Should have thought of that himself. Distracted, he guessed.

John misunderstood the look. "You don't have to tell us what they took. We don't need to know that." Though, it was obvious he could hack in any time. Not that he would. Maybe. "But you know what it was. Can you guess what else they might want? Would they want more of the same? Or would they want to fill in some gaps? Or expand on what they already have? We don't need to get involved with any of that. We can write a general straightforward trap for them. Your IT people can check it to make sure we haven't snuck anything in it, and they can modify it if need be. Then we can put the traps at the next likely location or locations and wait." John smiled to himself. No way would Jake's team be able to understand what the gang was doing.

And then thinking as he was talking, he continued, "I suppose we could write code to find the backdoors." And then shook his head. The others were also shaking their heads. "No, we can't do that. Too many variables."

Jake finally spoke. "I like your ideas. That look you just misinterpreted was not one of mistrust, but of respect. I should have thought of that. Where they might hit next. I'm pretty annoyed that a geek got there first." He said it with a smile. "My hesitation was that I just realized where they're heading. I want to think about it a little more and get my people to toss it around. See if they have more ideas or suggestions. And then I would feel very comfortable having you writing the code and applying it." Jake saw he was already getting a nod from Ron.

John looked pleased. Didn't expect anything reasonable from the jerk. But a compliment? That was a surprise. "Anyone have any more on Jake's problems? No? Then how about our own stuff?"

Sarah said the cloaking code had helped her, worked beautifully. "But I'm not sure we should sell it. It might be too dangerous in the wrong hands."

Peter suggested that someone else would write it eventually but agreed that it didn't have to be them. They didn't need to be responsible for the problems it would cause. "Meanwhile, why don't you work on an uncloaking device?" Peter suggested.

Several faces went blank as they looked inside their heads for possible codes and solutions.

"Well, gee, I like that idea," Kevin said. "That would be a challenge. Because if we can do it for our cloak, then maybe it will work against someone else's. In fact, it wouldn't hurt to test it and see if someone else is already using one." He was on a roll.

Cilla said she would leave that to Kevin and John; she was still working on her garden app.

"It's based on multiple types of flowers or vegetables for the home gardener. Well, maybe landscapers too. And maybe architects. Maybe I better give this some more thought. I've only just begun. Originally it was just for me, and then for any home gardener. I can easily add in subroutines to expand users. Or maybe they should be individual apps for the specialists. I'll let you know when it's ready for testing, but we might need to find someone outside our group to do the testing." She would use the simplified version herself as soon as she completed it.

At that point, Annie came in with lunch. *Lunch*, Cilla thought. It was only lunchtime? Already it felt like three days had passed since she got up this morning. And it was only lunchtime. She wanted potato salad. Annie's egg potato salad. She hoped there was some. She went over to hug Annie, and they talked for a few minutes about the accident and Blue.

Cilla sat on her rocker with a full plate. A plateful of hot cut-up chicken with pasta in a cream sauce, with lots of spinach because Annie knew she loved spinach. Chopped pears with cinnamon and pecans. And of course, potato salad. She settled in, starting with a forkful of the potato salad, and watched Peter and John at the table in the corner. They looked so happy. And Sarah and Michael. Sarah glowing even after being up all night, partly from her successful hacking, but mostly from just being near Michael, Cilla thought. They looked sweet together. She felt happy for all of them and hoped they would all fare better than she had with Jake.

And then she looked at Kevin and Penney. On opposite ends of the loveseat. Not touching. *But there is something going on there*, she thought. *Why did I never notice it before? Kevin and Penney? Why not?* She would have to pay more attention.

And then Jake came over and sat on the chair across from her. She couldn't just get up and walk away, could she? She could, but that would be weak, so she looked at him and waited for his next attack.

"Tell me about the guy you bought the condos from. Could he be mad enough to be doing this?"

It took her a minute to change tracks. From watching the lovebirds to wondering how Jake could think she had entered into a deal that would be so unfair as to make someone want to kill her.

"No, Jake." She said it patiently, as if to a small child. "No. He wanted to sell. He wanted his money. He had another investment, and he needed that money right then. He had purchased the condos when real estate was low and rented them both out. The renters each remodeled their own units. He rode the value up and then watched as the value started back down. His renters left, and he didn't want to be a landlord. He wanted to start his new project. I offered his asking price, in cash. He was ecstatic." She waved an arm.

"He actually came out of the deal with a nice profit and he knew it. He was walking away on air. And he didn't care that the value would go back up if he'd hung onto the units. He wanted out right then. He didn't enjoy being a landlord. So everyone came out a winner on that deal. Kevin handled the purchase and made a commission. Penney got to watch her client make money by selling a liability in a down market. And I got a great place to live and an investment with appreciation and income."

"OK," he said. "I'll need to look into your boyfriends. I'll need a list, names and addresses, when and how long you were with them, how you parted. I need to determine if one of them would want to harm you."

"Yes, Peter said that would be your next line of inquiry. Though Peter thought you would be more interested in lovers. Not boyfriends."

"Lovers? Plural? Christ, I've only been gone ten months. Lovers?"

"You just want to know about my love life, don't you? Any way you can. Will that make you feel less guilty for leaving me? You're just using these accidents as an excuse to find out who I've been with. You don't even have the guts to ask straight out. You have to use a con."

"Cilla," he said warningly.

"What? What are you going to do if I don't tell you? How will it satisfy you to know? Were you happy when you thought I was doing John and Peter? Will you even believe me?"

"I need to know you are safe."

She knew she would tell him. She was just delaying the inevitable. Wanted to make him work for it. And she had seen the hurt flash across his face when she had said lovers. What did that mean?

"There have been no lovers, Jake. There have been no boyfriends. The closest I have come to male companionship is Tiff. I told you once, I have always believed there would be one man for me. I loved that man. The one I married. Still do. Love the man whom I married. Not the man in front of me now. The man who believes I would take multiple lovers when I'm still married. The man I married would never even entertain that idea. No one wants to hurt me, Jake. No one can hurt me the way you did." Her voice was flat.

"And maybe you need to look at yourself and your motives," she went on. "Aren't you really just prying into my life? Using my supposed danger as your excuse?"

She looked down at her food. A few minutes ago, she was hungry for it; now just the sight of it made her feel sick. She started to get up to walk away when his cell squawked. Actually squawked. He looked worried as he took the cell from his pocket and looked at it. Touched it a few times. He looked at her, stunned.

"What?" she said. "Tell me. You're scaring me."

He looked back at the cell. "Someone just broke into your apartment."

At first she didn't understand, and then she panicked. "Tiff. Tiff's home alone." She looked ready to run.

He took her hand. "Not your apartment. Priscilla's apartment."

"Priscilla's? Why would anyone want to break into Priscilla's? How do you know that?" She took a breath. "Why am I asking stupid questions? I need to call security. The police? How do you know that? Tell me," she demanded. The others were gathering around.

"I'm getting video from the security system. I turned it on when I left. Jesus. They have guns. Don't send security. Call the cops. No sirens. I'm going over. Ron," he said, "someone is in Cilla's apartment. I'm going over. Stay here and coordinate. Call Cav."

Ron's wife, Jen, wouldn't be happy if he took Ron into danger. And Ron wasn't trained for police work. He was a desk jockey. So he would go in by himself. He was trained.

"Jesus," Kevin pulled out his cell and said, "Nine-one-one."

Cilla was out the door before she remembered she didn't have Blue. "I'll go with you."

"No."

She ignored him and got in the truck.

Sarah went to the computer to pull the video up and put it on the monitors. Priscilla's security was already programmed into the system, and they could give the police a running commentary from the gatehouse.

"I want you to stay in the truck when we get there," Jake told Cilla.

She didn't bother to argue, just jumped out as soon as he parked in front of the building. She went running through the door looking for Paul. When she didn't see him behind the desk, she headed for the office and almost tripped over him lying on the floor.

"Paul! Paul!" She knelt down and touched his shoulder and got no response and looked up questioningly at Jake.

It had taken Jake a minute to get his gun and holster out of the locked glove box. He had put it there when he went into the hospital to pick up Cilla. He was just clipping the holster onto his waistband in back as he came through the door. He ran to her and felt for a pulse. Then examined the bump on Paul's head.

"Pulse feels good. Looks like he was slugged. Just knocked out."

He took her chin and looked into her eyes. They were horrified.

"Listen to me, Cilla. You have to stay here. You shouldn't even be here. It's too dangerous. You need to wait here. Tell the cops I'm upstairs and armed so they don't shoot me. Tell them to cover the back."

"No. You can't go up there by yourself. You need to wait."

"We can't take that chance. This is my job, remember. This is what I do. Now promise me you'll wait here. Call an ambulance. OK? Promise me."

Stuttering, she said. "Oh—OK. Yes, I'll stay here with Paul. I'll call an ambulance." And she watched him pull out his elevator key and his gun. She shuddered, scared. Took a deep breath and called for the ambulance.

He checked his cell on the ride up. The two men were moving through the rooms, cutting cushions, tearing down drapes, slicing paintings, knocking over furniture, and breaking anything they could reach. He realized they were intent on destruction, not robbery.

The door was open, and he could see on the cell the men were each in a bedroom. He slipped the phone into a pocket, moved cautiously through the living room into the first bedroom. One man was emptying drawers and smashing them against the wall. The other guy must still be in the next room. Jake slipped up behind the guy, intending to wrap his arm around his throat, but the guy must have sensed him and whirled around. Jake grabbed his gun hand, and they danced a few steps.

Jake was gaining purchase when the second burglar came up behind him and kicked him hard in the leg. His bad leg. The worst part of his bad leg. He went down like a felled tree, his own gun bouncing out of his hand. But he kept hold of the first guy's gun hand and took the guy down with him. Where had the second man come from? Must have been in the bathroom. The pain from his leg was excruciating, but through a gray haze, he saw the second guy point his gun at him and used the last bit of his strength to drag the first guy on top of himself to use him as a shield.

The second burglar shot his partner. Jake felt the impact of the bullet as it went into the man on top of him. Then the burglar shot his partner again. He was getting ready to try for Jake a third time when the cops pounded in through the front door, shouting. The second burglar glanced toward the front of the apartment, then turned around and calmly put a third bullet into his buddy's head. A kill shot. He laughed once and ran out toward the back door.

Jake was still trying to get his breath when the cops charged into the room. He put his hands out, empty, and said, "I'm the owner. I'm the owner." Even though it was obvious that the guy on top of him—a dead guy, he was sure—was the one in the mask. "The other guy went out the kitchen."

Jake recognized the same cops from this morning, and they pulled the burglar off him. "The other guy shot him. Aiming for me," he bit out. Hurt to talk too. Sheriff Cavanaugh came in then. Looked over the scene. Grimaced.

"Your wife has already called for an ambulance. Let me get a second one for this guy." He'd heard Jake's statement as he came through the door and walked over to see how badly the guy was hurt.

The sergeant was already feeling for a pulse. "Doesn't look good. Looks like he's dead. No pulse. Two rounds in his chest, and of course the hole in his head is a good clue. Let's get the mask off him."

Cavanaugh pulled off the mask. "I recognize him, local thug for hire. Guess he picked the wrong person to work for. I have people downstairs by the back entrance," he said to Jake and then noticed Jake was still on the floor. "Jake, can you stand?"

"Give me a hand," Jake said, wincing. "She, I think the second guy was a she. She kicked me in my bad leg. Not sure I can stand yet."

Cavanaugh helped him up and then steadied him. Jake leaned on Cav until he felt he could put weight on his injured leg. The deputy returned his gun after he got a nod from the sheriff.

Jake stood on both feet and turned and saw that Cilla was standing there watching him. Just what he needed. Then she looked at the burglar and turned pale.

"Oh Christ, get her out of here," he said to Cavanaugh.

"You shouldn't be here, ma'am. Sarge will walk you out to the front room." She let him walk her out and collapsed on the cushion-less couch. Looked around, dazed. Noticed the gasoline can. "They were going to set a fire? Burn everything? Isn't this enough damage?"

Jake limped in. His progress was slow and painful. He sat on the arm of the couch. No way could he get down that low to sit with her.

"Looks like it," Cavanaugh said. "Almost a waste of time to destroy things if you're going to burn them. Lot of hate here." He looked at Jake and asked, "You want the EMTs to look at your leg, Jake?"

"No, it will stop hurting when it feels better." He tried to joke.

"Leg?" Cilla said. "Why are you limping? What does Cav so obviously know about your leg that I don't?"

"You told the officers you own this place?" Cavanaugh had heard that comment too.

"Wife owns it. So I sort of do. And it seemed like a good thing to say so they wouldn't shoot me or cuff me."

"Well, this is a third incident for you, Mrs. Jayden. Maybe not all coincidences, do you think?"

She just nodded. "But I don't know anyone who hates me this much. To destroy like this. And besides, anyone who knows me knows

I don't live here. I don't even like this condo. I live in the condo next door."

"Hmm. Would security tell someone who asked that you were in this apartment?"

"Yes, if they asked for Priscilla or Jayden. But they couldn't get up here without an elevator key card."

At that point the EMTs came in and went into the bedroom. "Both of you stay here," Cavanaugh said as he followed them. Watched them examine the guy on the floor. They merely shook their heads. "Need the wagon and coroner for this guy."

Cav looked at his cell, told it. "Christ." He listened some more before he went back to the living room and said to Jake, "She walked out. Right past my man. Took off the mask, shook out her hair, and strutted out. Shit. My man didn't know he was looking for a woman. We'll pull the video feeds from security here and get pictures." He was shaking his head in disgust.

"Mrs. Jayden, I think Jake is right about you being a target. But I don't think it's anyone you know."

He looked at Jake and continued, "Sheri's out of jail. That guy didn't kick you in the leg by accident. And I think you're right. It wasn't a guy, but a woman. Sheri. She knew what she was doing. Knew that a kick there would bring you down. Sheri knows that. And she just waltzed out of here."

Jake closed his eyes. Sheri. His fault. His fault that Cilla was being targeted. His fault. He had hoped Sheri's conviction and imprisonment would end it for him. That he could come back and restart his life. He hadn't understood Sheri's need for revenge.

Then he stopped castigating himself and thought back to her kicking him. "Yeah, that could have been Sheri. We can look at the video and—"

Oops. The video was still running. He got a quirky smile on his face and looked at Cavanaugh and said, "Ah, Cav? The security system here is sending video, right now, of us, of the whole apartment, back to the gatehouse."

Cavanaugh looked stunned. Said slowly, "Well, turn it off, Jake."

Cilla looked up at the camera and said, "Hi, Mom. Hi, Dad." And gave a little wave. Levity probably wasn't the best answer to the danger, but it brought a half grin and a covered chuckle from Cavanaugh.

The gang raised a cheer at her comment just before Jake cut the feed with his cell phone. They discussed turning the video feed back on, but decided against it. Probably only because Ron was there. Partly because watching a man get shot and killed was chilling. For a minute it looked like it was Jake being shot and killed. They had witnessed a murder. Real life was scary.

Cilla waited for Jake to put his cell away, and when he looked up she asked, "Why would Sheri want to hurt me, destroy my stuff? You left me for her. She was the winner here, I was the loser. This doesn't make any sense." Then she looked at Cavanaugh. "Out of prison? You said she was out of prison?"

But no one was listening to her. No one was answering her.

"How can she be out?" Jake demanded. "She was sentenced to life." He was angry, frustrated. And the pain left him in little control of his emotions. He was yelling at Cav.

"Before you say anything, I called Munson. Because I pretty much believed your wife when she said no one would want to hurt her. And all the evidence I had said the same thing. But I was also certain these were not accidents. The person I thought of immediately was Sheri. So I called Munson. And if you hadn't been so worried about Cilla, you would have done that," giving Jake an excuse.

"Sheri stabbed herself in her cell. The prison had a new trainee working, and he called an ambulance. All protocols and normal procedures were disregarded or overlooked. The ambulance took her to the emergency room."

"How is that even possible?" Jake thundered. "How could they take her out of the prison? Why not take her to the prison hospital?" Christ, he hurt.

"Don't yell at me. It was a major screwup. Munson doesn't think the guards were simply untrained new hires who panicked when they saw the blood. He thinks it was a planned prison break. Too many rules were ignored for her breakout to be accidental. At the hospital they left her alone with a technician. She stabbed him and took his uniform and walked out. The security cameras show her being picked up. The technician needed surgery but will be OK. He says her wound was superficial, not life threatening. All the mistakes and screwups put one very dangerous woman on the loose."

Jake listened stunned, finally started thinking. "You need to get someone on Juanita. Right away. Sheri will go after her first. Considers her a traitor for testifying against her."

"Hold on," Cavanaugh said and pulled out his cell. He had Munson on speed dial. He turned his back and murmured into his phone. Listened a while and then spoke again and closed the phone.

"Juanita is covered. That was Munson. He says he has an army around her. You know that he and his wife are fostering Juanita?" he asked. "Munson won't let anything happen to her."

Jake hurt. His leg throbbed. It was hard to think through the pain. But he put it aside, and said dangerously, "When did Sheri escape? Why didn't I know? Why wasn't I notified?"

"She's been out a week. Munson was just told. Only because he checked after I called. You and Munson not being notified is only another part of the cluster fuck. Munson's going to track down where the break in communications originated and chew out some poor excuse for an agent for not notifying either of you."

"That does a lot of good now. Better Munson deals with him than me. Cilla might have been killed because no one here knew Sheri was out."

Cilla was switching her attention from Jake to Cavanaugh, back to Jake again. She spoke into a moment of silence. "Back to my question. Why would Sheri come after me?"

Cavanaugh looked uncomfortable. Looked at Jake, who was not going to answer. Jake just shook his head helplessly and looked away with shame. When it became obvious Jake wasn't going to talk, Cavanaugh continued with the ball, offering Cilla a condensed version.

"Sheri and her brother were operating a white slavery ring. Jake stumbled onto her operation when he was working another case. He worked undercover with her and her brother, Lenny, for six weeks, finally busting up the ring. Sheri nearly killed him and Juanita. Jake made it possible for us to rescue about thirty children. Juanita was one of them. Webb was killed during the takedown, and Sheri apparently blames Jake for that. She swore she would come after him."

He's leaving a lot out, Cilla thought, but didn't press for more. It was obvious that neither man wanted to add anything. Later she would want the full details. And she wanted to know about the "leg" too and the pain that went with it. Instead, she looked around at the condo and said, "They couldn't have been here more than fifteen minutes, max, and yet they seemed to have destroyed pretty much everything in here. Can I walk through the rest?"

"I need to go check downstairs; one of the officers will walk with you. Don't touch anything."

She couldn't be allowed to walk through by herself, she thought. She didn't want to touch anything. Jake stayed behind, looking grim.

When they came back to the main room, she was shaking her head. She couldn't believe the thug had actually smashed one of the toilets, flooding the adjacent rooms.

Cav came in, and both Jake and Cilla looked at him, questioning.

"You're going to need to find another place for at least tonight. This is a crime scene and you can't stay here."

"I live next door," she said somberly. She wasn't sure she would feel safe there now, though. And she was worried about Tiff.

"No," Jake said. "You will not stay next door. You're coming with me. You need to be protected."

She gave that little thought. Be with Jake in a small apartment? Wasn't going to happen.

"I can go to the gatehouse. It's secure there. And my rental car is being delivered there." She looked at the sheriff and said, "I'll just go next door and get some clothes and stuff. And my cat. Can someone drive me?"

"I'll take you," Jake declared. "You're not getting out of my sight until Sheri is back in jail. And I'm going to arrange for a twenty-four-hour detail."

"Do you really think that's necessary? She's only one woman." He was scaring her.

"Yes." This came from Cavanaugh and Jake at the same time. Cavanaugh continued, "The woman is crazy, smart, and dangerous. Let Jake protect you. That's his job."

He turned to Jake. "I need to finish up here, and I'll check in with you at the gatehouse later."

Cilla shrugged. They both thought she was in danger and that Jake could and would protect her. So, she would be alone with Jake again for a while. Just what she needed, though he didn't look like he would be much protection right now. He went with her to get her stuff, still limping.

Fortunately, Cavanaugh had sent an officer along too. Jake couldn't carry anything. He could barely get himself around. The officer took her one suitcase, and she put Tiff in a carrying case she would bring. Tiff had been in the gatehouse before, so she knew he would be OK. He had food dishes and a litter box there. And the garden.

When they got to the truck, Jake tossed her the keys and said, "You drive."

She watched him drag himself in the passenger side, unlock the glove box and take out a bottle of pills. He mouthed two of them, dry, and put his head back with his eyes closed a moment.

"Drive," he said again not quite suppressing a moan. He kept watch while she drove, looking in the mirrors and out the window to make sure they weren't followed.

The gang was waiting anxiously. They had heard nothing more after the feed was cut. And Ron wouldn't tell them anything. Sarah ran over and hugged Cilla, held her tight. Peter took Tiff, spoke to him, and let him out.

As Jake limped into the gatehouse behind her, Michael offered to look at his leg, saying he had some experience with injuries. Jake only growled at him that it was fine, which didn't fool anyone. Especially when he sat down heavily with a sigh. They were all talking at once, asking questions. He held up his hand and repeated what Cavanaugh had said about the Webb operation. With a warning look at Ron. Then he told them he would be with Cilla from now on, guarding her. They would be staying at the gatehouse. He looked at Ron and instructed, "We'll need a team on-site by tomorrow morning for backup. They'll be here round the clock until I find a safe house." Ron nodded and pulled out his cell.

Cilla looked at him in surprise. "A safe house? You want to lock me in a safe house. For how long? I don't think so. I'll be fine here. There's plenty of security here. I'm not going to be locked up away from my friends and my work. You can't do that, and I won't let you."

He looked angry and was about to say something when both Kevin and Peter agreed with her. Either or both of them could supply bodyguards. They looked at each other and smiled. "We can compare names," Kevin said to Peter. "And Jake can make the final choices."

"If Cilla has to move, she can come to my compound," Peter said. "That's another option. But she's right. This is the best spot. The security is top of the line. Just look around. One of The Boys did it when he was home. It's state of the art. He did Cilla's condos too. He was just playing there.

"And something else I'm sure you have thought about," he said, looking at Jake. "If Sheri has been out a week, she could already know about the gang. You might be able to lock Cilla up in a safe house, but what about the other four? You need to protect them also. If Sheri knows Cilla is the route to you, she knows the four are the route to Cilla. She grabs one of them, and she gets Cilla. I don't know if she is aware of Michael or me, but if she grabs one of us, she has Sarah or John. You're going to need to keep us all safe, and this is the best place for that. It has facilities, a kitchen, and bedrooms. It's designed to house and feed eight to twelve people. It's just what you need. All of us and all your guards in one spot. Two buildings, house, and gatehouse. One property, fenced and gated.

"Now we're going to have to discuss how to keep Cilla safe with all of us coming and going. We don't want Sheri taking one of us hostage to get in here. We saw what she did. We saw that video." He shook his head. "The woman purposely shot her partner in an effort to get to you. And then killed him rather than leave him behind." Peter looked around and saw agreement.

"Jake, you're outvoted," Peter continued. "You know how stubborn Cilla can be. And I'm right."

"OK, OK, we can work together on protecting Cilla. And we do need to protect all of you. For this to work, you must all do exactly what we say. Can you do that? Lives are at stake here. Not just Cilla's." He winced as he tried to get more comfortable.

They all nodded.

"Ron will be in charge. This is his area of expertise: bodyguards, schedules, and procedures." He nodded at Ron, who said, "On it, Boss. I'll have two men here before midnight. More tomorrow."

Cilla looked at Jake and said, "That's settled. Now you have to do something for me. Let Michael take you into a bedroom and treat your leg." She saw he was getting ready to protest and talked over it. "You can't protect me or anyone else if you can't stand without pain. And it's obvious to everyone here you're in extreme pain. In spite of those pills you took in the truck."

"He can't help," Jake said shortly.

"Give him a chance. You won't know until he looks. It will be between the two of you. Doctor-patient confidentiality. Please. If you won't do it for me, do it because you are no good to Ron the way you are. You can't keep me safe if you can't walk." She was pretty sure that was the only threat that would work on him.

He gave up and followed Michael into the bedroom. "Drop your pants. Let me see." Michael took one look and frowned. "Sheri did this? This injury? I don't even want to know how. Not now. What are you taking for pain, oxycodone?"

"Yeah, and it's barely taking the edge off. From past experience it will kick in soon, and then it will take a couple of days for the leg to calm down. If it does. The doctors don't know if I'm going to keep it yet."

Michael gently felt the leg up and down, moving it and rotating the knee. "Do you have a brace?"

"Yes, heavy, awkward. And I can't really walk with it. Get in or out of the truck. I need to be able to move around."

"I might have an idea there. How about other drugs? What else are you taking?"

Jake told him, and Michael nodded his head. "I have a salve we'll try tonight. It should have a calming effect and won't interact with anything you're taking."

"Sure. Go for it. Cilla's right, I'm no good to anyone this way." Defeated.

Michael got a cream from his bag and gently rubbed it on the extensive bruised area surrounding an old wound and surgical scars.

Jake looked at him with surprise, "That's quick. It's warm. The pain is not so bad."

"Pretty amazing, isn't it? I haven't needed to try it myself, thank goodness, but it seems to be almost instantaneous in the relief it provides. Sheri didn't break the skin, but there is considerable bruising. I have some meds for that." He got a glass of water and shook out a pill for Jake. "I'll wrap it for now and then you sleep. I'll bring you a new brace tomorrow."

"I don't need to sleep. I need to be out there finding bodyguards for all of you."

"You're going to have to lie down and rest for a couple of hours, doctor's orders. Let Ron deal with getting bodyguards and setting everything up. You did put him in charge. And you did say he was capable. You can't do everything, and you can't do anything in your current state. Peter will help Ron. He has some good people. I've used them to protect some battered spouses and children."

He paused, "And you should tell Cilla about this. It isn't right for her not to know this. It isn't fair."

"Stay out of it. You're on shaky ground. I'm not that appreciative of your salve," Jake growled. He leaned back against the headboard and fell asleep.

Michael smiled. He'd given Jake a quick-acting sleeping pill. Rest would be one of the best medicines for the leg. He went back out to the main room.

"He's resting. Ron, he wants you to finish getting your protection teams in place. Do whatever it is you do. I have him knocked out for at least six hours. Peter can help you, he knows people."

"We also have to figure out where Sheri might go and/or be hiding," Ron said. "What her next move might be. Jake's our best help there. So that will be tomorrow."

Cilla had brought in a suitcase. And the cat was roaming around. Everyone was used to having Tiff there. Kind of an unofficial mascot. She put her case in John's room.

Ron said he already had four men who would be there within the hour. He and Peter were selecting eight more.

"From right now, no one will go out by himself. Two men will always go out with each of you. It will be tough for a few days, but live with it. It will keep you alive. No one leaves here alone. Am I clear?" he restated.

Tuesday

Jake woke slowly, a little groggy, with an unusual weight on his stomach. He reached one hand over to massage the heaviness and touched… fur? He got one eye open and looked down. The cat. The cat, Tiff, was curled on his stomach, looking at him, almost smugly, with his ears back, flat down the side of its head. Didn't that mean something, when a cat had his ears back? Mad? And Jake's hand was touching the cat's head. Jake moved his fingers slowly away, afraid the cat would scratch him again. But it just moved its head for Jake to rub behind its ear. Shut its eyes and purred. Pointed its ears up.

Thank goodness, Jake thought, he wasn't going to lose more blood here.

He realized his leg actually felt better—a dull throb, which he could deal with. He didn't dare turn his left wrist and check the time. Not with the cat on his chest. Looked like morning. Had he slept all night? He couldn't afford to waste that time. He should get moving. But he was a little afraid to stop rubbing the cat, so he lay there feeling almost well. The cat didn't look so mean with its eyes closed like that. It almost had a smile on its face. What would it do if Jake moved?

As if reading his mind, the cat opened its eyes and looked at him. Jake tried a little dialogue.

"Now what? Are we friends? You slept with me, we must be friends. Can I stop rubbing your ear?" The cat seemed to like what he was doing and tilted its head, giving Jake another area to rub. "So that's the way it works. OK." *This was almost like rubbing a woman*, Jake thought. Felt good. And then laughed at himself. "Hey, cat, I gotta go pee. OK?" He was talking to a cat now. Like it would understand.

Tiff stood up, and that kind of hurt. Before, the cat's weight was spread out over its whole body; now it was on four pillars. The cat raised its back as it stretched and then jumped off.

Jake breathed a sigh of relief and swung his legs out from under the light blanket someone had thrown over him last night. He was prepared for pain when he put his injured leg down, but still only had the dull throb, which felt good compared to the blinding pain last night. He could get used to this.

He went into the bathroom and took care of business. He was washing cat off his hand when he saw clean clothes folded on the counter with a shaving kit. New stuff in the kit. The clothes were probably Kevin's.

"OK. I'm taking a shower and getting cleaned up. A few more minutes won't matter. Screw the time."

Cilla was coming through the doorway when he came out of the bathroom. He could tell she was uneasy. Nervous.

"Good morning. Here's coffee. Tiff said you were up. I'm a little jealous. My cat abandoned me and slept with you last night. Ordinarily Tiff doesn't let strangers touch him. Only the gang. But then, I guess he only knows the gang."

Jake could understand why she was rambling. She was anxious. She wouldn't know what mood to expect from Jake this morning. And she was probably worried about him. She shouldn't be, but she was. Maybe because the cat had spent the night with him. Hadn't he read somewhere that cats could sense when someone needed help, companionship. Their presence appeared to be caring and supportive.

She put the coffee down and backed out as Michael came in.

"You drugged me," Jake said, finally figuring out why he had slept so long.

"Yes, I did. It comes with the painkiller. You needed the rest. Your leg needed to be immobile for a while, and you were not going to lie down voluntarily."

"How could you do that? Leave everyone out there unprotected? I needed to be working."

"No, you didn't. Everything is under control. Ron and Peter are handling everything and Cav is in constant contact. Now sit down and let me look at your leg."

He put on more salve, wrapped the bruise with another bandage, and then pulled a soft brace out of his bag. He'd been allowed to go get it last night. With Jen, Ron's wife, as bodyguard. She was the first of the guards to arrive. He smiled, "Ron's wife is here. At first I thought she was just a biker girlfriend. Black hair, cut close to her head. Almost a helmet. Tanned, muscled. She wore a black leather vest, no sleeves. Her tats showing. Black leather pants. She arrived on a black motorcycle. Cute, petite like Sarah."

"She is a biker chick. And tough as nails. One of the best bodyguards in the business," Jake told him.

"No problem, she makes me smile. We don't get many good looking biker chicks where I work. Now, your leg, I imagine your doctors told you to wear your brace, but I don't see it. Try this one. You'll find it comfortable; it fits close and provides support for the injured muscles and tendons. You'll like it. Even if you don't like it, you'll wear it. It will increase your chances of keeping your leg. Let's get it on, and you can practice walking."

When Jake hesitated, he said, "Don't argue, just do it. As long as you're here, in the gatehouse, you'll do what I say." He helped Jake strap on the brace and showed him how to adjust it.

Jake was surprised at how light and flexible it was, and still it provided the support he needed. Felt good.

He said it. "Feels good."

"It will fit fine under your pants too. You need to do some exercises; otherwise you'll run into trouble down the line." Michael demonstrated them and continued, "Just do them whenever you think of them. They'll help keep the leg and the muscles strong. Wear the brace every day. You can take it off at night. But keep up with the exercises. One really good thing about the brace? Next time Sheri kicks you, you won't go down, and she'll break a toe."

"Won't be a next time. She won't get that close again. She'll be dead. And why do you care about me anyhow?"

"As a doctor, I care about all my patients. You in particular? Cilla cares. And Sarah cares about Cilla. So I care. They're both generally really good judges of people. Though in your case, I'm not so sure they're right. Anyhow," he changed the subject, "your team is waiting for you, and I hear breakfast arriving."

Jake smelled the food as soon as they walked into the great room. Made him realize he was hungry. He looked around and saw Penney in the corner talking to Kevin. Ron and his wife, Jen, were talking to Cilla and watching her monitor. When he looked closer, he saw the cat draped over the top of it. Cilla looked tired. He imagined they all had been up most of the night. Had he spent the night in Cilla's bed? Where had she slept?

Jen was an experienced bodyguard, and he was happy to see her there. She would have been one of those on his list to contact. Ron knew the danger and had called her anyhow, so Jake didn't have to make that decision.

Jake knew nothing would be accomplished when there was hot food and felt heartened that Ron had at least part of a team already in place. That implied that he had taken care of the other necessary operations and setups.

Sarah and John came in talking to Jason and Rib, two bodyguards he would have contracted for protection. He was relieved to see them there. They all headed toward the food, and Michael went over to join them. Jake knew Rib would get there first. Rib was always first when there was food.

Even though he knew Ron had done the job, he couldn't help asking, "Did you put a guard on the condo?"

"Not yet. It's still a crime scene, but a couple of Peter's people will be working with security there. Hold on before you make any comments, we have a team in place and more on the way. Peter has access to some good men." He took Jake's arm and walked him to a corner. "How's the leg? Michael's not talking. But you're not limping this morning."

"It's OK. Michael did a good job. Though he shouldn't have drugged me."

"You needed the downtime. And Peter helped me. We got the job done without you. He's got some really good people, names you'll recognize. We worked together and covered most of the bases. The first team is here, as you can see. We have two of Peter's people at the gate and two more on the grounds. Peter also put a man on our offices. Jason is here, he took Peter home to get stuff. He and John are going to move into the main house and stay on the grounds. If they stayed at Peter's, they would be going back, and forth and we'd need more people. This way makes the guard work a little easier. Also, since the wedding announcement broke this morning, there's a mob of reporters at his compound.

"Cav has been here to pick up a copy of our security tape and dropped off a copy of the tape showing Sheri coming in with flowers and knocking out the security guard. You can look at it later. She must have followed you there. The guard said she asked for Priscilla Jayden. Said that's what it looked like on the card in the flowers too. He told her Three A and then said he'd deliver them. She got angry and insisted she'd take them up. When he wouldn't let her, she hit him and took his key card. That's all on the tape. And her walking out the back entrance? It's amazing. I would have let her walk too. What a body, fully displayed. You can look at that later too.

"Cav has his people pulling in anyone who had contact with the Webbs," Ron went on. "Either one of them. We, your team and the gang, are working the computer resources and feeding Cav whatever we get, which isn't much. Mostly we're just providing protection. Jen will be guarding Cilla."

"I'll be with Cilla," Jake declared.

"Listen to me, Jake. I'm running the op, and I say both you and Cilla get protection. You're not one hundred percent. Step back and look at the problem. It's you Sheri is after. We need a guard on you. And do you really want someone in your condition to be the only one guarding Cilla? Cilla and you both will be living here, but she gets her own guard. You do too. That's not open to discussion or debate.

"Kevin brought over clothes for you. I don't want any of our people going into your apartment or leading Sheri back here in case she doesn't know about this place. We have a team watching in case she tries to get in there."

Just then security announced Peter was back with another guard and Cavanaugh came through the gate behind them, and another man, identified himself as Dieffenbaker, was right behind him. Daffy? Daffodil? That was a name Jake recognized. A man with a larger-than-life reputation. He had never met him but Daffy was a legend in the security world.

"You got Daffy?" he asked, surprised.

Before Ron could answer, all the men came in together, and Jen ran over and jumped on the stranger. Wrapped her legs around his waist and hugged him. And he was a little guy. Well, little compared to some of the giants in the room, but he was about John's size, about five foot ten or five foot eleven. Slim but solid looking. Brown hair with eyes the same color.

"Hey, love," Daffy said to Jen. "Good to see you too." He let her down gently and reached to shake hands with Ron and then Rib. Looked like they were all old friends. Protection was a small community, and most of the players knew one another or knew of one another. Rather like the coder community, Jake suspected. He hadn't known that Ron knew Daffy, though. The new arrivals got some food.

Ron called for attention.

"OK, let's introduce everyone. This new guy is Dieffenbaker. Or Daffy. Some of you already know him. Daffy, Jake Jayden here, my boss, he's one of the primary targets. Cilla, his wife, is the other." The two men shook hands, Ron pointed out Rib and Jason, the sharp-shooter. And Sheriff Cavanaugh. They all nodded.

"And the rest of these folks are targets, simply by association with Cilla through Jake. The gang of five, they call themselves." He pointed them out one at a time. "Kevin owns this place. He, along with Sarah and John, are secondary targets. With Sarah is Michael. With John is Peter. The fifth gang member is Penney."

Daffy acknowledged them one by one. Stopped when he got to Penney. Tall. Red hair. Something about her. Red hair. A color he had never liked. Before. What was up with that? And she was looking back at him as though she knew him, had known him her whole life. Daffy seemed to realize he was starring, that Ron was still talking to him. He tore his gaze away from Penney and back to Ron and work.

"Here's the situation. I think you all know that Jake was instrumental in taking down that child slavery ring about nine months ago. The head of the ring, Webb, was killed, and his sister was sent to jail for life. She broke out of jail and she's looking for revenge. She's been out eight days. Long enough to know all the players, and where they live and work. Our contact at the FBI, Munson, thinks she had inside help escaping. No one in law enforcement was notified of the escape. Munson is looking into that also."

Cavanaugh broke in then and said, "Since Sheri's been out, she has killed four people that we know about. Two of them, we think because she was angry they were not prosecuted. The FBI didn't have enough evidence to charge them. Sheri shot one through both knees and then shot him in the face. The other guy was gut shot and left to bleed out. Same treatment to an unidentified woman who was unlucky enough to be with him. And last night she killed her partner rather than leave him behind to be arrested.

"We picked up another guy. Actually, he came in looking for protection. He's spilling everything he knows. Enough so that we can pick up the rest of the ring that we missed the first time. Which we are in the process of doing now. The guy is scared and begging for protection from Sheri and wants to be in solitary. Seems while Sheri was inside, she arranged the murder of one of her own men who had failed to protect her from Jake. Anyhow, this guy was afraid Sheri would come after him next, because he was supposed to snatch Juanita for her. Juanita is the fourteen-year-old that Jake rescued. She testified against Sheri. Sheri had some plans for that little girl."

Ron picked it up there. "Juanita is safe. Munson and his wife are fostering her, and she's surrounded by an army. Munson says there's no way anyone can get to her. Sheri is after Jake and is targeting anyone close to him. That's Cilla. The gang of five, and by association Peter and Michael, are links to Cilla. So we need to protect them all.

"Since Peter and John announced their wedding plans, the media has been camped out at his gate. Too much going on there and we don't want to be dealing with media every time we go in or out, so Peter and John will stay in the main house with Kevin. Peter has a good security crew protecting his own place. We don't have to worry about that. Same here. Kevin has a good team in place. He called them in last night.

"Jason, you'll be here in the gatehouse and float where needed. Sarah and Michael will be in the main house. They're both doctors with busy practices. They'll be the toughest to protect because they'll be working with the public. I have two medics coming to cover them inside the examination rooms."

Ron looked at Jason and Rib. "You two will be with them. I have two additional men coming. Get together and decide how you want to work it. Let the rest of us know. I don't want anyone leaving here alone.

"Penney thinks she can work from here, the gatehouse, but will have to go pick up some clothes and files." He was thinking he would put Daffy with her. He had seen some spark pass between the two of them. Wait and see.

"Jen and I will be with Cilla and Jake here in the gatehouse," he said. "There's another empty room here, and plenty more in the main house. Cavanaugh will send extra patrols around by the offices and residences, but can't watch them twenty-four/seven."

Cilla spoke up then. "We've all lived here at one time or another. The kitchen is well stocked, and the restaurants are used to delivering meals."

"I don't want any regular deliveries," Ron said. "It would be better to decide what you want, and then a couple of my men will go pick it up."

"Look," Penney said. "I'll do whatever you want. I already said that. The security video was terrifying."

"I can work here with just a few files from my home office. Most of my work is online. And I want my own clothes. I agree, Cilla might be at some risk, but I think the rest of this is serious overkill. Sheri coming after us is a stretch." She held up her hands. "I will bow to you professionals and do what you want. I won't be a problem."

"I don't want my friends in danger," Cilla interjected. "But—and don't think I am telling you how to do your job—but I don't think you're going to catch her this way. Sheri can just wait. Pick her own time and place. You're going to have to draw her out eventually. Why not just do it now?"

Ron looked at her with new respect. "I agree, but first I want to be sure everyone is safe. That is our primary goal. But you're right in your assessment, and we'll work on that when I'm sure everyone is protected."

Jake broke in and said, "Just put me out there and wait for her to come and get me. It's me she wants and my fault everyone's in danger. Use me for bait."

"I wish that would work, Jake. But from what we've seen and what she has done already, she wants to hurt you before she kills you. She's had opportunity for eight days to go after you, and she chose to go after Cilla. And she knows Cilla's friends. Would you say that Cilla was at fault if Sheri went after one of them? I don't think so. She could grab Michael, which would get her Sarah, which gets her Cilla. We can't do it your way. No one leaves the premises here alone. You included, Jake. Especially you. You are her prime target."

Daffy spoke up then. "You are forgetting the golden rule, Jayden. It's Sheri's fault. Not yours. Anyone who stumbled onto that operation would have done what you did. She's terrorizing even her associates. She's the one responsible for this danger in your lives. You're thinking like a victim here, and the fact that you are thinking like a victim means you should have no part in the decision making."

There was shocked silence in the room. Shock that Daffy had spoken so boldly. They waited to see what Jake would do.

But Jake couldn't argue with Daffy. He understood. He knew it wasn't his fault. He'd always known it. But somehow he still felt responsible for the turmoil. For not being able to find a better solution. But for the first time, he realized that maybe there had been no other way. Somehow Daffy was getting through to him where no one else had been able.

He looked at Daffy for a long moment while everyone else held his breath and then admitted, "You're right."

Ron nodded and then said, "Anyone have anything else?"

"Yeah," Rib said. "How come all the Midnight Plus One posters? And where did you get them? I haven't seen anything like them online. That game is awesome."

That brought another silence, this one not strained, while everyone waited for someone to speak up. Then a laugh went through the room and Cilla explained, "John wrote most of Midnight. The rest of us, the rest of the gang of five, we supplied plotlines and graphics. We all did a little of the coding. We're geeks."

"Wow. That game sold millions in the first twelve hours or so. You're not just geeks, you're filthy rich geeks."

That brought another laugh.

While the group of bodyguards was digesting that, Penney said, "Can I pick my own minder? Can I? Can I? Though I'm not sure if I want a pretty one," she looked at Daffy, "with a cool name. Or a macho one," looking at Jason, who turned red. Oops, so much for macho, he wasn't going to live that one down. "What are you guys? Guards, protectors, guardians?"

She looked around at the room full of men. Bodyguards, strong men. *Guardians*, she thought. *These men are guardians, protectors.*

"No, Penney. You don't get to pick," Ron said sternly. "I want Daffy on you. You two look like you might be a couple. And," smiling at Jason, he continued, "the macho one is your backup."

Penney thought, *yes, the pretty one, on me.* She could almost feel him on her. *That's what I want.* She smiled at Daffy with that thought in her eyes.

Daffy was hung up in the promise he thought he saw there. He had heard the same thing. Him. On her. Ron probably hadn't meant it that way, though. He smiled at her. Yes, he did like that red hair color.

"Sure, no one said this would be easy. So I get to guard them both. The girl and Pretty Boy." Jason looked at Daffy and laughed at him.

Daffy stared him down and then turned to Penney. "Whenever you are ready, ma'am," he said politely. *Keep it impersonal,* he told himself. *Can't do the job if you're thinking of being on her.* He had been impressed with her attitude, her humor.

Daffy had heard a little about Jake and didn't doubt that soon, Jake would be bait in a trap. After Ron planned the trap.

"Go now," Ron said. "And take the communications. Keep in touch. I want everyone back here and settled and safe in one hour."

The group watched Daffy and Penney head out. Rib went to talk to Sarah and Michael.

Jake walked over to Cilla. He acted as if he might be going to talk to her, explain. "Cilla," he started and then paused, "are you going to continue working on our espionage problem?"

She considered him. Took a deep breath, "That's it, Jake? You walked all the way across the room to tell me to go back to work on your problem? Yes, I'll get on that right now. I haven't forgotten that I have a friend in trouble, a friend who needs my help. And I know you and Ron have been busy, but you remember we needed more information from you. Can you check on that?" she asked as she turned away hurt and disappointed.

He caught her arm, and she turned around, looking up into his face. She could see the turmoil there.

"Look, I can't talk about it yet. OK? Soon. Soon we can sit down, and I will try to explain."

"You don't need to explain anything," she said. "No. I take that back, that was a really stupid thing for me to say. You have a lot to explain to me. Things that all your buddies know. Things that Cav knows. You have to tell me what happened, why you left, why you never called. You owe me at least that. They all think you are a hero and you might be. But you're a sorry excuse for a man, where I'm concerned. When are you going to be ready? Ten months is a long time to get ready. So when you do get ready, let me know. And until then, I would just prefer that you stay away from me. And," she added, looking down at her arm, "don't touch me again."

He let her go. "I'll get that information for you." He turned around and saw Ron shaking his head at him.

Daffy drove. Penney was all out of witty remarks. It just seemed so unreal. And Daffy? He made her insides shiver. She wasn't going to think about that. Instead she was deciding what she needed to get from her apartment. And the steps to get everything. A list of steps. Shut down the computer first. Just in case. Once it was off, no one could bring it back up. And she didn't save anything on the hard drive. Everything she did was automatically erased and then written over randomly. She did have some client lists on thumb drives. Coded. Those she would get as the computer shut itself down. Grab a tote, stuff it with undies, socks, running shoes, jeans, and T-shirts. Sleep in her T-shirt. There were toiletries at the gatehouse, and she didn't use makeup. A geek thing, she figured.

That would be it. Five minutes, tops. She wouldn't even need to e-mail her assistant because they usually communicated by texting and e-mail anyhow.

She directed him to her apartment on Main Street, a duplex she owned. She loved the bustle and almost constant buzz of activity here. Something was always happening. She wasn't like Cilla at all. Cilla wanted peace and quiet. Maybe if she was married, like Cilla, she would want to live on the beach. But for now, downtown was perfect.

Daffy? Where did he get that name, she wondered. A pretty face and a flower name, daffodil. Or was it daffy, like crazy? He didn't seem to mind the nickname. Like Penney the Freak, maybe. A badge of honor.

"You can park here or around back."

He parked in front. She started to get out, and he grabbed her arm. The contact was electrifying. Anywhere else but here, anytime else but now, he would pursue that reaction.

"We'll be five minutes max. You wait; you sit right where you are. I'll come around and open the door and help you out. Hook your right hand through my left arm. Don't pull. Leave my right arm loose. That's my gun hand. Do exactly as I tell you. If I say drop, drop to the ground. This is not a game. OK? Can you do that?" he asked, looking her in the eye.

"Yes. I know it's not a game. I will do whatever you say. You're scaring me. Is someone watching?"

"One of our people should be here. I don't see him or anyone else right now." He was watching a guy, two houses down, smoking on the corner. No one he knew. And anyone Ron hired would not be so obvious.

He spoke to Macho Man through his jawbone. "You see our guy?"
"No."

And then to Ron, "Our guy here yet?"

"If not, he'll be there soon. I'll check," Ron said as he worked his phones.

Daffy spoke calmly but sternly to Penney. "Act like we're just getting back from a late date. Ready?" He waited for her to nod and then went around and opened the door. Helping her out, he looked around but didn't see anything unusual. Just that one guy. Might be OK. He knew Jason would watch him.

He got her key and unlocked her door. And moved her inside the doorway. Pushed her gently into the jamb and whispered in her ear, "Wait here a moment." She nodded. He looked around the room. And then walked through each room, checking the closets, showers, and under the beds. Tested the back door, unlocked. He pulled his gun out and opened it slowly and looked out over the parking lot. No one there.

"Ron, I have an unlocked back door," he advised Ron and Jason. "No one here, though."

He put his gun away, locked the door, and came back to her. "Go get your stuff," he instructed and closed and locked the front door.

She went to the computer first to shut it down. It was awake. It shouldn't, couldn't be awake. She looked at Daffy. Terrified. He saw the look and came to her. She leaned against him.

"Someone's been in here. The computer's on," she whispered, partly because she didn't want anyone else to hear her, partly because she couldn't find her voice.

He didn't doubt her. "Come on, honey, let's get your stuff." He said it calmly, squeezing her hand gently.

He told Ron about the computer.

"OK, I need to shut the computer down first and get my files." She clicked it off and pulled out the client lists and thumb drives as she spoke. "It will just take a minute to get my stuff. Come with me." She kept hold of his hand, for comfort, and dragged him with her.

She was glad she had it all planned out, because she couldn't think. She was shaking. Grabbed the tote, threw in the files and thumb drives, underwear, jeans, and T-shirts. Two minutes.

"Done," she said.

He looped the tote over her shoulder, took her hand, and headed out. Opened the door slowly, looking outside and around. The guy was still smoking on the corner. He could have been the one who had been in the apartment. Daffy was opening her car door when four thugs came at them from between the buildings.

He saw the guy on the corner throw down his cigarette and race toward them, yelling, "Get her. Kill the guy."

The first thug swung at Daffy but never connected, because Daffy's kick to the groin bent him over, gasping.

"Get in the car and lock the door," he ordered as he pushed Penney inside the car. The second thug, right behind the first, walked into Daffy's fist as he shut the door. That was a mistake on the part of the crooks. They should have gone around the car and come at Daffy from different directions. And they came on too quick. The third thug tried a roundhouse punch and Daffy caught it, twisted it, and broke the arm. While the second thug was getting up, Daffy kicked him in the head. He went right down again. The first attacker was standing, bent over double, and the fourth guy? *How many of them were there? For one woman?* The fourth guy had a knife.

Daffy backed toward the front of the car, getting ready to pull his gun when he saw the door open and Penney get out. His shock must have shown in his face because the guy started to turn around and caught Penney's tote bag square in his face when she swung it. Daffy hit him in the kidney and then chopped him in his neck. And Penney? Penney used a judo kick on the first guy as he was trying to get his balance and stand up straight. He never saw what hit him.

And then Macho Man reached them. He'd been delayed taking out the cigarette guy.

"Well, you're just in time to save Pretty Boy and his date," Daffy said, bent over catching his breath.

"I was watching the dude on the corner. Never even saw these guys. They were out of sight down the alley. Sorry. You OK?" He was putting plastic hand ties on the men, both wrists and ankles. These guys weren't going anywhere. Daffy helped with the guy from the corner as soon as he got his breath.

"They must have a car around here somewhere. Call Sheriff Cavanaugh and get some troopers to take these guys in, look for the car. I'll get Penney back to the gatehouse."

He looked at her then. That was one of the bravest things he had ever seen. The woman had been so scared, she was shaking, and yet she had gotten out of the car and really walloped that thug. And where had she learned to kick like that?

"I don't know if I should yell at you for disobeying my orders, or give you a medal for one of the bravest things I have ever seen, lady. Where did you learn to kick like that?" he asked, and then, "Doesn't matter. Get in the car, we're getting out of here."

To Ron on his cell, he said, "We're leaving, slow and twisty, back to the gatehouse. I don't want anyone following us, though they probably know where we are anyhow." *And Penney needed time to get herself together*, he thought. She looked like she was going to be sick. Now was not the time to chastise her for getting out of the car. Later he would do that. He put her in the car gently, leaned over, and buckled her seat belt.

"Put your head down between your knees and take a deep breath," he said, gently giving her shoulder a little push. "It's the adrenaline. It will get better." He closed the door again and went around and got in himself and drove.

He kept an eye on the rearview and down the side streets, keeping Ron appraised of his progress. And rubbing Penney's shoulder. When she lifted her head, she had a little color in her cheeks. "Feeling better?"

"A little. Thank you."

"Just doing my job."

"No, you aren't. Thank you for protecting me, which is your job. Thank you for supporting me when I was too scared to move. Thank you for helping me into the car. I couldn't have done that by myself. Thank you for giving me a chance to get my wits together. For letting me save face." She said it all matter-of-factly.

He just looked at her in surprise. Who knew geeks understood the real world?

"Most people wouldn't have noticed that. But it's my job to protect your body and your mind. And lady, I'm not sure you needed me back there at all."

"I was scared to death," she admitted.

"And yet you were able to knock down two thugs. Scared doesn't count. It's what you do when you're scared that counts, and lady, you did it." She needed the positive reinforcement.

"But I almost threw up." She was ashamed; she could still feel her stomach turning.

"I have a buddy, one of the best. Ex-special ops? Special operations. He gets the shakes after every fight. Like a silly girl or a dog afraid of thunder. His whole body trembles. It's amazing. You put a martini in his hand, and you get a James Bond shaken-not-stirred cocktail. Nothing to be embarrassed about. And why would you pick out two things your body did to you that you have no control over and ignore the ones you can control? The fact that you decided to get out of the car, and did, and you decided to hit that guy with your purse, and you did. That you really kicked that last dude. I bet he feels that for three days."

"Before, when I was little…" She hesitated, but decided he could know more about her. "When I was little, I had to fight a lot. I always fought harder when I was the most scared. You know, if you're really scared, you have the most to lose, so you come out fighting and fight hard. And dirty." She took another breath. "Cilla taught me how. I think John taught her some, but she was born fighting dirty. She was small, like Sarah, and learned early to get in the first punch or be beaten."

He glanced over at her. "Cilla? Fights dirty?"

"She always said. 'Don't let them get you down on the ground, because you don't get up.' And she had this great move she called Jacaby, because that was the first bully she used it on."

Daffy waited, wondering. How could she know that? When she was little? And why would Penney need to learn? Why would Cilla need to teach Penney?

"Back then we had each other for protection. Later, I took kickboxing and judo. Some of them did too. But it's been a long time since I had to fight scared," she admitted.

"Well, I guarantee you that Macho Man is bragging on that kick right now to the cops. And the purse attack. Telling them a girl took out those thugs. And he'll be ragging on me too. Needing a girl to help me. Wait and see."

He saw she was calmed down and said quietly into his mouthpiece, "OK, Ron, we're coming in."

He had to show ID to get past the guard, which was good. As soon as they got in the door, Ron demanded details.

Cilla grabbed Penney, drawing her close. "You OK?" she asked. Sarah and Michael were right beside her. Patting Penney. Comforting her. They took her over to the couch and sat down with her.

Daffy gave a short and sweet report; he knew a more thorough debriefing would come later. When he got to the part where Penney got out of the car, he veered into storytelling and a demonstration. Of the purse and kick. Some of his amazement and respect bled through, as he meant it to. To reinforce what he had said in the car. The group on the couch was paying close attention.

A cheer went up for "our hero."

Penney looked at Daffy, but he was only grinning back at her because it was her they were cheering. She was blushing; that was sweet. It was good she had her friends gathered around her.

"Tell us the full story and don't leave out a single detail," Sarah ordered her.

She looked her thanks to Daffy.

He went over to caucus with Ron and Jake, and give the real debriefing. "They were waiting for her. They had already been in her apartment. You'll have to ask her how she knew, because they left it neat. The guy on the corner must have seen us drive up and told them to get out and wait. They wanted her, not me. And they wanted her alive. Otherwise we'd both be dead. I never saw them coming. And she really put a hurt on a couple of them."

"Did she really kick that guy in the balls?" Jake asked Daffy.

"A thing of beauty. That is some brave woman. She got out of the car, shaking so bad, she could barely stand, and let that guy have it across the face with her bag. And then kicked that other guy. A perfect spinning back kick. I don't think I have ever seen anything like that before. I mean, Jen can do it. But Jen is a stone-cold professional. This woman, she's a geek."

He stopped; he just didn't have the words to describe his feelings. "She apologized to me for being scared." He shook his head. "That is one tough mama," he said with respect and admiration. He felt a connection with her. Surprised him.

Jake smiled. "Yeah. I can remember her telling me what she thought of Lenny in front of his sister. And she was scared of Lenny too. The gang of five? They're all like that. Geeks, freaks. Brave geeks. Solid. Every one of them." He paused thinking about that and then continued.

"Here's how I read it. Hindsight: Sheri would go after Penney first. Penney really disliked Lenny. She warned me against him, like I said, right in front of Sheri. Didn't back down. And Lenny hated her. No love lost there. And Sheri knows how important Penney is to Cilla. So, she would be a prime target. I wasn't thinking. I screwed up."

Ron got angry. "Don't start blaming yourself again, Jake. We didn't expect Sheri to be this far ahead of us. Damn. I really had hoped we were being over cautious. But looks like Sheri is at least one step ahead of us. At least we can optimize what we have."

"This is our base, our central area, and we can all work out of here. There are certainly enough electronics. Let's get electronics in each of their residences. Better late than too late. We need to know if someone breaks in. And two teams to go out and get provisions. Two teams, one to do the work, the other for backup. Send a security team with backup to Sarah's office.

"I wonder if Sheri knows about Michael," he continued. "We better not take a chance. Get someone over to his home too. He works at the clinic. That should be OK. Maybe. The cops can watch that. And they probably have a security guard. I'll check. I'll have Peter notify his people. We'll beef up Kevin's security. Though I think he has top of the line already. Jake, you can check. We can put in temporary cameras and sensors if we need to.

"And none of the gang leaves here without two teams. Five guys to grab Penney is overkill, and we want to be ready the next time."

Ron was listening to his phone. Put it on speaker and said, "Repeat that for all of us, Cavanaugh, I have you on speaker."

"We got the car. And there appear to be only the five of them. They're on their way to the station. Doesn't look like anyone saw anything here. Too early in the morning for anyone to be up. They could have got her and no one would know it. We found your guy. Knocked out and tied up in his car. He's OK. Feels a little stupid, though. And he should. You want him to stay here? Or should I send him back to you?"

"Send him back here," Ron said. "I'll get someone else over there, maybe two someones. And this guy might be one of them. Depends on how he handles being chewed out. Handles his screwup. If he own up to making a mistake, I'll keep him on. But if he offers up excuses, he's gone. I'll pay him off and send him on his way. Won't be dependable if he can't admit he screwed up."

"Hey, Pretty Boy, hear you had to have a girl rescue you," Cavanaugh ragged Daffy over the phone. "Macho Man is explaining how she saved you."

The room got silent. Daffy looked at Penney, who was listening. Everyone was listening.

"You ever need anyone to save your butt, Cav, I'll send her over," Daffy said. "But for now I'm keeping her by my side. She did Macho Man's job. Took out those thugs while he was playing with Cigarette Guy." He lobbed that back at them. "Tell him I said that."

Penney beamed. Sarah clapped her on the back.

"You the man," Sarah said. "You the man. We're going to have to find a new nickname for you. I'll work on it."

"After we got in the car, I was so scared and he was so calm. He made me feel so brave," Penney was telling the story her way. "I was sitting there shaking and feeling like a fool and a coward, and he just told me how brave I was. I keep thinking about him. About him and me. Him on me." She gasped and put a hand over her mouth. "Did I say that out loud? It's OK. I think I'll keep him. On me. That picture's in my mind again." She giggled. Actually giggled. It was a reaction she was sure, the giggle. After the near abduction and the video from last night.

They had watched the video again when Cavanaugh came by. Cilla had been scared to death she'd said even though she knew how it ended and that Jake was OK. She had thought she was going to be physically sick when Sheri fired that last round. But she'd held it together. Penney had held her hand.

Cilla had said, "Oh, my God Penney, I don't know how you could have watched that without knowing the outcome. I'm terrified and I know the ending."

"It's not near as bad to watch it now as it was when it happened, Cilla. We were all so scared. You know I love Jake. You two were so good together. I hate that Sheri. Hate her."

"You and me both, Penney. And it sounds like there's more to the story then we know. No one is talking."

Cilla changed the subject. She didn't want to think about what Jake hadn't told her. "What's going on with you and Kevin? And how come I'm only just noticing?"

"We had a thing going for a while. Friends with privileges. Whenever one or the other one of us was feeling lonely. But we stopped a long time ago. Didn't seem right. And there was no passion. No zing. You know, what you see between Michael and Sarah. And between John and Peter. So we just stopped. Still good friends though. We weren't trying to keep it a secret."

"OK. Back to Daffy. He isn't really a pretty boy, Penney, he is so rugged. But, Daffy? I'm not so sure about that name. He looks brave and strong. And you say he's sweet. Go for it, Penney," she urged. "One of us ought to be able to have some fun. Get a good guy." Then she changed the subject again.

"I have a software proposal I have to finish and submit to a client. And then I'll work on the spy stuff. You could check with Ron or Jake and get us the information we need on those client firms. When they get done with their private conference." She nodded toward them.

Ron was saying, "Jake, you need to sit down and tell us everything you know about Sheri. And Lenny. We need to know where she can go for help. Who she can bully or buy. You know most of that. Call it a debriefing. And maybe Cilla should sit in on it. She should hear it." Ron got back to business.

"No, not Cilla. I am not talking with Cilla listening."

"OK. Let me get the rest of this set up, then we can meet in one of the bedrooms. Daffy and Jen too. Am I forgetting anything?"

"Shit," Jake said. "Of course we are. The house. Our house. Sheri knows where that is. I was just over there Sunday. Didn't look like any-one had been there in a while. But I wasn't looking for signs of Sheri. I better get over there."

He stood up, but Ron stopped him. "No. No, I think I'll have Cav meet one of our teams there." They stared each other down.

"OK." Jake was thinking again. He knew Ron was right. Cav could do a safety check. Jake was the target, and he belonged here, protected. He sat down.

"She hadn't been in there. I'm sure of that. Nothing was disturbed."

The guardians were alone now; they had gone into one of the bedrooms. For privacy, they said. Jake was telling his story. "I wasn't even undercover," Jake began. "I was having a heart-to-heart talk with a scumbag who we knew worked as muscle for a guy selling some secret diagrams, not military, just industrial. We knew when the sale would take place, day and time, but not who would be there or where it would be. We had been alerted by one of the possible buyers. He had just turned state's evidence and used the sale to trade for a lighter sentence. Even though this scumbag was pretty far down in the hierarchy, it had taken me two weeks to get close to him. We were just a couple of lowlifes having a drink at the bar and comparing jobs. I had him just drunk enough that he finally leaked the site, and I was getting ready to wander off when Lenny and Sheri clapped him on the back and he followed them over to a booth. I watched in the mirror as they talked."

Jake paused and said, "You know all this. They were only in the bar to meet him. I never saw them in the bar except for that one night. And that scumbag is dead."

"Keep on going," Ron instructed.

"I had a simple cover. I was supposed to be just another muscle for hire. It was supposed to be just a simple make friends, get the info, get out. Nothing elaborate." And that's all Jake had when he got mixed up with Sheri. He was using his own name and his real office. His job, if anyone asked, was a low-level guard and driver. That was all he needed to get the information on the sale. So, because Jake had miscalculated, he had to go into Sheri's operation without good cover. That's how Sheri got to Cilla.

"Anyhow, after they left, he came back and offered me a job. Make a pickup, transport the merchandise, and then make the delivery. I could have said no, but I was curious. I wanted to be around him until the sale. And he was nervous. I had never seen him nervous. He was afraid of her. Not Lenny. But Sheri.

"The scumbag vouched for me, and we went over to another club a week later for a meet. We sat at a table. Sheri did all the talking. Lenny just smirked. She liked what she saw and wanted me to drive her around. She needed to check me out. Neither of them talked to anyone else while I was there. Lenny walked us to the door and let it slip that they were getting some mighty fine merchandise. Bring a high price. His would be a freebie, though. Bragging. After he was done with his 'perk' they would have to take a loss on the used merchandise. That's when it began to sound like people, white slavery, not merchandise. I wasn't even thinking child predators."

Then Jake couldn't walk away. Had to act like muscle with a side job and a wife. He tried to downplay Cilla. Sheri had seen the way he looked at Cilla. He had tried to convince Sheri that Cilla was his meal ticket. A rich little boring geek. In the short time he had known Sheri; he had heard her reputation for destroying people. He'd had to distance himself from Cilla.

So he had distracted Sheri with a tale of an open marriage and all the money he wanted, as long as he was discreet. He would lose it all if anything happened to Cilla. There was no love, just love of money. Apparently the only person he had convinced was Cilla. Sheri didn't care if it was love or love of money that he felt for Cilla; either would be reason for her to go after Cilla. He had really screwed up.

"And you don't need to know all this. No way can we track all the people who went to that club. Everyone who was involved with the porn ring is dead or in jail."

"They meet anyone? Talk to anyone? Did any of them know what was going on?" Ron asked.

"I didn't go back inside the club again. She always went to different places. Didn't have a hangout. She told me to bring Cilla and come for a show in yet another club."

Jake had a flash of a man with a knowing leer, almost drooling.

"Hudson. George Hudson," he said slowly. "That guy on TV? George 'Lease My Car' Hudson. I've been trying to figure out why he looks familiar. I saw him. Two times. Talking to Sheri. Hudson was licking his lips. He knew what she did. That she sold children. He wasn't at the auction."

Jake paused, seeing it come back into focus. "He wasn't at the auction because he was buying Juanita outright. That's what I heard when Sheri had me staked in the barn. She called someone and told him not to bother coming to the auction because his special order was damaged. Juanita, she was talking about Juanita. I didn't understand at the time." He closed his eyes. Yeah, it made sense, anyway he looked at it.

"But my gut feeling isn't enough to go after him. Though, I guess Cav could make a courtesy call. To let him know Sheri is out and see how he handles it."

Ron made the call to Cavanaugh. Told him about Hudson.

"He's going to follow up and get back to us. What about where you took Sheri? Dropped her off? Picked her up? Office? Condo?"

"No. Never anywhere she did business. It was mostly stuff to demean me. And to demonstrate her power. Have me watch while she verbally destroyed some helpless assistant. She liked to make people suck up to keep a job. Or run out crying. I never saw any physical beatings with my own eyes, though one time I took two men to the emergency room after she was through with them. She'd messed them both up bad.

"She didn't want a man, but she did want every man to want her. So mostly I drove her, shopped with her, and carried her packages. Helped her decide which pair of shoes she should buy. Which pair of panties. Made me watch while she changed her clothes." That had been about the worst. She demanded he accompany her into the dressing room. She loved to get naked in front of him. Watch his reaction. She could spend hours trying on clothes. He wanted to shower just thinking of it.

"Don't look at me like that," he said when Daffy raised his eyebrows. "It wasn't fun. You wouldn't have liked it. She loved to belittle Cilla. Frumpy, boring geek, she called her. And I let her. Encouraged her. Joined her. Anything to make her believe Cilla meant nothing to me. She would remind me endlessly that I was dependent on the frump's good wishes for my job and income." He wasn't sure which was the worst, when she insisted he take Cilla to the club or the day she set it up for Cilla to find them having a cozy lunch together. Either. Both.

"No, I never drove her anywhere on business or to a meet. That's it; she never met with anyone. Took me everywhere with her, like her pet. I always picked her up in front of her condo or her office. They found a lot of information in her office, after they took her down. She kept track of all her contacts and their weaknesses. Munson will have that. Have him e-mail it. Or ship it overnight."

As they broke up, Ron said to Jake. "You need to talk to her. Don't look at me like that. You need to talk to her. Give her some credit for understanding. Suck it up. Take a chance. This isn't fair to her."

Jake just shook his head and walked out. Of course she was the first person he saw, but she was at her computer, staring at the monitor and rubbing the cat in her lap. The cat watched him escape outdoors.

Cavanaugh showed up about three hours later with the young officer, Jones, from the car wreck. By that time Jake was cooled off and inside watching the gang at work. Ron hadn't yet given them the list of names. They were working on their own ideas.

Penney offered them coffee. Cavanaugh thanked her and sat down. He looked exhausted. Dark lines in his face. He rubbed his eyes. The officer stood by the door. He looked a little green. And a little in awe as Cavanaugh introduced him. Some of these people were legends in the protection sector. Penney made him sit down.

"Did Hudson give you anything?" Ron asked.

"Hudson is dead. Looks like she went at him with her weapon of choice. Gun." Cavanaugh looked at Jake. "She took a long time with him. You don't need the details. Jesus. That woman is sick. Left him to bleed out."

Cav drank some coffee, trying to get the picture out of his head.

"He apparently let her in. Any idea why she would do that to him?" he asked Jake.

"It never took much to tick her off. Any slight, real or imagined, could do it. She has a vicious streak. And likes to humiliate and hurt people any way she can. I think he might have gotten kids from her.

She could blame him for Juanita. I have a feeling Juanita was for him. Did Hudson have a wife? Maid? Kids? Lord, I hope not."

"Wife and kids. They left him just before your bust. We've been through his house. The place was trashed the same as yours. He had a wine cellar. Every bottle was smashed. We couldn't find any of his files, records, bank accounts. Maybe that's what she wanted. He probably has a safe, but we haven't found it yet. Still clearing the crime scene."

"What about a safe room?" Daffy asked. "People like that have a safe room."

Cavanaugh looked at him. "Jesus. How could I not think of that? I really need some sleep. Hold on." He called someone and told him to start looking for a hidden room.

Jones spoke up as Cavanaugh was talking into his cell. "Look in the cellar. The wine cellar. Behind the wine racks. See if the racks pull away from the wall. That's where those sickos hide their safe rooms. Either the cellar or in the bedroom."

Everyone looked at him. Cavanaugh, flabbergasted, said to Jones, "Behind the wine racks? Pull out the wine racks?" he asked incredulously. The detective on the other end of the phone thought it was an instruction.

"Yes, it's a common hiding place," Jones said.

"And you know this how? You have been on the job one week." Jesus. Looking back, the kid had been exposed to a lot for his first week.

"It's a common hiding place in romance novels," he defended himself. Everyone was still looking at him, and he said defensively, "What? My sister reads them. Adventure romance. Suspense. She tells me the plotlines."

"Yeah, sure, *she* reads them," Cav said with the emphasis on *she*.

Cavanaugh looked at him. "I didn't see anything that looked like a locked room. But I didn't go into the cellar. Jesus. Romance novels." His phone was yelling at him and he was listening. Looking at Jones in amazement. Now everyone was looking at Cav.

"OK," he said and then again, "OK. You have an ambulance coming? Good and a social worker? Children's services? OK. Look for Hudson's files. They might be what Sheri wanted. The safe room would be a good spot for them. If he was protecting his family, he wouldn't give the files to her."

He disconnected the call. "Well, they found a room hidden behind a moving wine rack in the cellar." He looked at Jones and shook his head, disgusted. "And we would never have looked there. Sarge heard me talking about movable wine racks, and thought I was telling him to look there. Wife and two kids. Apparently they came back. Been locked in the safe room a couple of days. They're OK, just hungry and dehydrated. Why have a safe room with no food or water? No exit for God's sake. Hudson had them locked in there from the outside. No cell phone inside there either. Idiot. They would have died in there and no one would have known." He shook his head again.

"Health wise, they don't look too bad, but they're scared, tired, and hungry. They'll be transported to the hospital and met by children's services. Someone with experience with kids. Jesus." He paused and then continued, "And I got Nora Roberts over here, one week on the job, and he's the only one who can find them. Because he reads romance novels. Nora Roberts," he said, disgusted.

"Sister," Jones claimed. "Sister reads them. And they're adventure romance, not romance. She makes that distinction."

"Sure, Nora," Cavanaugh said, smiling for the first time.

"No. Not Nora." Sarah said. She knew just how deadly nicknames could be. How much damage they could do. They could follow someone all their lives. "Sherlock. Sherlock Holmes." And then she pointed to Daffy. "Sherlock, meet Daffy, or as we are calling you today, Pretty Boy."

Daffy understood what she was doing and nodded his head. "Sherlock," he acknowledged.

"And over there is Macho Man."

Daffy got in on it and pointed at Penney. "Legs," is all he said.

Penney got gooey eyed. "I've gotten used to Penney the Freak, but I like Legs better." It made her feel sexy and beautiful. She went over and hugged Jones. She wanted to hug Daffy, but was afraid to touch him. She remembered what it felt like when he'd touched her arm in front of her apartment.

She shook Jones's hand. "I think the name Sherlock is perfect for Jones. Pleased to meet you, Sherlock. That is sooo cool. Thanks for saving those two kids."

Sarah's cell rang then, and as she looked at it, Michael's went off. "Hospital?" she asked him.

"Yeah. Two kids are being transported. What are the chances it's the same two kids? Let's go. We can go together."

"Hold on," Ron said at the same time Jake said, "No."

"What?" Michael asked.

"Wait. Sit down a minute. You can't go anywhere until we talk this out."

"Those kids might need help," Sarah said. "You can't stop us."

"Just wait. A few minutes are all I need. Be getting your stuff together if that makes you feel better. But you're not going anywhere until I get your bodyguards and backup teams organized." He looked at Jake, "Are you thinking what I am?"

"Yes. Is this one of Sheri's plans? Is that why she tortured Hudson? To find the kids and use them as bait for Sarah or Michael?"

"You said you didn't think she knew about us," Sarah disputed. "And it doesn't make any difference whether she planned it or not. We're the best those kids will get. They need us."

"We don't know if Sheri does know about you," Ron said. "Or if she was looking for something else. Or if she just enjoyed torturing Hudson. We may be giving her way too much credit. It doesn't matter. We can't take any chances. We have to treat it as a possible attempt at abduction. Especially since they went after Penney. Do the kids have to go to the hospital? Is there an alternative site for them?"

"No," Sarah said. "They need to be examined at the hospital, and they might need attention twenty-four/seven. That's why we set up SC Digital. To raise the capital for a facility for kids in need. There is no other place now. When Sarah's Child opens, we will have teams on duty twenty-four/seven. We'll have beds for kids. The occasional abused parent. Mostly we will have a safe place."

"OK. Just checking our options." He looked at his men. "I need a four-man team to go to the hospital and do a reconnaissance. Keep an eye out for Sheri. Make sure it's safe. And then stand watch. When they give us the all clear, Michael and Sarah can go with their guards."

Now he looked at Sarah again. "I'll get your medics over here from the main house. They'll go with you too." Ron turned to do that.

"Daffy, I want you with Sarah and her medic for now. Macho Man, I want you with Michael and his medic. The medics drive. And there will be two more teams to back you up." He turned to Jake. "Tell them the rules while I get everyone lined up."

Jake took up the instruction. "Michael, Sarah, do whatever Daffy or Macho Man say. When they say it. No questions, just act. Your lives, their lives, might depend on instant obedience. You saw how quick everything went south at Priscilla's condo. Keep close to Daffy and Jason. Don't take any chances. Never get out of their sight. Even in the examining room. Make sure they can always see you. OK? That's all you have to do. They'll do the rest. And the medics will always be with you too.

"Now I have a question. Does the fact that both you and Michael were called mean that the two kids are a boy and a girl?"

"Most likely. Michael for the boy, me for the girl. They try to match up the sexes. Does it make a difference?"

"I don't know. Maybe. I don't know."

And then Cavanaugh said to Ron, who was off the phone, "How did we miss Hudson when we rounded up that ring? We need access to the FBI's records. We need to go over the reports with a fine-tooth comb. Make sure there's no one else still out there."

"Munson is overnighting copies of everything he has," Ron said. "Should be here by morning. We had already decided we had to go back through all the files, looking for anyone Sheri could be working with. Now we'll look for more Hudsons. Try to track down every buyer. Hard to believe Munson could miss something like that. Miss Hudson."

"Not Munson. He wasn't the FBI's agent in charge. He's espionage and terrorism. He had to turn that trafficking operation over to Collins. Munson went with you to the hospital because Collins took over the operation," Cav corrected him.

"Huh. Didn't know that. But that's not the only thing they missed," Jake said, thinking. "Sheri escapes. How? No one knows Sheri's out. Why? Someone dropped the ball there. Just like someone missed Hudson ten months ago."

Both men looked at him speculatively. Cavanaugh finally said, "What are you saying?"

"Just saying. Getting to be too many things that were missed or overlooked. Laying that out there. Maybe when we go through the files, we'll find an explanation," Jake finished, shrugging.

The surveillance team was sent out, with Ron and Jake making plans and hammering out details for security at the hospital. Should they bring in the hospital security? Cavanagh said he would give them a heads-up; he was buddies with their chief of security.

Cilla watched Jake with these men. These tough, strong men. He fit right in. And he was respected. It was obvious by the way they listened to him and accepted his conclusions. He didn't have any trouble talking to them. He just had trouble talking to his wife.

She turned around and went over to Penney, who was still holding Jones's hand from the Sherlock introduction. It was cute.

"I have an idea for a module to find backdoors. One that deals with most of the variables. We'll still need to examine a lot of individual code, but the module will get us close," she told Penney. "You know once we get into the code and find the backdoor, we could lock down that back entrance and protect the network and divert anyone trying to use that entrance to our own duplicated site. One with our own version of secret information. The criminals would never know they have been relocated. And we could feed them some good stuff. Like maybe some schematics from the game, from Midnight Plus One. Those would fool anyone except maybe a weapon designer. We made them pretty real. It will be fun; John will really get off on it."

Cilla could see Penney thinking. Thinking about the bogus information they could put on the site, Cilla was certain. "We could do some good fake secrets stuff based on the game. Sure, it would be fun. Let's run it by Sarah before she goes and get Kevin and John over here. They need to know about your module to find the backdoor. And you're right; they'll want to play too."

Penney talked with her hands. She suddenly realized she was still attached to Jones. And Daffy was looking at her. He winked at her with a smile and turned back to Ron, missing her blush.

Jones took the opportunity to ask, "Midnight. That's you guys? That's why the posters are all over the walls?"

Penney was still beside him and said quietly, "I'll tell you all about it later. Let's go play. You can come with us and play with Midnight Plus One, maybe even get a look at the sequel." She dragged him over to Cilla's work area. "Have you played the game yet, Sherlock?"

He looked at her like she was crazy. "You folks have had me busy almost nonstop since the game was released."

She was a little taken aback at his time line and said, "Gosh, it seems like months. So much has happened." Jake being back. Sheri loose. The condo raid. Daffy. Daffy made her feel warm all over. And a little bit tingly? "Come on, you can play it here on this computer, and Cilla and I will be geek talking right beside you."

"You guys really wrote it?" he asked, amazed.

"Well, John wrote it and the rest of us contributed ideas and modules and graphics. You'll meet John soon."

Kevin, John, and Peter came in with the medics and their guards. For a few minutes, it was confusion as everyone tried to explain what was happening. But Ron quickly got them quiet and explained what they were doing and why.

There was shock and concern when they heard about the attack on Penney. The three men went over to comfort Penney and reassure themselves of her safety. Cilla introduced the new arrivals to Jones and then told John, Kevin, and Peter what she was thinking about backdoors. She apologized to Jones. "Sorry to talk geek in front of you, but this is a project I've been working on and I can't hold my idea in. I always have to share right away, and we have to do it in geek talk."

John agreed, saying, "Yeah, don't worry, we'll be back to English soon." Cilla explained how her code should be able to find the back entrance, and John agreed that it could work. "Good thinking. Set it up and we'll test it."

Daffy watched the gang work together. It was apparent these people really liked *one another*. It was obvious in the way they offered support and encouragement. Their compassion spoke of how hard their childhoods must have been for them to develop this level of attachment. He wasn't going to use the word love, even though that was what it looked like. They acted like family. Siblings. It made him a little uneasy how much these people did care for one another.

Then they were all looking at him. Penney was telling them how he had saved her. He became the object of their gratitude, which he sidestepped by telling them how Penney had saved herself and him also. It made for a good tale.

"Legs is responsible for me now," he said as he elaborated on his story. "She saved my life."

Sarah was anxious about the children, but Ron wouldn't let them go without his support personnel in place first. Jake suggested she call the hospital and check out the family's status. Maybe she could do some long-distance treatment. She called immediately. Walked over into the corner as she talked quietly into her phone. Then they heard her, not yelling, but using her "I'm the boss" tone.

"Don't you dare separate those children. You'll panic them. Let them stay together. They need each other. Put them in the same treatment room with their mom and wait for me and Michael to get there before you touch them. Is that clear?" She waited for a response. "Give them some food and some milk; it's possible they haven't had anything for a while."

She hung up, shaking her head, and came back to the group.

"The kids were terrified. I could hear them screaming in the background. The aides were trying to separate them and put them in different cubicles." Still shaking her head at the idiocy, she looked at Jake and said, "Thanks for letting me call. We probably saved those kids some unnecessary distress, and the residents will wait for Michael and me before they do anything else. The kids appear to be physically fine, and a half hour more or less won't hurt them."

Ron gave the go-ahead for the medical teams to leave.

Daffy came by on his way out and kidded Penney, "You want to come and watch my back, darling?" And then, serious, he reminded her, "Don't go anywhere without me." He winked at her and added, "You're mine." She turned pink again.

"She doesn't leave this building until I get back," Daffy said to Jones. "You don't leave her side. And watch out for those legs. They're not calling her Legs just because they're gorgeous." He turned back to Penney, winked at her one more time as he walked out.

"Now you have another story you have to tell me. Was that Daffy?" Jones asked Penney, amazed and a little awestruck. "Really? I got to meet Daffy? And you called him Pretty Boy and got away with it?"

"He knows who he is. He can handle a silly new nickname. And he knows that Daffy is too good a name for his buddies to give it up and trade it for Pretty Boy. Take a lesson from him; let a nickname roll off you, and people will stop using it. When they get no reaction, they'll get bored. Sarah saved you from Nora. Sherlock is a good strong name. Be thankful."

Jones looked at her a minute and then smiled. "OK, Mom, I know that sticks and stones ditty. It could be worse; they could be calling me Suzy. Show me that game," he instructed.

"Ooh, two new nicknames in ten minutes, Legs and Mom," Penney cooed.

"Back to business," Cilla reminded her. "We need the information from Jake about where these hackers may go next." She and John approached Jake. "Are you going to give us the names of the other companies?" John asked. "So we can check their networks."

"Get them from Ron," he said shortly, and turned and walked away.

John looked at Cilla. "What's wrong with him? I thought he wanted to do this."

"Doesn't want to be near me," she said sadly. "I don't care. This isn't my Jake. My Jake had died."

John was watching her closely. He saw the hurt.

"I'm going to work on the code," she said. "Penney will help." She looked at Penney and saw that her eyes were a little glazed over. "Once she gets over those winks she got from Daffy." She laughed and said to Penney, "Control to Legs. Control to Legs."

Penney started and looked guilty. "Oh, his winks are an intoxicating weapon. That man has everything I need." And she whispered almost to herself, "On me, Pretty Boy. On me. A promise?"

"Well, he's gone for now, help me with this code. And later we can help John with the game schematics. I wonder if maybe we can just hide the real schematics, take them off-line, and substitute ours. No, we don't know who has seen them. It would be better to put up a mirror site. Confuse everyone with too much information. If they discover some are fake, we may be able to convince them everything is fake. We need to look at all the possibilities. We could have the code ready when John gets the names we need."

Penney sat Jones down with Midnight +1. "We'll be right here beside you. Probably lost in coding, so if you need me, you may have to reach out and touch." She smiled at him. "And I want to meet your sister."

"First tell me what a backdoor is," Jones said.

Penney thought a minute and then explained, "The simplest one and probably the simplest way. You know how you need to use a name and password to get into your e-mail?"

When he nodded, she said, "Well, a coder can just hard code, um, include a name and password for himself in the code. Then he can always get into a site."

The next couple of hours were quiet. Cilla worked on code that just wrote itself. Penney offered an occasional comment or suggestion, encouraging her.

"It will do it. It will do ninety percent of the hard work, and we can sift through what's left. This is good. This is good, Cilla."

John and Kevin were working on the game schematics. Cilla was aware of them egging each other on. She heard, "This is some serious piece of hardware. The laser gun is awesome. We ought to sell this stuff ourselves. Oops, John, you missed a decimal in the dimensions there. This is fantastic. Wow. Look at this, guys. Look at this gun. And come see John's electromagnetic pulsar."

They went over and looked. "I haven't seen that pulsar transmitter before," Cilla said. "Where did that come from?"

"Brand new in the sequel. And there's an ion generator too. But these are the new and improved versions. We're making them for the hacker to steal. You gotta see what we've done. I can't wait for those thieves to steal this. I want to see what they think."

They all kept an eye on the clock, waiting for Sarah's call as they kept working. It was another two hours before it finally came.

"We're on our way back. Things are better than expected. The kids are scared and hungry. A little food and maybe some milkshakes, and they should be fine, physically. Now that they are out of the room, they should recover with no lingering effects."

"The wife overheard a call Hudson got from Sheri. We think it was the night of the auction. Mrs. Hudson heard enough to realize he was a pedophile. He was angry because his selected treat was not available. She accused him and he admitted he liked young girls, but he said his daughter was too young. Mrs. Hudson grabbed the kids and went home to her mother the next day.

"She came back for one day to pack up all their things and arrange for movers. She says Hudson saw Sheri drive up, and he locked them in the safe room. Told them to be quiet. And he never came back. The inside lock didn't work, and they didn't have a cell. They were getting desperate. The wife thinks it's been two days. No food, water from the bathroom sink. We are going to get a happy ending out of this one."

The gang continued working while waiting for Sarah to return. Jake was watching them work and listening. He had nothing else to do. Their comments back and forth were entertaining.

"You know, Cilla, you can test your code for a back entrance," John said. "Try it on Midnight Plus One. It would be interesting to see if you can find mine."

"You built a backdoor? In our game? "She was a little surprised. "And you didn't tell us?" Annoyed because she hadn't caught it.

"Sarah found it," he said defensively. Only realizing now that he might have done something wrong.

"Well, I don't think I'm angry that you did that without telling us, but I'm irritated because I didn't see it," Cilla said. And then after a pause, she asked, "Does Peter know?"

John looked shocked. And then chagrined and maybe nervous. It was obvious to Cilla he hadn't even thought about the backdoor after he put it there. He had never mentioned it to Peter, even after Peter bought both games. Now, should he be worried that Peter might get the wrong idea about his code?

"Good point. I never even thought of that." John looked around and saw Peter and went over. Hesitantly.

She watched him approach Peter and draw him away. John's body language screamed distress and anxiety. She saw puzzlement and then anger on Peter's face and heard him say, "Don't ever…" His voice faded out, as he appeared to be admonishing John. Then he grabbed him and hugged him.

"Silly," they heard. "We love each other. We trust each other. How could you think I wouldn't understand? We should never be scared to discuss things with each other." They were both smiling as they came over to Cilla and Penney.

"So there's a secret backdoor into my games, huh?" he asked.

"You put one in the sequel too?" Penney asked. "Oh, of course you did. Are you going to take them out?"

"No, he isn't. I think it's a good idea. Never know when you might need something like that," Peter said with a smile.

"So what was that chewing out we saw over there a bit ago?" Only Penney would be brave enough to ask that.

"That was me chewing John out for not trusting me to trust him," Peter told them. "As if I expect him to be some sort of comic book superhero with no flaws or black marks. Like me," he added joking.

Cilla hoped Jake was listening to that interchange. It might help him understand that where there is love there is trust. Where there is trust, there is communication. She looked around to see him watching with a confused look.

"That's it! That's who it is!" John exclaimed, calling her attention back.

"Who?"

"The hacker. The spy. Mark, Mark Blackit. Remember how he used to call himself the Black Markit, and we used to kid him and call him the Black Mark? Back when we worked with him on Tigertale? In school, Cilla. We worked with him on that one project in school."

"Yeah. The jerk," Cilla acknowledged, and then her eyes got wide and she groaned. Put her hands to her head, grabbing her hair between her fingers. "Arghhh."

"Headache? Do you have a headache? Are you OK?" Penney asked, concerned. Looking around for help. Jones was right there, watching, puzzled. Waiting to see how Cilla would respond. Ready to jump in if needed.

"I can't believe I was so stupid. I should have recognized that code. The guy was an idiot. This all fits him. Pompous website. Spurts of pretty good code mixed in with trash. How could I have not remembered?" She looked at John and said, "My backdoor code, my module. We don't need it. We don't need to do multiple scans for numerous variables. We know what the backdoor looks like. At least in Tigertale we do. He bragged on it enough. I bet he used the same code over and over again. Why would he change it? All we have to do is scan for that same module he put in Tigertale."

"Huh. You're right."

Cilla called up Tigertale and found the backdoor module. "I got it. Here it is. I'll just plug in a search in the code for Jake's company…" She paused while she did it. "Here it is. This is the back entrance he used. More proof it was him. We can close it down and put up our own mirror site."

"Let me Google him. I bet he has a Facebook page. He's the type to brag on everything he does. Always needing attention and praise. Yeah, here it is Mark Blackit, Hacker."

She quickly read the main points on his page. "Fool."

"Wait a minute. Let me try Black Markit too, maybe he has two pages. Oh my God, I don't believe this. Ron. Jake." She called them. "We found him, we found your spy."

They came over with Cavanaugh, who had just come in. Jones leaned over to look too.

"Remember we said the code looked familiar?" Cilla said. "We worked with the guy who wrote it. His name is Mark Blackit. We worked with him in school, on a class project called Tigertale. A digital comic book."

She looked at John. "That's why you remembered, John. Peter said comic book heroes with no black marks. Mark Blackit and digital comic book hero and trashy code. You put it all together."

"Yeah," John said. "We barely completed the project because he wanted to be in charge. He thought he knew everything, but his code kept crashing. He did almost everything wrong. A real idiot. He called himself the Black Markit."

Cilla picked up the dialogue. "And Jake? Now we can tell you which one of your government contract businesses he's going to hack next."

"How?" Ron asked. "We haven't shared any information with you yet."

"You don't need to," Cilla said as she looked up. "Just nod your head if you recognize any of these names." She had barely made it past the second one when both Ron and Jake tried to shut her up and take away her iPad.

"Stop." She pulled back from them. "It's all here online. Those companies and the two already hacked and two more. He has a list here of every place he worked, where he helped write code. There, on the large screen." She pointed.

"He has them all here," John said. "We don't need your help, Ron. Now all we have to do is look at the code for each of these companies and find his backdoor. Simple."

"I don't see any security on his site at all," Cilla said. "I can't believe it. And here, look at all his friends. I'll bet they're all on some government watch list. Man, this guy never learned how to keep something private. Bragging. He's bragging."

"This is classified. Top secret. And he has it on his Facebook page?" Jake thundered, outraged. "I'll put this guy away forever. He'll never see the light of day. He will never touch another computer."

"Oh, oh," Cilla said quietly. "Look." She put up the Black Markit web page.

"Oh my God," Jake sat. It was unbelievable. Everything was there. A list of all the weapons being developed at the two hacked sites. Hints of more that might become available. "He is going to sell them for a price. He's auctioning off the weapons? He's selling them online?"

Cilla continued to the next page, which contained directions on how to purchase samples of the designs, for a price. The room was now silent as she worked her way through the pages and found samples of the hacked data.

"He's going to sell them here, right on his own website. How stupid can that be? I'll copy it. He probably has a tracker on the site. Though he probably doesn't track where the hits are coming from. We should be OK, we've got good security. He won't be able to find us." She quietly went to work, copying what they needed and erasing her tracks.

She put the homepage back up. "He's promising more. Soon. John, we better finish work on our substitute mirror pages and schematics. As soon as we locate the backdoors on these networks, we can lock the sites down and put up our mirror sites with our schematics. But I haven't finished the code yet."

"Goddamn it. Goddamn it." Jake stalked, complaining. "This guy is an idiot. He has this classified stuff up here for the whole world to see and copy? It's a wonder these production plants haven't been bombed. How long has this been up? We might never get a handle on this."

John, meanwhile, had been looking at the site history. "The list only went up today, and I can block these pages right now, if you give the word. Or I can block out the whole site. Or we can just watch and track anyone who comes here. I would recommend tracking. We can do that legally. The complete plans don't appear to be published here yet. Just the partials. You need to get a warrant, really, to be legal. But I can do stopgap, legally."

"Let's track it. For now."

John pushed some keys and said, "Done. And we have full access. I can go back in the history and get you a list of everyone who has been here, and which pages he went to, and for how long."

"Do that too. Let's see how bad it is. God, I don't believe it. National security information published on Facebook."

Sarah and Michael came back then with Daffy and the guards. The gang filled them in on developments.

"Jake, don't get your hopes up that we'll be able to identify all these people," John said. "Some of these hits are bound to be professionals, and they're not going to be as stupid as Blackit and use real names and addresses. They'll do what we did. Set up fake email accounts to get into Facebook."

While John was tracking, Jake looked at Ron, shaking his head, and said, "I have screwed everything up. Sheri, Hudson and his family, the hacker. Take me off of everything. We can't trust my judgment anymore. Anything I do could be wrong. Even anything I don't do."

"Well, listen to the sissy whining," Daffy said.

There was a horrified silence while Jake just looked at him like he couldn't believe what he had heard.

"Listen to yourself. Poor me, I did this and some bad thing happened. Poor me." His tone was insulting and belittling. "Let me get you a hankie."

Jake jumped at Daffy and was already throwing a punch when Ron caught his arm and John body blocked him. John? Body blocked him?

Daffy smiled. But he still took a step back. "OK. This is more like it. This is the Jake Jayden I've heard all the stories about. Not that sniveling weakling I just saw. Do you actually believe you can see into the future and have control over how a psychotic crazy bitch is going to act? Predict it from your hospital bed? Give me a break. How can you know an FBI agent might go bad? How can you know someone has left a child predator off a list? Or how can you predict that an idiot will make national secrets public?"

He had Jake's attention now. They were all looking at him. Jake was listening. For the first time in a long time, Jake was listening and understanding there were things he couldn't control and was not responsible for.

"You need to find the crazy bitch," Daffy continued. "To do that, you need to know who helped her. There were just a few too many coincidences during her escape. That was a little too neat. Who arranged for the new guards to be on duty that day? For no one with any experience to be around? For the doctor and nurse to be off-site? Who decided to send her to the hospital? Where did her transportation come from after she escaped? While I'm asking questions, how about Hudson? How did his name disappear from the crazy bitch's files? If Hudson was going to buy a kid, where is that record?

"And speaking of Hudson, Jake, if you hadn't seen him in his brand-new TV ad, if you hadn't remembered him from two sightings ten months ago and made the connection, his wife and kids might have starved to death before anybody found them. If anybody ever did find them. You can't beat yourself up for that. That was damn good logical police work you did. And while I'm asking questions, don't you wonder if there are more Hudson's out there?"

Daffy looked around and then directly at Cavanaugh and Ron. "These mistakes are in-house. Someone altered those files. Who had access to them? Who could do that? And is the person who arranged for Sheri to break out the same one who neglected to notify any of you that Sheri was out?"

"Wasn't any of my people," Cavanaugh said. "We were not allowed anywhere near the arrest. The FBI froze us out. They even took Sheri. All we got were a few underlings and the dead guys."

Ron nodded. "As soon as Jake got hurt, they kicked us off the case."

"Shut up, Jake," Daffy said when it looked like Jake was going to say something. "That wasn't your fault. You were doing your job. You didn't screw up when you decided to put your life on the line to save an innocent girl. You are not responsible for what happened after you were hurt. When the FBI takes over, they take over. Pay attention. Start thinking like a cop again. And while you are thinking, remember the thirty or so children you are responsible for saving. You alone are responsible for that."

"Sooo," Daffy dragged that out, "It will be interesting to see which version of the files we actually get. They should be here soon?"

"You know, we might be looking at more than one person here," Jake said. He was finally thinking again. Thanks to Daffy's jabs. He smiled at Daffy, who seemed to understand his thanks. Everyone looked at Jake, he didn't have to explain.

"Sure, you have the higher-up managing the case the way he wants it to be handled," Daffy said. "And you could have one or maybe more underlings for the cover-ups. In fact, those underlings don't even need to be crooked. They might just be following orders. So we probably don't want to keep updating the FBI on your progress. And what about Munson? Didn't you say he was fostering one of those girls? What better cover for a predator?"

"No," Ron stated. "No, I know him; I know his wife, his kids. No way any of those kids is abused. I'd stake my life on it. Besides," Ron continued, slowly, hesitantly, "Munson talked to me. Well, maybe he talked to me. Maybe he leaked some stuff. About the case status. He was locked out too and didn't like it. He's in national security. This was kidnapping and selling of children across state lines. Not his department."

"It's not Munson," Jake stated.

The intercom squawked, "FBI agent in charge, Munson, to see Jake Jayden."

They looked at each other.

"Send him in," Ron said.

"You might have to stake your life on it sooner than you expected." Daffy reminded them of what they had just said.

Munson came in and looked around. He knew Ron and Jake. Some of the bodyguards. Had seen Cavanaugh, but never met him. They were all looking at him with more than curiosity. A little animosity and suspicion.

He nodded and said, "It looks like you guys have reached the same conclusions I have."

Daffy took it. "And those are?"

"We have a double agent in the FBI. Might have two or three, and one or more might also be a child predator. Too much is happening that can't be explained. Yes, I can see you've reached the same conclusion. That's why I'm here. Hand delivering these files. No one back at the office knows I'm here. As far as anyone is concerned, I'm on leave, at the shore. My family is in a safe place." He was looking at Jake when he said that and stopped because Jake was nodding his head.

"And," Munson continued, "I have copies of the original digital files. I took them directly off Sheri's hard drives. My department made the original bust and we kept the original hard drives. When AIC Collins took over, he got everything we had, but I wouldn't give him the hard drives. Only copies. He insisted the originals be locked up. No one knows I made this copy." He handed over the thumb drive, which Ron passed to John.

"I also have copies of what is in Collins's official files." He handed over a second thumb. "I don't think you'll find them both the same."

Ron handed the second thumb to Sarah with instructions to find Hudson.

"I don't know these people," Munson said. "Are they authorized to look at those files?"

Ron laughed. "These are our civilian computer geeks. You'll get to meet them soon maybe."

Just then John said, "I have Hudson in the original files."

They all looked at Sarah and waited. "No, I don't. He isn't here in the official file."

"Who is Hudson?" Munson asked.

"Do you have a file named 'Invest'?" John asked, ignoring Munson's question.

"No."

"Shit. That's it then. Someone altered our files. Shit." Munson hit the desk.

"Mine's 389 K," John said. "Let me put it up. Might be able to pull out more missing names. Then Ron or someone can take it the next step. God, I hate this. That's a lot of K, kilobytes, of information. Not enough for pictures, but a lot of names. It's going to be a lot of kids. Hold on, pass worded. I have a program to decode that." He called it up.

"Hard copies. Do the hard copies contain sign-out sheets?" Jake asked Munson.

"Yes, but I'm not sure we can trust those. A guy this high up? He could grab files and not sign them out."

"We can find time stamps for the deletions and try to match those to names," John said. "But I don't think we'll be able to come up with a name for you. The computer can do this work by itself. Give it about ten minutes."

Ron looked at Munson. It was obvious he would still need to offer something more tangible to be fully accepted.

Jake supplied that. "Your wife, Sally, and kids are in a safe place?" he asked.

"Safe place with bodyguards, childhood friends," Munson added. Jake would understand.

"Tell these guys a name they'll recognize," Jake suggested.

Munson looked at him, thinking. "If I give you a name, then everyone knows Sally's connection."

"But they'll still be safe. No one is going up against those men. Share that name, it will convince the people in this room who don't know you. What is her childhood friend's name?"

Now they were all looking at Munson. It took a long time.

"Heatherton," he spit out.

Cilla saw the shock on the faces.

Daffy said quietly, "She's with Heathertons?"

Munson nodded.

"Those are some scary dudes," Daffy said with a tone of respect. "Dangerous. She knows them? She's with them?" he asked Munson.

Munson nodded again. Jake had been right. The tension level in the room dropped as acceptance went around and the men relaxed. That one name, Heatherton, put Munson on the side of the good guys, the side of the angels. It was his validation with the men in this room. Heathertons were legend.

"Where are they?" Ron asked.

Munson just looked at him again and finally said, "Safe."

Jones started to ask a question and Penney elbowed him quiet. "Later," she whispered. Cilla looked at them; pointing to herself. She would be there when Penney shared.

John called for their attention. The computer had finished its search. "Ah, folks, if you all are finished with the dramatics, I have that list. Only four names are on the 'Invest' list, with occupations. The extra Ks are thumbnails, picture clips, not names. That's good." He pointed to the large screen.

"Ah shit. That's Collins. AIC Collins. That explains a lot. Why didn't he delete that?" Munson was disgusted and sickened. And then answered his own question. "He couldn't get his hands on the original. Only the copy. So he made sure I buried the original. No one could touch it. Everyone worked off his copy. Had to be. You can work it that way. I have a few times."

"And Hudson is listed here too. As a used car salesman."

"I know Vittors," Kevin said. The third name on the list. "I sold him his home and a shopping center. Checked him out and he seemed OK. I didn't find any criminal history, but I didn't look. I just checked his financials. He's a financial advisor, like it says."

"So you know where he lives," Daffy said. "And the layout of his house. And where he keeps his money. Where it comes from and where he spends it." A statement, not a question. Based on what he had seen of this gang, he was sure of those facts. "And I wouldn't be surprised if you knew a lot more than that."

Kevin didn't even look embarrassed. "Might. The same way Munson might have leaked stuff to Ron."

Now it was Munson's turn to look at Ron. A look of disbelief that Ron had shared that information. "You told them that?"

"Well, they were thinking bad things about you. I was trying to explain how I knew we could trust you. And I didn't say you actually leaked anything." He looked sternly at Kevin. "I said you might have leaked some stuff, maybe," he defended himself.

"Here's the last one, Sanforth," John said. The four were listed on the screen.

"Hmm, another financial advisor," Penney said. "Two financial advisors on a list of four people. I wonder if the connection is money rather than white slavery."

"Who are you?" Munson asked in his FBI interrogation voice.

"Penney, Penney the Freak. But you can just call me Legs." She held out her hand to shake. Smiled when Daffy came over to stand beside her. As if she needed protection. "I'm one of this geek gang of five. These are the other members of the gang. John and Sarah, Kevin and Cilla." She introduced them one by one. Name and profession and relationship. "You're sitting in our office. I am also a financial advisor. Not just an advisor, but the best financial advisor in the state. Ask anyone in the field."

Then she continued thoughtfully, "This might be naïve, but do you really think a sexual predator could be in charge of that unit in the FBI? John, Google Vittors and Sanforth."

As he was doing that, she told him, "Now, look at assets." Penney pointed at Munson and said, "Don't pay attention to anything we're doing now. It might not be totally legal."

"It is, though," John said. "They have everything up here, free and clear."

"And look at Hudson's assets, real estate, like Vittors and Sanforth." John had Googled him also.

"And the common link, Vital Forth Investments. They have a lot of funds and holdings. A financial investment company and advisors I have never heard of. Makes me think I would want to take a close look at their books, their activities, and their investors." Penney was talking as she was thinking. "You know, this could simply be investment fraud, a Ponzi scheme, or money laundering. The file is named Invest. Makes sense. I'd know about Vital Forth if it were an investment firm. If it were legal. And I would know if it were a Ponzi scheme. I would have heard of it. So by my process of elimination, these people are connected by money laundering."

"Continue, we're listening," Munson said.

"Where do they get their money? From investors? Who are their investors? Where do they get their investors? I would guess that Sheri might be an investor. Brought in by Hudson, maybe?" Penney was connecting the dots.

"My first guess would have been a Ponzi scheme," Penney continued, still thinking out loud. "But you know what? With Sheri involved, I bet it really is money laundering. That would make more sense. Would she be stupid enough to get involved in a Ponzi scheme? You know better than me. But from what I've heard about her, she's too smart. You need one of your famous FBI task forces on these accounts," she finished.

Munson wasn't the only one stunned.

Penney looked at Kevin and said, "You didn't come to me for help with Vittors. Probably, looking at just one investor, you wouldn't see a pattern. But when you see the three of them up there together, then you got to wonder."

"Vital Forth is up on the middle screen," said Sarah, who had been following along.

Munson was the first to point out, "There's Collins. And yes, this I can believe, money. He was bought. The child predator thing, I was having trouble with that, but money fits. And money will be easy enough to follow."

"Sheri would have a lot of money to invest," Penney said. "She probably researched Vittors and Vital Forth. Probably found them through Hudson. Thought her money was safe. And now Sheri is out and wanting her money. She might be looking for revenge on Jake, but she also wants her money. She could be going after the money holders. That could be what happened to Hudson. Sheri looking for her money."

"You know, Penney could be right," Munson agreed. "This could actually be two different crimes. It would explain why Collins didn't pull the plug on us until after the bust. He didn't know we were after one of Vital Forth's investors. That would explain a lot. Because if he were a predator and knew Sheri, he would have taken over the op sooner. All he could do was take over after we made the bust. Probably right after Sheri made her one phone call. Probably threatened Hudson and Vittors and Collins with exposure. Collins called real quickly after that." He was thinking of the timing.

"He told me to stand down, he was taking over. I told him we had her hard drives and he made sure I locked up them up, issuing only copies. Copies for him. From which he had carefully deleted names and files."

They sat there digesting the ideas.

Munson looked at Jake. "I can't do anything. I'm on leave. And Collins would be watching me anyhow. I'm thinking we need Gibbs. Ryan Gibbs. He's Special Agent in Charge of Crime Data and Forensic Accounting. He can look into Vital Forth and check on Collins."

"He's on leave too. Had to go home and help out family," Jake said. "But I got his number. Doesn't matter where he is, he can still direct us to the right people." Jake looked around for agreement and got it.

"I know him," Daffy said. "Worked with him before. He's a good man, and he is far enough up in the hierarchy that he can help with everything. All your problems. Ryan can help with Black Markit too. And he might be on leave, but he just handled two big busts in Florida."

Even Cavanaugh nodded. "I heard about those busts. The sheriff down there is a buddy of mine. Said Gibbs had the FBI Art Theft Department and Florida Law Enforcement working with his local cops just like they were a well-trained team. They all worked together on both cases, the federal art theft and the local drug trafficking, and shared the glory when they made the busts. Gibbs pulled it off. Everyone came away happy."

While Jake placed the call, Cavanaugh told the rest of them about the two busts in Florida. "Would you believe they hid the drugs in the soap, thinking the dogs wouldn't be able to smell them? Some crooks are just stupid. All you'd have to do is check it out on the web." They were all laughing at the idea. Well, the guardians were. The gang was looking the information up on the web.

Jake walked outdoors to make the call. When Gibbs answered, he said, "Hey, Ryan, what are you up to?"

"I'm on leave, Jake. Call someone else if you want something."

"The way I hear it, you just solved two big cases while on leave."

"Did not, just helped out the locals. Where did you hear that?"

"Right here. The local sheriff was talking about you. Making busts single-handed." Now Jake was just pulling his chain.

"Huh. What do you want, Jake?"

"Got a problem and need some help." He was serious now.

"Call Munson. He's your controller."

"He told me to call you. He's here. On leave too."

"I didn't hear that. Everything OK with him?"

"No." Jake paused for effect. "His family is with Heathertons." Jake waited.

There was a long silence and then, "I'm listening." Gibbs sounded like he had all the time in the world now.

"We think we found a collaborator in the FBI." Jake gave him a short version, with all the facts he needed to know. Not about the gang of five, or Midnight Plus One, or his wife. "Munson took leave to work with us."

There was a very long silence on Gibbs's end. Then, "I'll get back to you." And he disconnected.

Everyone looked up expectantly when Jake walked back indoors. "I told him. He hung up. Probably going to do a discreet check of the facts. And then I imagine he'll be calling you, Munson. I might have mentioned Sally's friends."

Jake and Ron told Munson about the black market websites. Munson's jaw dropped. "You have got to be kidding." John had made hard copies of the web pages, which they gave to Munson. "Oh man, I picked a bad time to go on leave. Ryan will have to help here. If he ever decides to call back."

Just then Jake's phone chirped. He looked at it and said, "No name." Put it to his ear and said, "Yeah?"

"Who is your local contact there?"

Jake mouthed *Ryan* to them and said, "Sheriff's department, Cavanaugh."

"Call him and tell him to give you a reference for me."

"He's right here, hold on," and then to Cavanaugh, "Do you have a reference for Ryan?"

"Rogers," Cavanaugh said. "He knows David Rogers, the sheriff down there. He'll vouch for me."

Jake repeated the name and Ryan hung up. "Well, at least he's still thinking about us."

Annie came in with two guards and dinner for everyone. For these men, work stopped when the food came. Geeks either forgot to eat or stuffed whatever they could reach into their mouths.

"We can use the time to make some decisions," Ron said. "We have a lot of strings here and at least three different problems. We need to decide who will work on what and if there is a priority." He stopped and looked at Annie, who was sitting with Kevin.

Before he could say anything, Kevin stated, "Annie's family. She stays."

Munson looked at Jake, who nodded. "Fine, she stays. Will there be more family members coming?" he asked rudely.

"Oh yeah." Kevin gave as good as he got. "There are more family members, and if any of them show up, they'll stay also." Munson looked around at the gang. All were agreeing.

Jake hadn't known Annie was family. He hadn't known there were more members. What type of detective was he? Didn't even know his own wife's family. He hadn't pressed her about her friends. She had seemed reluctant to talk about them. Maybe he should have insisted. Maybe he should have done a lot of things. Fuck it.

"Go ahead, Ron," he said. "We'll deal with other family members if or when they arrive." Shaking his head.

"First, we have the original security breaches that made Jake contact Cilla. Those that pointed to Conrad. We now know that was someone named Blackit, not Conrad. Blackit has a website where he brags that he worked on writing the code for multiple classified sites and lists them here by name. That page links to another page where he has put limited secret information up for bid. Information Blackit was able to steal because when he helped write the code, he inserted a secret backdoor that allows him to enter the restricted networks. The internal intranet communications of the company."

Ron looked at John and asked, "You have tracking devices on Blackit's web pages and on our classified networks?"

"No. They're ready. Just waiting for warrants to make it legal. Everything we have found so far is readily available to the public. We're almost in a gray area now. The mirror sites are up with our improved schematics and ready to go."

"So that is number one for Ryan. Get those warrants. As soon as he calls back, Jake, you need to get him working on them. We need to assign a team to shut down Blackit and follow up on each and every hit on his websites. It would be nice to be able to make arrests during an actual transfer of top-secret information for money. That team will be FBI, or us, or some combination of letter agencies. Let's get Ryan to help us work on that too."

To John again, Ron said, "John, you get with Jake and me on those substitute pages. We probably should see them. We'll get Ryan to OK them. John, you'll run the technology side." He looked around for agreement and got it.

"OK," John said. "Everything is here, ready for you."

"Second, we have Sheri and everything that comes with her," Ron said. "Protecting everyone in this room is the priority. We need to find her and take her down. Hopefully before she can murder anyone else." Again he got agreement. "That should be Cavanaugh's job, with…I want to say Jake and Daffy."

He looked at Jake. "Can you do it, Jake? And before you answer, you need to remember that lives will depend on you being objective. Can you work with Daffy? He will partner with Cavanaugh. You will report to both of them. Can you do that?"

"I don't have a problem with that arrangement. I think it will work better that way. If Daffy will put up with me." Any of Jake's men could run any operation, and it wouldn't be the first time Jake took orders from one of his own men. And putting Daffy in charge was a good idea. Jake couldn't trust himself to be objective or impartial where either Sheri or Cilla was concerned, but he could follow orders.

Daffy nodded.

"Third, we have Collins," Ron said. "We need Ryan for that too. As lead on that one. He is the only one of us who can work from within the FBI structure on Collins and any other agents who might be dirty.

"Fourth, as a subcategory to Collins and Sheri, we have Vittors and Sanforth, along with Vital Forth. Penney will do the forensic accounting we need." He looked at Penney. "Can you?"

"Depends," she said. "If you want records and balance sheets you can use for trial, then you need to get me warrants. Maybe Cav can do that. Get the warrants. It would be outside of the FBI, and your man Collins might not be looking for a warrant from that direction. After that I can probably find everything legally. I bet it's all online where each of them can watch the other. Probably with passwords. I can break them easily."

Daffy acknowledged this woman had a head on her shoulders that was not only beautiful, but smart. Always thinking. Logically. He smiled at her causing a tinge of pink again when she noticed him looking.

"Cav? How soon can you get us warrants?" Ron asked.

"I'll get started when we break up. Might not be able to get a judge until the morning. I might wake someone up. My priorities are probably to make sure Vittors and Sanforth are still alive. I'll have a few of my guys sit on their houses tonight. Sheri might wander by."

"I can find places they frequent locally," Sarah said to Cavanaugh. "Restaurants, bars, hangouts. You might be able to talk to people who know them." Tracking people was her specialty.

"OK," Cavanaugh agreed. "Give me a minute to get two cars sitting on their homes first. Then I'll see what you have."

"I can check real estate for Vital Forth," Kevin said. "Don't need any warrants for that."

"Sounds good, any other comments?" Ron looked around.

"I want to know that all the perverts, scum, have been arrested and that they are in jail," Cilla stated. "I want to be assured that every single kid is back home and safe. I'll check all the victims first for any who might still be missing. I want to be sure there are no names missing from the second file. Then I'll check all the crooks with public records for status and convictions. That's the kind of grunt work I do best." She dared anyone to say no.

"Good idea. I want you all to make yourselves available if any of the law enforcement folks need your expertise. Is that OK? And we have to know the status of each of these situations as soon as you find something. We could keep a list and timeline on a whiteboard," Ron suggested.

The gang nodded. Sarah already had the information on Sanforth and Vittors and their hangouts. While waiting for Cavanaugh, she went over to help Cilla. "Two can work this faster. Make a copy of the CD, I'll run through the children and add them to your database. I understand the legalese better."

They went to work setting up a program with a database that would self-populate from a public records search. Cilla wanted convictions, length of sentence, prison. The kids database should include name, age, sex, and placement with family or foster care. In the morning they could compare with the FBI's completed case file.

Kevin kept his seat and tapped his tablet, using his own real estate software and multiple listings. His job was to go back to the date Vital Forth was incorporated, about five years prior. That would be well before Sheri went down. Depending on what he found, he was to go even further back. Collins, Vittors, Sanforth, and Vital Forth were included in his search. He talked his way through for Penney's benefit, who was doing the accounting research across from him.

John huddled with Munson, Ron, Jake, and Daffy to explain what he planned for the fake schematics.

Meanwhile Cilla worked on her task. When she raised her head, Kevin, Jones, John, and Peter were gone. Cavanaugh too. He'd gotten what he needed from Sarah and took off. He wanted to look at each house and maybe go to one or two of the hangouts with Jones. He had a judge working on warrants for Vital Forth, and Penney had added warrants for each man's finances also.

Sarah was assigning sleeping arrangements, working from a list. She and Michael would be in the big house, along with Peter and John. Kevin of course. And all their guards. Annie would get everyone set up.

In the gatehouse Penney and Cilla would be in their own rooms. Ron and Jen would be in a third. Jake, because of his leg, would get the fourth. Daffy and Munson would be on pullout couches. Plenty of room.

"Annie is bringing breakfast at seven, and everyone staying in the main house will come with her," Sarah said.

"I'll make coffee at six," Cilla offered. She was the early riser of the group.

Penney was still working on the accounting when the rest turned in. Daffy stayed with her. "You could finish that in the morning, you know," he said to her.

"It's done now. I was just double-checking everything. I'm going to sit back with a small brandy and rest my brain before I try to sleep."

He got them both a brandy and sat beside her. The cat jumped into her lap and curled up.

"How did you all get together, the gang?" he asked

"We were all outcasts. Poor. Different. Quiet. We were geeks, thinkers, and we were loners. None of us trusted. We had learned not to trust. We were pretty much ignored or forgotten by our parents, if we were lucky. If we even had parents." She paused.

"Cilla saved us. She rescued us. And then gave us the power, the self-confidence, to save ourselves. She had parents. Not bad parents, just oblivious. Didn't seem to know she was around unless they were drunk. Then, for some reason, they had to beat on her. Who knows? She doesn't talk about it, and there's more to it than that, but that's her story. She was a computer junkie. Always in the computer lab. She loves programming. Cilla's a watcher. She watches people, and she has an intuitive understanding of people. She watched John. He was in the lab a lot too. She decided he was like her. They hooked up in sixth grade. Not hooked up hooked up. Got together. They were both twelve then.

"John lived with an aunt part time, when she wasn't turning tricks. He spent a lot of time on the streets. Whenever he got in trouble, Cilla hid him in her bedroom. She snuck him food, treated cuts and bruises. Got him clean clothes. One time he stayed there for two weeks. Her folks never even knew. His aunt never missed him. That was the beginning. They were the first two. The first two members of the gang.

"They found me the next year. I had a dad. Not a bad guy. He left me alone; I was lucky. He was an investment counselor. He was seldom home, but when he was home, he was always talking to himself about this stock or that bond or that business. I eavesdropped. He never actually talked to me; it was like I wasn't there. He had a computer, and I used it to go online and learn about the things he discussed with himself. And while I was at it, I learned some hacking. Don't laugh. I'm not as good as the others, but I get by.

"I was alone. Cilla saw me. They just started hanging with me. Before I knew it, I was the third.

"Kevin showed up a couple of months later. He had been kicked out of another private school and ended up in our public school. He wasn't quiet. Always acting up. In trouble. He'd been held back a grade, not because he was stupid, but because he was bored. He was an outsider, a spoiled kid who was always writing stuff. Cilla said he was one of us. Even though he was rich, or maybe because he was rich, he was a loner. His parents were never home. He was either at boarding school or with the housekeeper, Annie. She raised him. Now we were four.

"And that's when Cilla found Sarah. As bad as any of us had it? Nothing compared to Sarah. Sarah had it worse. No parents. She was moved around foster homes, one crueler than the other. Abused, beaten, and forgotten, when she was lucky. She never admitted to rape. She never admitted to anything we couldn't see for ourselves. We could see a lot. The teachers never noticed when she came in with a black eye or her arm in a cast. Cilla said we had to help her. Kids. We were what? Thirteen? Sarah was so small, tiny. Timid. Brutalized. So we pulled her into our gang. Protected her. Sheltered her.

"She's the fifth. Sarah wants Sarah's Child so she can protect children like she was. Like John. The gang is going to make sure she gets it. And Michael, we found Michael for her this year while searching for a medical doctor for Sarah's Child. He was perfect for Sarah's Child. And then perfect for Sarah. That's another story, or stories.

"Cilla always seems to know who needs help and how to help them. She made plans, wrote lists. Kept us safe. Encouraged us when we were down." Penney stopped, remembering.

Daffy reached over, put his arm around her, and pulled her closer beside him. She rested her head on his shoulder. He rested his chin on her hair. It felt so right. She fit perfectly. "Go on." He wanted to know more about this woman, a woman whom Penney admired. He had a feeling Penney didn't admire too many people. A geek. A millionaire. A protector of the helpless.

"With Kevin we got the gatehouse. It was abandoned back then, but a great place for us to hide out and hang and be safe. We couldn't all hide in Cilla's bedroom. When it wasn't safe to go home, or to stay home, we lived in the gatehouse. Cilla too sometimes.

"And with Kevin we got Annie. She looked out for us. Whatever we needed, she got. She knew first aid. That helped when we got hurt. She is a cross between a mom and a big sister. She got us a couple of computers from the main house, and we were in heaven. And safe. We used her as a surrogate whenever one of us needed adult representation in school. We could make any official document we needed. We did too.

"There are more of us. More than five. We tried to save the world. Cilla did." Penney laughed. "Even before Sarah's Child. Over the years we have added three or four kids. Kids like us. Some just lost, some hurt, like Sarah. Worse. Becca, she's older, she lived here most of her senior year of high school. And the Boys. Twins, we called them, because they were the same age and came together. But different as night and day.

"We all grew up, moved on. We stay in touch, though, because we're family. We know we always have one another. One of us will be there.

"I don't remember where Cilla found Jake. That's a lie, I do, but that's not my story to tell. You'll have to get that from her or Jake. But they were beautiful together for a while. That look she has now? The sad, hard, blank, 'you can't hurt me' look? Jake taught her that. Even after what we all went through, she was an innocent. Not naïve. Innocent. She could always laugh. Until Jake left. He was gone a month. A month before we figured it out. John did. He looked at her one day and said, 'Where's Jake?'

"We moved her out of that house. It was killing her, being alone there. The bit of her that Jake hadn't already killed. We put her in here and made her take charge of decorating for SC Digital. Gave her work." She motioned around the room. "Did a good job, didn't she? Kevin did the kitchen. The rest is Cilla. She hasn't gotten over Jake. I don't think she ever will. But she's learned to live without him. Function on her own again. She's strong. Was starting to come back to life. Then he came back. Was it just last week?

"I know, I can tell Jake did something that makes him a man in your eyes. A hero. But we don't know that. Until this week we knew nothing. All we know is what he did to Cilla. I want to pound him so bad. Every time I look at him, I want to pound him, hurt him." She stopped. She wasn't going to cry or get angry. It was too nice here. She was comfortable snuggled up to Daffy. Changed the subject.

"Now, tell me about Heathertons. Who, what are they? I told Jones I would explain everything, and I don't know anything. And I don't want to disappoint him."

"No one knows much. Think Superman, Spiderman, Batman, the Seals, Rangers, and Special Forces, all rolled into one. And multiply that by, no one is sure how many. No one knows where they live. And you only hear about them when one of the letter agencies needs expert help. They're the stuff of legends. I didn't know Munson knew them. Jake was a surprise too. Wouldn't think he was deep enough into protection to hear about them. Heathertons always come through too. Kind of like your gang of five, only on steroids and with weapons."

Penney twisted around to look at him. "Why do you speak about them in the third person when it is so obvious that you are one of them?"

He went still and now it was his turn to look at her. "How can you think that?"

"I was watching you. You didn't fool me for a minute."

"You are an amazing woman. I knew that the minute I saw you. You're probably going to belong to me. Soon. Forever."

"Works for me," she said. "I feel the same way. It's strange, I didn't know I was waiting for anyone until I saw you, and then I knew you are the one. Cilla always said there would be one man for me. She didn't promise, but she was right."

He leaned down for a kiss. Just a taste. Quick. Barely brushed her lips. Afraid he would be caught if he lingered.

"Later," he promised. "After this is over. I'm on the job now, and I can't protect you if I'm sleeping with you. And don't mention Heathertons anymore." He leaned over again and this time he got caught in the kiss as she opened beneath his lips. He kissed her thoroughly as his tongue stroked inside. He started to lay her back down on the couch, but Tiff growled. He stopped himself. Broke it off. He had forgotten the cat. Thank goodness the cat was there. He gazed at her with smoking eyes that held such promise, ravishing her face. Licking her taste on his lips. Trying to get his body back under control.

She was laughing at him. He looked in such pain.

"Go to bed," he said roughly. "Go to bed." He thought they better get this wrapped up soon, or he would find himself sleeping with his client.

Wednesday

Cilla was up even earlier than normal. She was anxious to check her program. Breathed a sigh of relief when she found only two blank spaces. Two men not accounted for. They were not purposely left out, she saw, but had jumped bail. And all the children appeared to be home with their families. That was good. She made the coffee.

She looked down at herself, dressed in her puffy blue sweats. *Good enough to go out into the garden*, she thought. She did some warm-up exercises and then slid into Tai Chi as the sun rose. Stopped thinking and lost herself in the form. The fluid motion and balance always soothed. She repeated all the postures and bowed to the sun. Took a deep breath to face the day and turned to find Daffy behind her, dressed only in gray sweatpants. She didn't generally notice men, but maybe because she knew Penney was interested, she looked him over. And this was one fine specimen. Broad shouldered, ripped muscles. A warrior. Probably a good thing he kept his clothes on most of the time. She smiled.

"I made coffee," she said.

"I found it. Saw you out here and came to watch. Did the second Tai Chi form with you. Brought you coffee." He held it out.

"Thank you."

"What is your specialty? I know Penney's."

"I write business software. Business specific software." She saw he was still puzzled. "You've heard of QuickBooks, haven't you?

The software program small businesses use to track sales, income, and inventory?" When he nodded, she continued, "My programs are small, only what the client needs to run his particular business. Plus the specifics for his field. QuickBooks is one size fits all, but that might be too cumbersome for a non-technical person. Or not detailed enough in some specific areas. Some people want a program that has been tweaked just for their business and their style."

"Is there a market for that? I mean, obviously there is, but enough to make a living?"

"Oh, more than enough. I always have to turn down jobs. I just do the ones that really capture my interest or provide a challenge. And I'm always available if my clients have a problem. Which isn't very often, because I am very good at what I do and with the customers I pick." She laughed again.

It was a cheerful sound, out here in the garden.

"Could you write a program for a bodyguard?" he asked. "How would you do that?"

"Sit down with you. Discuss your income and expenses. Find out what you wanted to track, buy, save. Discuss your long-term and short-term goals. I am guessing, though, that you wouldn't need my services. I think you know exactly what your income is and where it goes. I'll bet you have a tidy sum of money socked away, waiting until you feel you're ready to retire. Start a family. So I would recommend that you see a financial advisor. Someone like Penney," she said with a smirk.

He looked at her, questioning.

"I'm guessing you're a saver. That you have your future mapped out." She took a breath. "I've seen the way you look at Penney. The way you watch her. You should know I'm fairly protective of Penney, by the way."

"The way I hear it, you are protective of the whole gang. Are you warning me off?"

"Me? Me, the woman who couldn't even hold on to a man she was madly in love with? You think I would tell someone else about love? Abandonment, maybe. I'm an expert on abandonment and desertion. I thought I had learned all about those growing up, but those were just the introductory courses." She stopped herself.

"I've seen how Penney watches you. I would guess you two are already seriously involved. And I think maybe you have filled in that blank space on your long-range plan. The one waiting for the name of your wife. No, I told Penney to go for it. Grab it, enjoy it, take a chance. Love, lust, whichever, is great. If it goes bad, the gang will pick up the pieces. They did for me. But while it's good, I hope it is as good as what Jake and I had." She wasn't surprised to find that she believed that.

He saw the hurt; it matched the pain in her voice. "It must be hard to be in the same room with him."

"I sound like a loser, don't I? But I'm not. I can deal, at least for a few days. Besides, this Jake is not the happy, warm man I loved. I don't know this Jake. I can't read beyond the cold anger that turns to disgust when he looks at me."

"I've seen the same expression, except I thought that Jake's anger and disgust were at himself, not at you." He changed the subject.

"What about me?" he asked. "What do you see when you look at me?"

"One of us," she said immediately. "You would have been one of the gang. Not a hacker, but a lost child." She saw the shock in his face. "I'm sorry, I shouldn't have said that."

"I asked. Thank you. I'd like to think I could qualify to be one of you. Jake was an idiot to let you go."

"No, just a man with no support group. He has Ron. And you've helped him a lot, I think. He seems to hear you. Maybe Sarah could help him," she said thoughtfully. "I'll have to ask her." Because Cilla couldn't. It was him or herself, and she couldn't save them both. She knew she could save herself, had saved herself, but wasn't sure he even knew he needed to be saved.

"We better go back in. Here comes the group from the main house." She pointed them out.

Even though all the commotion was at the front door, Penney watched them come in together and smiled at them both. Jake was behind Penney. He looked angry. This morning his anger was hot. Because she had been with Daffy?

Jake had seen her with Daffy in the garden. He was jealous. Because he wanted to be in the garden with her. But couldn't. Not until he worked up the courage to talk to her. He had watched Peter and John. Seen the worry, even fright, in John's eyes when he thought he had crossed a line. Watched him go talk to Peter. Immediately. As soon as he realized there might be a problem. A geek, facing problems and consequences that Jake himself was afraid to face.

Jake had watched the two of them and was moved by Peter's understanding and compassion. It had hit home. He had heard what Daffy said. Ron had said the same thing many times, but this was the first time Jake actually heard it. He had to talk to Cilla. Take his chances. He had to know how she would react. It was hell being shut up in the same room with her. It was worse to watch her with another man. It had been different at her place. Why was that? Because then he was only concerned with the security breach? Her source of income? Her lover? He didn't like her out in the garden with Daffy. He went outside to be alone with his anger.

Cilla watched him go out and followed him. He turned and looked at her. His pain was almost physical. She caught her breath. She followed him out.

"You know, we could talk. You could talk to me, clear the air. If you could tell me what happened, and why, we might not hurt so bad. Right now, from what I can see, you hurt as badly as I do. Could it possibly hurt any worse if you told me what happened? Explained why you left? Trust me."

She held her breath to see what he would do. Begged him, "Trust me, Jake."

"Knowing that you hate me? Hate what I did? That would be worse than thinking you hate me but hoping you didn't."

"How could I hate you? If I could, would that be worse than what you are doing to yourself, wondering, fearing? Look at you. How could it be worse? Talk to me," she begged again. "Please. Tell me what happened. Those men inside? They know. Why can't I know? Take a chance. Make me hate you. I dare you to. You couldn't do anything to make me hate you."

He gave up, couldn't hold the fear of her rejection inside anymore. He would be as strong as John had been.

"OK, let's walk, my leg is stiffening up." He turned, deciding where to start. To finally end his own pain. At the beginning.

"I bumped into Sheri's organization when I was looking into another matter. The thing I was working on and the man I dealt with, I didn't need a fake name. I wasn't undercover. It was a simple information for cash transaction. And suddenly I was in the middle of wicked evil. With no cover, no fallback. I had to make my story up as I went along. I told them I sometimes did some arm breaking because it was fun. That I was married to a very rich, plain, boring woman and had this unimportant job with her father, who also provided our home."

When Jake looked at her now, he saw only how much she loved the man she thought he was. He had loved her so much. His Cilla. He loved everything about her.

"Sheri bought it, because Sheri equated a woman without makeup to a woman without power, not realizing the reverse was true for you. She couldn't see your inner strength shining through. Sheri was a malicious, depraved woman. She terrified me. She stopped at no evil. She loved to hurt people, physically if possible. But emotionally worked for her too. She didn't really want a man physically. I never did anything with her. I told her I was dysfunctional and couldn't get it up. I explained I couldn't be seen with her, or your father would break me. You remember that day you found me with her in what appeared to be a very intimate luncheon?"

"Yes," Cilla whispered. She had been heartbroken.

"Sheri arranged that. It was a command performance for me. She wounded us both that day. I believe it gave her a sexual high. When you ran out, she laughed. I couldn't go after you; she would have known you were important to me if I had. It killed me to sit there and laugh with her.

"Once they called me in to take a guy to the hospital when she was done punishing him. I don't know how one human being could do that to another. She just smiled and said my geek wife could look that way. She terrified me.

"That was when I trained myself to stop seeing you. I knew if Sheri understood how much you meant to me, she'd hurt you, if only to hurt me. I thought if she believed you meant nothing to me, she would leave you alone. I had to stop looking at you, so she wouldn't see my love."

He remembered. She had asked him why he had stopped looking at her, stopped seeing her. At first he had just looked puzzled and said, "I see you. I'm looking at you now."

And when she said, "No, you're not. Not the way you used to," his face had gone from puzzled to blank. All expression gone. Worse than not seeing her. He was lying to her then.

"Each time I didn't see you, I hurt you, and something inside me became empty, cold, dead. When I could no longer bear to hurt you, I left, and then there was nothing in me. I was stone.

"It got tougher as I got in deeper and deeper. It got dirtier and dirtier. But I couldn't leave; we knew there were at least fifteen kids who would be sold in a week or two. If I could just hang in, we could rescue them. I couldn't walk out on those kids, so I walked out on you." He couldn't touch her. He felt so dirty.

"But finally, one day she told me to be ready; they were having their auction that night. I could see the end; all I had to do was let our guys know where and when. But they blindfolded me. Didn't trust me totally, though they still needed my muscle. I had my cell with its GPS, but had to wait before turning it on.

"They took me to a farm. A farmhouse and barn. The sale would be in the house. The merchandise, the girls, was in the barn. We all went to the barn so Sheri could show off her girls. All prime meat, she said. One of the girls had escaped earlier. The guy on guard duty at the time? Sheri punished him; he was dead, in the barn. Sheri was saving the girl for later, for her men to play with. A guy had broken her arm dragging her back. Sheri wanted her men to beat and rape the child right there and then in front of the whole crew and the other children as a warning."

He took a deep breath. "I couldn't stand by and let it happen. Lenny shot me as I tried to pull the child away. I fell with the girl under me, trying to curl myself around her. Sheri shot me, and I played dead with the girl locked under me. Didn't have to do a lot of playing. The bullets had done some damage.

"Sheri grabbed a pitchfork and stuck it through my leg and into the ground. Jumped on it, pinning me. She laughed when I screamed, and she said, 'Leave them there. The bitch will be real submissive when we get back. And Jakey baby,' she said to me, 'when we come back, you can watch us play with the bitch. And then we're going to go visit your wife, bring her back here. You can watch as my men party with her. She'll be the gift that keeps on giving. If you're still alive, that is. If not, you won't be the first dead person lying around here.' Then they all went into the house to prepare for the auction, less this one girl. And me.

"I couldn't get my phone," Jake was remembering. *He'd asked the girl, "What's your name, sweetheart?" In a whisper. That's all he had strength for.*

"Juanita," she whispered, scared.

"Can you reach my pocket, Juanita? Can you get my phone?" She had struggled to move that small bit, and Jake had felt every motion. When she got the phone, he told her to turn it on. And then to hit the speed dial. Munson answered right away. "Jake?"

"Yes," he whispered. "It's going down in an hour. We're at a farm, I don't know where. Protect Cilla. Guard Cilla."

"Are you OK?"

"No, hurt," he said, and he'd passed out.

"The girl, Juanita, got the phone. Munson talked to Juanita, had her repeat what I said. Had her tell him where I was, how I was hurt. Told her how to slow down the bleeding. He talked to her for an hour. Kept her calm. Juanita saved me. She saved me that night. We saved each other.

"They tracked us by the phone GPS. The SWAT team came in. There was a firefight. Some of the bad guys got shot, including Lenny. They got the buyers, rescued the girls. Called ambulances for me and Juanita. For all the girls."

He took a breath. "I wouldn't let them tell you. I was awake long enough to make them promise not to call you.

"I spent a long time in the hospital. The leg got infected. The pitchfork. Each time I almost got better, I had a relapse. Juanita came a couple of times to visit. Munson and Sally brought her. They kept her.

"I finally got well enough to get out. I came back here about three weeks ago."

Cilla just looked at him. "I don't understand. Why didn't you tell me? How could you not tell me?"

"I couldn't. I couldn't talk about it with you. Sheri had shattered my self-confidence, self-respect. And then later, I didn't know how. I felt so dirty. Stupid. I almost blew the whole deal that night."

She didn't understand, "Blew what whole deal? How?"

"Stepping in to protect Juanita. There should have been another way to do that."

"How can you blame yourself for that? You saved an innocent girl. You shut down a white slavery ring. No one could expect you to stand by and watch an innocent child be raped. Beaten. Why would you think that? Don't be an idiot. If you want to be an idiot, think about how you hurt me. Left me. Never said a word. Those things make you an idiot, Jake. Not saving an innocent." She was angry now at his grief.

"I know. I know in my head what you say is right. But still I wonder. Still I think I could have, should have, done something differently. There must have been another way."

He looked at her anxiously. "Do you hate me? Can you forgive me?"

"I don't hate you, Jake. That is something else you should understand. I love you. Loved you and lost you." She had loved being in love. Loved their house. Loved her gardens. But most of all, she loved him being in love with her. Loved that he looked at her with that secret smile that said *mine, all mine.* He had said he loved his geek. She was so lucky. His love was like life's blood for her. It exhilarated her. Like blood for a vampire, she guessed. If there were vampires. That's what it was like. So when he stopped seeing her, she stopped thriving. She wilted. And then she had cried for all she had lost.

They walked together quietly for a while. *Did he want her back? Is that what he was telling her now?*

"I'm sorry," he said. "Sorry for it all. What I did then. How I have behaved since I came back. I love you. I have always loved you. You are my life. The air I breathe. Without you I am empty and cold and angry."

He took a deep breath. "Do you think you could ever forgive me?" he asked.

"Oh, Jake, forgive you? I love you." She stroked both hands over his face and took a deep breath. "You hurt me so bad. You broke my heart. But I still loved you. Have always loved you. You can't kill that. If you want me back, I am not going to walk away. I'm not going to sulk or make you grovel. I want you back. The Jake I married, though. I can forgive that sad, angry man you have been showing me the past few days. But I want the original Jake to spend my life with."

"The anger was at myself. My weakness. I never meant those hateful things I said. I was trying to protect myself. From knowing that I had lost you. I didn't ever believe you were with another man. I know you would never do that. I was angry at myself for being afraid to talk to you. I didn't want you to see my failures. I didn't want you to see me helpless in a hospital bed. I didn't know if I would lose the leg. Didn't want you to have to deal with that. And I didn't want your pity. Seems so stupid. I was willing to lose you rather than face you. I was afraid you would despise me and send me away, so I walked away before you could. Dumb. My anger was at me for walking away. Never at you. I love you, Cilla."

It clicked then. "That's why Sheri is after me. To hurt you!" she exclaimed.

"Yes. She knows if she hurts you, she will destroy me. I never fooled her for a minute. She never believed I didn't love you. You are the only one I fooled."

"It might take me some time to learn to trust again, Jake. My heart knows you love me. My brain might need more time."

He touched her face, lifted her chin. Looked in her eyes and kissed her softly. "OK. I can wait," he said with relief. He had been so sure she would hate him. Not want him. Not give him a chance. He hadn't dared tell her. Couldn't chance her revulsion. Had forgotten her sweetness. Now here she was saying she loved him, even after the cruel way he had treated her. The cold inside of him started to thaw.

"You have to promise to always talk to me. People who love each other talk out their problems. They trust each other," she said as she wiped away a tear.

They stood together, rocking back and forth, Cilla crying softly into his shoulder.

"Yes. I'll talk. I won't leave again, I promise."

"I know. I know you won't." She giggled, surprising both of them. "Besides, if you did, Peter would punch you again." She laughed out loud. "Do you believe he did that? I don't. He's the big brother I never had."

Jake rubbed his jaw. "Still hurts. I'm glad you had someone looking out for you. I like him. Him and John together? Amazing." Amazing what he had learned watching their interchange about trust. That helped make him see, finally. Understand. Hear.

Inside the gatehouse Penney said, "Thank goodness." She didn't have to explain, because she wasn't the only one who had seen Cilla follow Jake into the garden. She wasn't the only one watching them. "I feel like cheering. Oops, they're coming in."

Penney ran to Cilla and hugged her, but she wasn't ready to forgive Jake yet.

Cavanaugh and Jones came in then, looking exhausted. Both brightened when they saw the food and attacked the buffet.

Ron gave everyone a chance to eat first and then got down to business, calling on Cilla first for her results. She was still wondering about cops and food, but brought her attention back.

"Only two men are missing, Axel Blaine and Juan Garcia. They jumped bail. The kids are all accounted for. I still have to look through the final case files to see if any new creeps or children were turned up. I'll do that after breakfast."

Cavanaugh spoke up then, a forkful of waffle almost in his mouth. "Axel Blaine is the guy Sheri killed in your condo the other night. So that just leaves Garcia on the loose." He put the fork down and pulled out a notebook. "No sign of Sheri, but Sanforth has been among the missing for two days. We made discreet enquiries at his favorite nightspots—thank you, Sarah, for your help there. The bar staff was actually wondering where he was. Unusual for him not to be there. I figure Sheri could have moved on him after Hudson. The timing is right. One of my teams followed Vittors home. He left a gay club with another man. Safe at home for now."

He looked at Daffy and Jake. "I'm lining up my SWAT team now to go in after Sanforth. Another health and safety check. We'll be ready in about another hour. Thought maybe you and Jake might want to be there."

"We'll go in right behind your swat team," Daffy said. "Me and Jake."

"OK. I expected that."

"Maybe Sheri will be with Sanforth," Ron suggested.

"No, I have a bad feeling about Sanforth," Cav said. "I don't think we'll find Sheri there. No signs of life at the house, and the neighbors haven't seen Sanforth for two days.

"I have your warrants, Penney." He walked over to give them to her and stopped short when he saw her holding hands with Daffy. Looked at both of them and shook his head sadly. "Damn," he said softly. Gave Daffy a thumbs-up and handed over the papers. "Your work, Penney, finding the link between Sheri and Forth, convinced the judge. Those are for everything financial at Forth, which includes detail on Vittors, Sanforth, Hudson, and Sheri. And Collins."

Munson's phone buzzed. He looked at it and said, "Ryan."

"About time you got back to us," he complained and then listened and put the phone away. "He's landing at the airfield and wants me to pick him up."

"Take your car and Jason, Macho Man," Ron ordered. "And fill Ryan in on everything." He looked around, "Anyone have anything else? OK. Penney has the finances, Cilla and Sarah will finish up the children. John, get hard copies of the websites for Ryan. Jake, I have a vest for you. And Daffy, you still have his back."

Penney watched Daffy get his vest out of his duffle. This was his job, and she had seen him in action. Had heard he was the best. When he turned toward her and saw the look on her face, he walked over to her and put his hand on her cheek.

"This is my job, honey. You understand? This is what I do. Protect the innocent. I am very, very good at my job because I am very careful." He turned her face up and asked, "Is this going to be a problem for us?"

"No. No. I just didn't connect the dots. I saw the vest and all of a sudden it hit me. I'm OK. Let me help you with that thing. Show me how."

He smiled at her and said, "I could do it myself, but it will feel better if you help. You are incredible, you know that?" He kissed her, couldn't help himself. A long, slow, comforting kiss.

Jake was heading to the bedroom with Jen to get the vest when Michael caught up with them, saying, "You're not going anywhere until I look at your leg."

Jake didn't waste time arguing, just laughed, and walked into the bedroom.

Cilla started toward them, but slowed to watch Penney. Penney wasn't scared? Cilla was terrified. She stood in the doorway.

"Should you be doing this?" she asked. They all looked at her. Jen handed her the vest, saying, "You help him," as she edged out of the room. Michael was checking his leg.

"Ron wouldn't let me go, if he didn't think I could do it," Jake said.

"But he works for you," Cilla said. "You're his boss."

"Doesn't matter. He's in charge of the op. He makes all the decisions."

"What about your leg?" she asked nervously.

"He's ready to go," Michael said. "Leg looks good." Then he also left.

Jake took both her hands in his. He had seen the worry. He handed her the vest and said, "Help me with this?"

"I don't know anything about those, and it looks like you just slip it over your head and pull the straps."

"That's my girl," he said. "Help me." He gave her the old Jake smile.

Neither one said anything as she slipped it over his head. There was an awkward moment when it looked like he would kiss her. She leaned away.

"Don't send me into battle without a kiss. I'll be OK. And I couldn't have anyone better than Daffy to watch my six." He leaned over and took his kiss gently.

Of course she kissed him back. And then got an extra one for herself.

She felt a change in him, but couldn't tell what it was. Maybe he was just a little bit less on edge. A little bit less stiff. She watched as he joined Cav and Daffy. They were all wearing vests, but only the cops were armed. Was that right?

Penney came and held her hand. "They'll be OK." Cilla knew Penney believed it, so she just nodded agreement. Now it would be sit and wait. Or sit, work, and wait. OK, she could do this. Put the fear away. Get on with living.

"I like him. I like your Daffy," Cilla said, smiling.

"Me too. Feels so right, Cilla. Feels like this is the guy. This is the one. He feels it too. Almost scary how quick it happened. For both of us."

Sarah came over and asked, "Lust or love?"

"Love, I think. With a lot of lust thrown in," Penney confirmed with a smile and got a gleeful hug from Sarah.

"Oh, the best combination," she agreed.

Jake and Daffy watched as the SWAT team went in hard, front and back. Cav and Jones went in right behind the teams. They could hear the men kicking in doors and yelling "clear." After it was quiet for a few minutes, Jones came out. "Sheriff says to come on in."

Cavanaugh was in the living room, looking down at Sanforth. "I'm having my surveillance team do a health and safety check on Vittors." Cops did health and safety checks all the time. Usually, when some friend or relative calls concerned because he can't reach a loved one and asks the police to check and make sure everything is OK. "I hate being one step behind this broad. Looks like he's been dead about twenty-four hours."

Cav walked off, talking into his radio. He walked back, disgusted. "I'm trying to get a warrant on Vittors, but I don't have enough. Think the fibbies can help?"

Jake looked at Daffy, pulled out his cell, and called Ron with the request.

"You're on speakerphone," Ron said. "I'm turning you over to Ryan; we just walked in the door."

"What's happening, Jake?" Ryan asked.

"SWAT team went in hard. Sanforth's dead. He looks the same as Hudson. About twenty-four hours ago. Cavanaugh is having his men do a health and safety on Vittors. He wants to bring Vittors in, but needs a warrant. Can you get one? Cavanaugh's afraid if we leave Vittors out there. he'll end up like Sanforth and Hudson."

"Have it right here. A sealed warrant. Tell Cavanaugh to go pick him up and let us know how it turns out."

"OK. Daffy and I are coming back in now. Nothing we can do here."

Cilla was relieved to hear Jake sound so normal and told herself to relax.

Ryan sighed, saw the remnants of breakfast, and looked hopeful. "Mind if I get breakfast? I've been on the go most all night."

"Sure, I'll have seconds with you. Want to update us?" Ron asked.

Ryan looked around at all the faces watching him and said, "Us? Everyone?"

"All of us. We're all in this mess together."

"I was afraid of that. Let me get some eats first." He filled a plate. Sat down with a sigh at the table.

Cilla offered Ryan coffee, and when it was accepted, she brought it over and sat down with one for herself too. He thanked her and ate a few mouthfuls, and washed them down with the coffee.

Jake and Daffy arrived then and immediately went for coffee. Jake sat by Cilla, putting his arm over her shoulder. Her heart almost stopped when he smiled at her. Actually smiled. Made her feel warm and loved again. He was more relaxed, the harsh lines gone from his face. He looked like the old Jake. It was hard to believe that talking could make such a difference. She almost didn't notice Daffy go sit with Penney.

Cilla had expected Ryan to be another tough, dangerous man. Not this friendly, soft, easygoing guy. But as she listened, she realized this man was another warrior. His strength was hidden under an exterior of soft middle age. Not old. Not soft as in gone to fat, but smooth. And what was it with cops and food?

She watched Ryan's eyes get hard as he spoke. He started with, "Collins is dirty. He is already being looked at by IA, Internal Affairs. Very quietly. He has been spending a lot of money, more than he's making. He is also buying drugs. Using. I gave IA a heads-up about Vital Forth. They'll be contacting you. Munson, you'll share whatever you have here?" he asked Munson, who nodded. "IA will do some tracking of their own, but don't expect them to share." He looked over at Penney and said with a smile, "I hear you are as good as our people, and you share."

"You heard wrong. I'm better than your people. I probably have everything right here you will need. What do you want to know?"

He laughed a full strong laugh. "Yep, that's what I heard about your gang. Let me finish with IA, and then we can look at your results. IA is almost ready to make arrests in the jailbreak. From the warden on down. Collins paid for it and didn't even try to hide it. Stupid jerk. He will be going down for that and any repercussions caused by Sheri.

"FBI, IA, and FinCEN, Financial Crimes Enforcement Network—who knows, maybe even ICE—will be handling Collins, Vittors, and Vital Forth. They will also examine how Hudson and Sanforth fit into the picture. I would like you to help them wherever they need it." He looked around. "All of you. I can't go through channels without alerting Collins. These guys can work from the outside. The locals will deal with Sheri, they're on scene. Cavanaugh has a really good reputation in law enforcement."

It was obvious Ryan wanted these people working with him, wanted them sharing. He was dealing with them as equals.

"We need any connection between Vital Forth and Collins and Sheri that you can find. Do you do forensic accounting?" he asked Penney.

"I have most of the current stuff and some ideas about how they are working the money laundering. I have payments going from Vital Forth to Collins. Nothing coming in from him. Though I can't be totally sure, because no names are used. I printed the dates and amounts. I also put them up on the main screen." Penney pointed to the screen and handed over the hard copies.

"With Sheri, I matched up dates that we know she had income, and the deposits are on that screen with the amounts. Only a few withdrawals. I think what Vital Forth is doing is too cute. Look at Sheri's account. They backdated stock purchases in her account. Say Sheri gave them one hundred thousand dollars. Vital Forth backdates their stock purchase, maybe fifteen or twenty years ago in the amount of ten thousand dollars. Then they list the stocks as sold for one hundred thousand. So now it looks like Sheri made a ninety thousand dollar profit.

"And even better, because it's in an offshore account, there's no tax. And the money looks clean. No one is examining the records to see if Vital Forth or Sheri actually made those stock purchases. Vital Forth was not even in business back then.

"Or they might show her as buying some recent stock right before it took off, and the SEC won't be looking at them for insider trading because they never actually made the trades. FBI, IRS, SEC, any of them could get the accounts. Or I can do it. Cav got me the warrants. I printed the transactions I found so far.

"On the third screen is Hudson. And here are his printouts. We know this account number is Hudson, because Cav found his information in a desk drawer in the safe room. I haven't found the source of his funds yet. It's not in his tax returns.

"I'm looking now at the other investors, because I'm thinking that probably all the investors are dirty. Mob money is what I'm guessing. They are the only ones with this kind of money. For now I'm listing them by ID number with the total amounts on the last screen. I'm assuming that the funds realized by the stock sales are the actual deposits, not the sales."

Ryan was almost speechless. "Can I hire you?"

"You can't afford me. But this is kind of fun in a kinky way, so you might be able to subcontract me for special research."

Ryan was nodding, "Oh yeah, we'll be subcontracting you. Can you find a connection between Vital and the mob? How did they get together? And how did Collins get in the mix?"

"I looked at Vittors," John said. "He's the son of a mob accountant. They sent him to school. He came out and set up Vital Forth and went directly to work laundering money. Looks like he expanded his base with Sheri. I haven't found the link to Collins or Hudson, but I expect I'll find a relationship between the men. Maybe as kids growing up or in school, college. I'm still looking."

Ryan looked at Cilla; "Munson says you're checking Sheri's records and files for anyone not prosecuted? Or children still missing?"

"Sarah and I, we just finished. It looks like Collins did his job there except for those three money men and the money laundering." She looked at Kevin. "Kev's got information on the real estate purchases. Tell them Kev."

"Vital Forth has purchased a lot of real estate. I'll print addresses, amounts, and dates for you. I'll send you digital files."

Ryan asked about the security breaches. He wanted details they hadn't shared with him yet. Munson nodded to Jake to fill him in. Jake gave a concise outline, from the original hacking to the gang's ploy to capture the thieves. "They need a warrant to put it into effect. And we need to get it done before the auction starts."

Ryan held up his hand and pulled out his cell. Dialed and talked for a minute, an exact recap of Jake's report. He listened a minute and handed the phone to John. "Tell him what you want."

John jumped up and explained excitedly into the cell. After a lot of back and forth, because John wanted to make sure all the legalities were covered, he handed the phone back to Ryan, who put it away. "He's going to fax them to your account."

Ryan pulled out his laptop, called up the network printer. "Your warrants are printing now," he said. "Now show me how this is going to work."

"The warrants will let us access the sites and follow any lead we find." John turned back to his computer. "We have the plan ready to go with the push of this button. Let me do that, and I'll explain what we have done and plan to do." He dramatically pushed the key with a drum roll from Kevin. Then John took up the tale, pointing to the screen to emphasize some points, as Ryan listened with half a smile. The young man was so excited, he could barely sit still.

"We, Kevin and I, needed access to the website so we could see what Blackit was offering and who was buying. First we opened anonymous e-mail accounts. We used those to set up our own Facebook pages, and then used the individual Facebook pages to friend Blackit. Blackit's Facebook page is on the main screen up there." He pointed to it. "Note that he lists all of the companies for which he helped write code. These include both of your hacked classified sites and two more of your classified sites, as well as a half-dozen other sites. His pages are mostly devoted to how important he is, and they are public and unprotected, so we didn't need warrants to view them. Only one page has privacy and I'll get to that.

"We Googled all his 'friends.' Most have legitimate IDs, e-mail addresses, and Facebook pages and appear to be fairly innocuous. We gave their names to Munson, along with the information we found. I recommend you do the same type of research on their Facebook pages and their friends, going down at least another layer. We didn't have time for that. I don't think you'll find anything, but it's just good thorough procedure.

"We backtracked all the hits to the site. Folks who just looked and passed on. We eliminated them after we followed their tracks and didn't find anything suspicious. Munson has that info also, digital and hard copy.

"That left eight friends we couldn't identify. I think these eight probably did just what we did, set up fake e-mail accounts using fake names. We didn't find anything on these friends in Google, nor were they on any social network. We didn't need a warrant for any of that.

"Black Markit's page leading to the samples has some limited privacy. We used our fake e-mail addresses to log in. We found our eight mysterious friends had logged in also, as well as two more unidentified people who never appeared on the homepage. From there we followed the link to this auction page. Black Markit is holding the auction on Twitter." John put the samples page up on the third screen.

They had known it would be bad, but no one had expected it to be this bad. At the top of the page was an explanation of the auction procedure. It said, "Below are four weapons that are now being built by top-secret companies. If you want to bid on any of these weapons, click on this link to see the sample schematics. To prove our good faith, you may buy a partial set of the drawings for one thousand. We have the complete originals. Shortly after you purchase the sample, you will be e-mailed a place, date, and time to bid on these weapons. Bidding will open for each weapon at one million dollars and will remain open for one hour. At the end of that time, the winner will deposit the amount in our numbered account and will receive a complete set of schematics."

Below that explanation the page was divided into four sections. Two weapons from each of the hacked companies. Each section contained a weapon name, a description of its capabilities, and a picture. There was also a schematic with a link labeled, "Bid on this? More info."

"If you click on the link, you access the option to purchase the samples." John demonstrated.

"Oh man," Munson said. "Did you buy the samples?"

"Yes, both Kevin and I did. I bought all four. Kevin selected one. We did this about six hours apart and from different machines, routing through multiple ISPs. Simple stuff and legal. We each paid our money, and we have the account number where we wired the funds. Blackit apparently has only the one account. We both got copies of your top-secret schematics. Proves he had them, and that he's definitely selling them. He made a nice piece of change with the samples. Four thousand from me, one thousand from Kevin. We needed the warrant to see who else bought samples."

A loud siren, like a tornado warning, filled the air.

"Hold it," John said. He sounded thrilled. "No way. He's got our game schematics. He just downloaded them from our fake mirror sites. We got those up just in time." He high fived Kevin.

"We knew where he was going and thanks to Cilla, we had the alternate mirror sites with the links to our fake weapons ready to go," he told everyone. "We got that warrant just in time. He just took the bait." He looked at Jake. "Cilla locked down the networks immediately. The ones Blackit had written the backdoor codes for. He couldn't get in. As soon as I pushed that button, our mirror sites became accessible, with our schematics. That's what he just took. Let's see how long it takes him to get them up on the auction sample page. We'll come back to that.

"While we're waiting, your warrant gave us the legal right to backtrack the eight plus two friends who went to the sample page. We were set up to run that automatically when we got the warrants. Looks like we have backtracked six of them. I'll put them on the monitor on the left. These are probably not real names, but the computer addresses are legitimate. We can follow those. So we still need to find four.

"Now here is our plan. When we get the e-mail for the auction, we'll each enter and bid. You can bid on any weapon. Each bidder can see all the tweeted bids, and we should be able to track the other buyers from Twitter. The bidding will take time, and they won't be able to hide from us. Would have been really difficult if Blackit had used different auction pages for each weapon. Of course, then he would have had trouble watching the bidding. So he made it easy on himself and us.

"When the bidding is over, the website will appear to crash. Blackit will get a spoofed website. He won't see any difference. The funds will be diverted and deposited into an account set up by us and Munson. We have authority to do that with the warrant.

"We'll spoof Blackit's e-mail and send the winners schematics for our own weapons in Midnight Plus Plus. That's our sequel to Midnight Plus One. We will also 'accidentally' send the plans to the losers. We're hoping when each bidder sees our drawings, they will realize they have been conned and circular file your secret schematics, along with our fake ones. Each of the e-mails we send will contain a sniffer we'll place in the drawings. The sniffer will report back to us. Kind of an 'I am here. I am here.' I'm sure the physical locations we have now are accurate, but this will be a double-check. The sniffers will also let us find the two people we've not been able to identify. One of them is in Europe, which I guess will bring in another letter agency. And if any of the people forward the packets, we can follow those too."

Ryan was impressed, not only with the work they had done, but also with how thoroughly they had covered all the specifics.

"I like it," Ryan said. "Good plan. Seems to cover all the bases. I can call a good guy in the bureau and get a recommendation for someone in DHS, Homeland Security, ICE. They'll make arrests at the physical addresses. I need you to share this information and these addresses with them. Munson will work with you."

"No, problem," John said and then added, "This is too cool. I wish I could see their faces when they figure out our drawings are fake." He proudly showed Ryan the diagrams. "I can't wait to see how this actually works, and the computer will let us know as soon as we get a hit."

"Huh," was all Ryan said as he made a call for eight more warrants. He printed them from his laptop. He ate some more as he watched the forms spit out and then asked, "What do you mean by game? And schematics?"

"Munson didn't tell you, I guess," John said. "That's our new game, Midnight Plus One. We just made a hundred million dollars off that Friday night."

Ryan choked on his coffee. They all laughed.

"Our sequel game is Midnight Plus Plus. Plus plus is sort of a programming term for a sequel or a new improved version. That's where the weapon schematics came from. See the weapon in Cilla's hands there?" He pointed to the poster with Cilla in a skintight red jumpsuit. Ryan realized two things. He hadn't noticed the weapon, which was a realistic version of a current laser gun he knew was under development. He hadn't noticed the weapon, because his eyes had been captured by the woman. And even though he was a trained investigator, he hadn't connected the woman in the poster to this girl next door, who was now mopping up his coffee.

"Yeah, I get that a lot. Yes, it is me. I guess I clean up nice. But this is the me I prefer. It's a lot more comfortable." She gave him an understanding smile. "Spilled your coffee."

Ryan appreciated that she didn't tell him to close his mouth which was still hanging open. He was a little embarrassed. He hadn't connected the posters to the game or the game to these people. It had been a long time since he had been caught off guard like that. *Must be getting old*, he thought.

"Would be awful hard to live with a woman like that," he said and pointed to the poster. "But you, I would keep around forever." He smiled gently.

Cilla held Jake's hand. "Thanks," she told him and changed the subject. "How did you get here so quick?"

"Charter plane. FBI special."

Cav called in then to say they had found Vittors alive and were taking him downtown—his boyfriend too. Since Ryan was an expert interrogator, Cav wondered if he would want to work on Vittors.

A slow evil smile spread across Ryan's face, he was ready with a simple plan. First, scare Vittors with Sheri. She would get him if they set him loose. Kill him the same way she killed Hudson and Sanforth. Second, get him to talk about Collins. Third, get him to turn on the mob.

Two hours later Ryan was handing Penney the names to match the ID numbers in Vital Forth. He was telling them that all it took was a photo of Sanforth to break down Vittors. He didn't ask for a lawyer or for leniency or a trade. Just begged them to protect him. He spilled everything. His fear of the mob was no match for his fear of Sheri.

"You'll find Collins there and Sheri," Ryan said. "It is just as you thought. Not all the money actually went through the firm. They just produced the paperwork to show trades and explain the cash.

"Vittors, as Vital Forth, had access to Collin's gambling notes through the mob. Sheri put pressure on Vittors when she got busted. She didn't call her lawyer the night she was arrested; she called Vittors and threatened him. Threatened to trade Vital Forth with the feds for a reduced sentence. He convinced her to wait and immediately called Collins and put pressure on him. Collins took over the investigation. Sheri kept quiet, because they promised her she wouldn't go to jail. All bets were off when she was convicted, and then Collins had to break her out. Vittors didn't know she was free until he saw the photos. That's all it took.

"IA will share Vittors and Vital Forth. They'll work with FinCEN and Munson. They got us warrants for all the accounts based on the names Vittors gave up. If it is OK with you, Penney, will you forward your research to them? You made this possible. And I want to keep you on the job. I'll arrange status for you. And see you get paid."

"OK. Who would have thought that the feds would pay me?" She laughed.

"Cav and Jones are finishing up at the station," he continued. "They're going to grab some downtime. Cav left a couple of men at Vittors's house, hoping Sheri would show up. Sheri hasn't been able to get to Vittors because he has been out of town."

"Um, folks?" John said. "Black Markit is holding the auction tomorrow night at nine o'clock. And our schematics are now up for sale."

"We're covered, right?" Munson asked nervously. "You have everything set up to track the bids? And they don't get the real thing, but your schematics?"

"Yeah, yeah. We got it under control. Everything will work just the way I told you. Me and Kevin will track them; they can't hide from us. At least not for long. Our schematics will have that little sniffer installed. We'll get 'em." John actually giggled. "Smooth, small, silent. Way too cool." Then he got serious again. "Our warrant covers following back through the numbered accounts of anyone who purchases samples. And the bidders too. The judge gave us everything we needed. Thanks, Ryan."

"Well, you ordered it and walked the judge through it," Ryan said. "Helps that you're an attorney. So everything you can find should be covered in that warrant. We have another that Homeland wrote. We got all the letters of the alphabet working this. You guys in this room? I don't know how you did it, but you have just about every law enforcement agency backing you up and looking at this setup with envy."

Ryan was shaking his head. "Makes my two busts last month look like small potatoes. I didn't know that as soon as I took leave, I would wind up enmeshed in multiple stings with multiple agencies. Homeland already has Blackit staked out and has arrest warrants for everyone bidding at the auction. All the agencies are working together. Except that the guy from FinCEN is kind of an asshole," Ryan said to Munson. "You have any problems with him, let me know. He knows you're lead on this, and I already read him the riot act about cooperating. If he doesn't, he's gone. He knows it too."

Cilla wondered how she had ever thought of this man as soft. She already felt sorry for the "asshole" from FinCEN. Ryan was scary.

Cavanaugh came in then, with Jones, looking even more bedraggled.

"Sheri parked on a side street, and got in Vittors's back door," Cavanaugh said. "Apparently had a key. My men braced her, but she ran out and got to her car, shooting all the way. Garcia was waiting with the engine running and they took off. There was a high-speed chase along the coast highway. Garcia lost control and they went through the guardrail and down into the water. Tow truck is pulling the car out now. Looks like Garcia was killed instantly. Buckled in, but no airbag. They stole the wrong car. Sheri's body was apparently washed out and taken by the current. They're still searching for her. Hard to imagine she could have gotten out alive. But I don't like not having a body."

"Anyone she can reach out to is either dead or in jail," Ron said. "That we know of. Right?"

"Well, that's the problem. That we know of," Daffy said. "We don't know who else she can go to that's local. Or who she might have met in jail. What about those men at Penney's apartment? Do we know who they are? We're still on full alert until Sheri's body shows up. We can't let our guard down. She's been too far ahead of us for too long. And I am not leaving Penney alone until the bitch is dead. "

"Yup. That's true. We're not going to let our guard down until we have a body," Ron agreed. "We need to make plans because Michael and Sarah want to work tomorrow. The medics and the guards will go with them. Same as before. The rest of us probably should get some rest; tomorrow will be a long day."

Jake asked Cilla to walk with him in the garden. "Daffy said Penney told him how all of you got to be a gang. I don't even know that. How can I not know? I guess I never asked. Why did I never ask? All I wanted was to get you into bed and then keep you there. I'm sorry. Again. For not paying more attention." He held her close. "You know, Daffy thinks you walk on water. I know you walk on water."

She looked at him in shock. "It's kind of cute to think that a tough guy like Daffy has a crush on me. I noticed. And no, you did pay attention to me. And well, the bed part, that was pretty mutual," she said with a grin. "I wanted that more than you did. But you did ask me about the gang. More than once. I just never told you. It seemed too personal and like bragging somehow. So I always just said we met in school. You're not the only one who didn't communicate. Did Daffy tell you how we met?"

"Yes. I'm sorry I didn't pay more attention. I will in the future. I didn't know there were more of you, though. More than five. Tell me about them. It is way past time for me to ask questions and learn about your family. My family too."

"Well, Rebecca, Becca, she's a cop, the next town over. She always wanted to be a cop. We hid her in the gatehouse for almost a year. She lived here while she got her high school degree. Did Daffy tell you about Sarah?"

"Yeah." Disgusted.

"Well, Becca had it as bad. Worse. She was older than us. Lived with evil longer. But she's beautiful. And smart. And a great cop. She's a detective. I'm so proud of her. We can go and visit when this gets over. You'll like her."

"What about her parents? Oh, silly question. You all really had it tough. I never realized. I thought you were just friends, not desperate and dependent on one another for survival. What happened when the teachers called, when she lived here?"

"Annie. Annie talked to them. We couldn't have done it without Annie. She is not just a housekeeper. She's our mother. Big sister. Confidant. She made it possible for us to work with the legal system that was supposed to protect us. We created all the legal documents Becca needed to make it look like she was still in Children's Services.

"Then there are The Boys too. We sometimes call them The Twins. They're a couple of years younger than us. We got them at the same time. Like John, they were living on the streets. Actually safer there than at home. The two partnered up when they discovered they couldn't beat each other to death. Tough guys. Big. Both in the military, different branches, different fields. But we all stay in touch.

I have a book. A sort of scrapbook with their stories. The scrapbook, with all the gang members in it. Our successes. I didn't track any of the stuff before we got together. For me, life began then. It's at the house. I forgot all about it until just now. I walked out without it. Without anything."

"I'm sorry, I am just so sorry. I am responsible for you leaving our home. Leaving everything behind. I wasn't rational when I left," he was remorseful.

She faced him and put her fingers on his lips.

"Stop. You have already apologized. I didn't say that to stab or cut. I said it as a simple fact. We were apart for ten months. That's a long time. That's as long as we were together. Things happened during that time, and they are going to come up in conversation. You can't keep apologizing. Opening that wound. Put it behind you. It's done. It's over; there is no going back. Leave it and begin anew. That's what I'm doing. I have you back, that's all that counts."

She looked at him to see if he understood and stepped back when he nodded.

"You might need to talk with someone. Sarah said she would help. You can talk to her or she can recommend someone. Or not. You know what you need."

"Right now, I need you." He gathered her close and she could feel his need. "No, not that way, not now. Soon. Right now, I just need you close. Just knowing I can have you is enough."

She rubbed against him and laughed at him. "Sure, big boy, you keep on telling yourself that. And tell it to that guy poking into me. But you're right, now is not the time. Too many people around. And all watching. Though they would probably cheer if we got it on, it doesn't seem right just now." She could wait.

"I'll have to go back and get that scrapbook. I want to keep that. Someday one of them will want to see it. And Becca and The Boys are in it too. You can see them. They are so handsome."

"I'd like to see the book," he agreed. "There is so much I don't know about the gang. It is time to learn. You sound so proud. A little like a mother. And maybe a sister."

"Jake?" She held her hand up. "I left my ring there. In the house. I couldn't wear it." She was a little scared to tell him. Waited for his reaction.

"I was there, in the house. I walked through. I saw your ring. I have it." He pulled it out of his pocket. She held up her hand for him to put it back on her finger, but instead he took her hand, turned it over, and kissed her palm. He placed the ring on his kiss and folded her fingers around it.

"I think you should have a new one. I want you to have a new one. For our new beginning. And it should match your necklace." The one she apparently never took off. "You love that necklace. And I bet you bought it for yourself. At one of your thrift shops. I finally started thinking. Stopped wallowing in guilt and looked around and saw a whole world. And I knew no one had bought you that necklace."

"We need a new home too. For the new start. I understand the bad memories in that house outweigh the good ones. We need a new home." He whispered, "I hope we can keep the dining room table, though."

"I like those ideas. New ring, new home, new life together. You're right. I couldn't live in that house again. We can stay in the condo until we find something. I have been looking for a place on the beach with a big yard. Small house, not a mansion. I want a garden, and Tiff wants a yard."

"Big enough for kids?" he asked.

Her face lit up. "Oh yes, big enough for kids," she said softly, holding him tight.

"I don't know if Tiff likes me," Jake said. "Though he hasn't hurt me since the first time we met. I can make friends."

"Buy him tuna. He's easy."

Jake laughed. "You never cease to amaze me. And the gang. You are an amazing group of people. What you're doing for Sarah's Child is beyond belief. I want to add my share of the money, the money you put in my account. I want to add it to the pot."

Cilla looked at him in shock. "No. That's kind of you. Thoughtful. But that is my share of the funds. I already paid taxes on it. I have already put a portion back in. No one expects you to do that."

"I want to. I want to help kids like Juanita."

She was going to argue and then remembered Juanita. She nodded her head. Understanding that it wasn't just a gesture, it was from the heart.

"OK. We can tell the gang in the morning. You can donate it in Juanita's name." She guessed she would have to take the initiative. "I changed my mind. I want you to come to my room with me. To my bed. To love me. Now."

She waited. "You know you want to. And I can feel you want to. No one will care that we're happy." She reached out and led him inside.

Daffy had watched Penney as Jake and Cilla left. He was holding her close, on the couch again. His hand under her shirt, just feeling her skin.

"Think they'll make it?" he asked.

"Oh yes." She nuzzled his ear because it was right there, and his hand was doing strange things to her breathing. "Cilla can convince anyone to do anything she wants. Before, he wouldn't talk. But now, now that he's talking? Now they can do it. Just wait and see."

"And us?" he asked, slowly pulling her shirt out of her jeans.

"Us? I think our future is written. I feel like I have known you forever. Been waiting for you. I didn't know I could feel like this. I have no choice but to be with you. It's strange, because I feel so certain this is the way it's supposed to be."

"Me too. I can't wait to get this job over. And get you alone. And in bed. Naked."

His hand reached her breast, and she stopped breathing. He found her mouth and teased it open. Knew he was going to have to stop. Soon. But the longer he kissed her, the more he wanted. And she was totally responsive. Pushing into his hand. She moaned into his mouth. He could taste her. He could have her under him, didn't really need her completely naked. He rolled her back and…came to his senses. Stopped.

"You drive me crazy," he growled. "Just wait."

"Is that a promise? Or a threat? Wait a minute, I don't care. Either one sounds good. Just get this job over. Get Cilla safe. Otherwise, you're going to ruin your reputation and have sex with a client. I can't wait too much longer. That's a warning." She pulled her shirt down. How had it gotten pulled up, out of her pants like that? Like she didn't know the answer. Like she hadn't enjoyed every second.

"Go sit on the other side of the couch," he ordered. "Start planning a wedding. Do we run off to Vegas? Or have a big hoopla with all the families?" He saw the hurt.

He grabbed her. "I wasn't serious," he said quickly. "About Vegas. No Vegas. I am serious about a wedding. Us. You feel that way too, don't you?"

He held his breath. Was he wrong? Had he misread her?

She looked amazed. "You're serious. You want to get married. We barely know each other."

"Are you saying no?" he asked, more scared than he could ever remember being.

"I always thought I would never get married. But that first time I saw you, I heard wedding bells." She giggled. "Of course I will marry you. Soon."

"Here. It will be here. At the gatehouse. A quiet wedding. You and your gang, they're your family. Your friends. I have no family. Maybe a couple of guys. From that group we can't talk about."

"The gatehouse is perfect. Thank you." She leaned in and gave him a soft kiss, careful to stay out of reach of his hands. "We haven't talked about you. Only me. Why do you not have a family?"

But Cilla and Jake came in then. Penney was glad she had her shirt tucked in. Daffy looked embarrassed.

She nodded at them. "He just told me to move to this end of the couch and start planning our wedding. How's that for romantic?" she said smugly with a huge smile. Daffy turned red.

Cilla squealed and hugged her. "When? Where?"

"Here, at the gatehouse." She looked at Daffy, "After his guard job is over?"

He nodded. "However long it will take you to get everyone here, no longer."

"We're all here except for Becca. She'll make it. We can arrange around her. The Boys will need to get leave, and if they're on assignment, they might not be able to make it. But they'll come if they can. What about you?"

"Jen, Ryan, a couple of those guys we talked about before and their wives. No problem."

"Let's not forget Cavanaugh and Jones, Munson, maybe his wife and family if they are close by," Penney added.

"Soon, real soon," he reminded her.

For a moment Penney was scared. She knew nothing about this man. Except she loved him. How could she? After only a few days? Well, almost at first sight, if she remembered correctly. They hadn't even talked about his family yet, or how he grew up, or his favorite color. But she looked at him and knew. This was right. This would work.

"Annie will be so excited. She can plan the wedding. I'm going to call her." Penney looked at Daffy again.

He smiled and said, "Yes, tell everyone to hold two weeks from today open. Or pick the day. Job done or not, we're getting married."

"Ah, Penney, it's two in the morning," Cilla said. "You might want to wait until morning."

"Right. I'll tell Annie and the guys later. At breakfast." She jumped up and grabbed Cilla's hand. "Come on, let's go plan."

Cilla turned to look at Jake, resigned. Her face said it all – that she had kind of hoped he would be coming to her room that she expected him to be taking her to bed. She held her breath. Which Jake would she see when she turned around?

"Go," the Jake she loved said.

"Uh-oh." Penney looked as if she just really saw the two of them and realized she might be interrupting some plans. "No, we can plan in the morning."

"Go," he repeated. "The mood is lost now anyhow."

Cilla walked to him and said, "Sorry. I love you. You know I love you, right?" She waited for his acknowledgement. At this stage of their relationship, she needed him to be sure of that.

He smiled. "Tomorrow," he promised. "We have forever."

She placed a soft kiss on his lips and danced away quickly to run with Penney, giggling.

Jake frowned at Daffy. "I was just about to get laid. Couldn't you pick a better time to propose?"

"Tell me about it."

"You two guys really going to do it? You and Penney? You're not going to hurt her, are you?"

"What are you, the father of the bride? Of course I'm not going to hurt her. I love her. I'm already part of the gang family. I should be asking you. Are you going to hurt Cilla again, 'cause I have to tell you, I love that woman too. Next to Penney she is the most amazing woman I know. And that includes Jen. I don't want to see you hurt her again."

"Well, that speech took care of my boner. Thanks." He sagged onto the couch beside Daffy. "Man, I'm only going to say this once, and I'll swear I never said it. But thank you for knocking some sense into me. Your censures were on the mark, and the insults helped me see some sense. I almost ruined us, Cilla and me, because I got confused about victims. Because I didn't understand how tough Cilla is. Now, I'm going to bed. Alone. Thanks to you." He stood up and walked off.

Daffy sat awhile longer. Thinking he did have a family, now. Because of Penney. He had Cilla. Even Jake. Smiled to himself. Married. Him. Oh, man, was he ever in for it. They hadn't even talked about where they would live. He shook his head, opened the couch, and got ready for bed.

Thursday

Cilla made coffee again and Daffy joined her outside. Penney came out with them for Tai Chi. Jake didn't even watch them. He hadn't slept much. He sat with his back to the windows and watched the news. Some new scandal.

The group came from the main house with breakfast. Annie laid all the food out, and it was immediately attacked.

The three came in from the garden just as Cav came in with Jones. Cilla was sure all cops had an instinct for knowing when there was food. Smiled to herself. Just like a module in coding. A code loop that would read the input (food is served) and automatically return (cops gather to eat). So far it complied and worked everytime.

Penney was sitting with Daffy; they were whispering to each other. When everyone had finished eating and over the murmurs, Penney stood.

"Before you get started, I have an announcement," she said and reached down to grab Daffy's hand. "Daffy and I are getting married. In two weeks. Right here in the gatehouse. Eleven a.m. You all are invited."

There was a stunned silence; Peter was the first to reach her. "Wow, you're quick," he said, hugging her. "You will beat me and John. We haven't even set a date."

"We could make it a double wedding," she offered.

"No, you deserve your own wedding," he replied as he glanced at John and saw his agreement. "As do John and I. And ours will have a lot of baggage." He smiled at her.

Jen, aghast, complained loudly, "Daffy, you have only known her what? Four days? Five? Isn't this kind of quick?"

Daffy just raised an eyebrow at her and said quietly, "And it took you how long to get Ron?"

She had the grace to blush, because she'd had Ron in her bed a lot quicker than four days. And in her heart. "I guess we guardians all work quick." She got up and gave him a kiss. "I am so happy for you. And now you will be part of my family for real. Not just a brother in arms." She hugged him again. And then hugged Penney. Ron got up and shook hands.

"A wedding here? Do I get to plan the wedding?" Annie asked hopefully. "Please say yes."

"Yes, Annie, we are depending on you for this. All of it. You will be my maid of honor, and Cilla and Sarah my bridesmaids. It will be a real ceremony. And someone has to pick out dresses, because I don't even know how to begin to do that. But nothing too fancy. A simple backyard, garden ceremony."

The women went off together, and the men just shook their heads and went for seconds.

It rained. All day. Putting a somber cast on their activities. Everyone waited for the auction. Another auction. *Funny*, Cilla thought, *first an auction of human beings, children, and now an auction of state secrets, weapons.*

Even though John kept them all updated, Cilla could almost understand the stress that Jake had been under waiting for his case to break. Waiting for the auction was unnerving. And there was no place to go and work off energy. So the gang worked on the sequel. Every time she looked up, she saw Jake watching her and her insides clenched. Maybe tonight, she hoped.

Cilla listened in as the guardians, as she had begun to think of them, got to telling tales. Jake asked about the art theft ring Ryan had just busted. And the drugs in the soap?

"For a guy on leave, you've been pretty busy. Two major busts. How did you manage that?"

"I didn't," Ryan said. "Just coordinated. Had our FBI Art Theft Department and FDLE helping each other. FDLE and the locals were working on the drug traffickers. Two major crimes in the same small area at the same time, with three agencies. A nice quiet area, family oriented. Good people. The crooks were outsiders. It was interesting. We were successful in both stings only because of the help we got from a pregnant lady."

He sang her praises. Looked at Jake and said, "She reminds me a little of your Cilla. Strong and brave. Smart."

Jake smiled a little smugly at that.

Cilla thought, *me? Strong and brave? He thinks that of me?* It made her sit up a little straighter.

Ryan told them his tale and then they discussed how poorly agencies generally worked together.

"You made it work down there with the feds, state, and the locals. But you can't even communicate within your own FBI bureaucracy now?" Daffy asked.

"That's mostly because it's internal affairs. IA doesn't share with anyone. Just the nature of the beast. And with Collins, you really can't blame them. Someone that high up in the system on the take means there might be more. IA will keep it close to the vest. Even from me."

And then Jake had to explain how he had got mixed up with Sheri. This story seemed to be easier for him with each telling. He couldn't have talked about it even a day ago. Today it was cathartic. Apparently it became more therapeutic with each telling.

And of course, they got sidetracked onto Midnight.

By evening, when the weather cleared, Cilla said, "I'd like to go to the main house and swim. I know it's petty, but I really need to get out of here and get some exercise. I'm stifling here. My brain is shutting down, but my body is on overdrive. I need to move."

"I'll go with you," Jake said immediately, hoping to get her alone.

Daffy and Jen both looked at him sternly. "OK. OK. Jen can come and watch Cilla. And Daffy can watch me. They don't need to swim. I'm just going to watch."

"I want to swim too," Penney said. "I'm with you on needing some exercise. My brain has gone dead." And she could be near Daffy. The others decided they could go too. Penney noticed Cilla looked gloomy.

"What's wrong, Cilla?"

"I don't have a suit; I was just going to sneak up there by myself."

"Oh, I don't either; it was not something I had thought of packing," Penney suddenly realized.

"I have suits in the bungalow at the pool," Kevin said. "We should be able to outfit everyone. I'll barbecue, and Peter? Want to help? Annie has potato salad and desserts. Maybe we can just forget everything for a few hours. It will be a good break. Exercise and food, always a good combination."

Cilla couldn't help it. She thought, *oh good, I still might get that potato salad after all.*

Penney and Cilla did laps while the rest played in the water. Jake watched Cilla. Jen watched also. Daffy watched everything. The other guards were walking the property.

The smell of roasting chicken and ribs finally got the gang out of the water, showered and dressed.

They ate outdoors by the pool. Desultory conversations on the weather, exercise, food. Jake staying close to Cilla, Daffy close to Penney. Jen laughed, and pointed the two pairs out to Ron.

"Finally he's talking to her. She's listening. I knew she would. She loves him. Even after he left her like that, she still loves him. It's so sweet. And Daffy? He's a goner."

They went back to the gatehouse to wait for the auction, bringing the leftovers with them. John had six hits on the website and was able to backtrack all but one. He and Sarah were going to work on them.

Cavanaugh came by late. He brought Jones with him.

"I have nothing. I could have called," Cavanaugh said as he headed directly for the leftovers, got a plate, and sat down. "I just came for the food. At least I don't have anyone new dead."

Jones copied him, move for move.

Daffy asked about the men outside Penney's apartment again, and Cav pulled out his notebook.

"They worked for Garcia. Cheap thugs. We're trying to track down the whole gang."

Ryan walked in from the bedroom area in time to hear that. "IA just told me that Sheri has called Collins three times today."

"She's alive?" Jake said at the same time as Daffy said angrily, "They're just telling you now?"

"I told you they wouldn't keep us informed. I'm surprised they called at all. Apparently someone felt we should let you know, Cav, since you're looking for her body. Guess you can call off your search crew. Anyhow, IA recorded the calls, and Collins is supposed to meet Sheri. They have a place and a time tomorrow morning, which they are not sharing with me. IA will be set up there waiting. They'll let us know when it's over. They think it will be that easy, but I'm not so sure. Sheri seems to always be a step ahead."

"They tell you where she's calling from?" Daffy again.

"She wasn't on long enough to trace. And using a throwaway. Now turned off. Sounds like Collins is going. She threatened him again. And since he engineered the escape, she has him by the short hairs."

"I don't like it," Jake objected. "I don't believe it. Sheri isn't that stupid. I don't think she's going to be sitting there waiting for someone to come in and ask her nicely to go back to jail. If she has a prearranged spot at a prearranged time, she has a backup plan. Even if she set it up herself. She won't be there."

"If Jake says she won't be there, she won't be there," Daffy said. "I'm here to protect Penney until I see that woman's cold, dead body, I'm not leaving her alone."

Ron stood up then. "We keep the guards. Nothing has changed. No one goes out alone or without setting it up with me first. Period." He looked around. "When one of us sees Sheri in jail or dead, then I'll release the guards. Not till."

He got acknowledgement from everybody.

Nine o'clock finally arrived. John had the auction on the main monitor, and, as each bidder came online, he and Sarah backtracked each to his source on a different monitor. As soon as they ascertained a physical location, Munson passed it on to the field agents. Penney would track the money. It was a little like watching Midnight sell, only the consequences now were enormous.

"Blackit is an idiot," John said. "This site is wide open. And he's running the auction from home. Should be in a cyber café. Or a spoofed website. I would expect a spy to have more sense than this. If the bidders had any hacking ability, they could get what they wanted without even paying for it; those drawings were saved on Blackit's site. Don't worry, we replaced them with ours."

John laughed. "And these bidders are wide open too. Might as well have flashing arrows leading to their locations. As soon as Penney gets account numbers, it should be all over for them. And we still have the sniffers on the drawings."

"Well, maybe because Blackit is so obviously out of his league, these guys have let down their guard," Cilla suggested.

"Homeland is outside his house," Munson said. "They'll pick him and his equipment up as soon as the auction is over. I'm keeping them advised in real time. I already sent them the addresses we have. They're located all around the country. Except for that one in Europe. Homeland or FBI has arrest warrants, and their teams are ready to move."

The auction minimum bid was far too low. The weapons were worth ten times the one million, and the bidding was enthusiastic. John had the winning bid for one of the weapons. He wanted to be sure that his e-mails worked as expected and that his funds ended up in Munson's account.

He was almost not surprised when he received an e-mail from Blackit offering him the drawings for the other weapons.

"Look at this," he told the others. "Blackit is going to let me buy the other weapons for my top bid. Guess it's a good thing we spoofed his site. Idiot."

"Me too," Kevin said. "I can buy any weapon, even though I didn't have a winning bid. This guy is a real jerk."

An hour after the last bid was made and the last group of schematics sent, Homeland reported that all the snakes had been corralled.

"OK," Ron said. "Good job, everyone. That's it for tonight. Leave all the sniffers up, and probably Homeland and or FinCEN will be by to talk to us tomorrow. Let's call it a night."

The main house group headed home, and the gatehouse settled into the nighttime routine.

Penney looked longingly at Daffy. She gave him an innocent good-night kiss, careful not to get too close or hold the kiss too long. Last night, alone, had been tough even with the excitement of a wedding. She was sure Daffy's night had been as bad.

Cilla and Jake went out into the garden. Jake spun her around and held her close.

"You folks are fucking amazing. Sorry about the language, but I can't think of a decent way to say it. You make me so proud." He turned her face up to him and kissed her. Gently at first. Kissed the corner of her mouth. Licked across her upper lip. Kissed the other corner. Teased her mouth open and entered, toying with her tongue. Broke it off to catch his breath.

"I love you," he said. "You know that, don't you? I have always loved you. There has never been anyone else for me but you. I want you so bad. I want us to go back to how we were when I lost my faith, my reason, and my confidence." Saying those words, speaking his thoughts, was one of the hardest things he had ever done.

"I love you too, Jake. Let's go inside," she whispered. She led the way. "But tonight we just ignore anyone on the couch. Come." She breathed a sigh of relief when she saw Daffy asleep, alone, on the couch, and led Jake into her bedroom. Giggling like a schoolgirl. She felt like a schoolgirl.

Daffy smiled when the door closed behind them, rolled over, and went to sleep, as Tiff jumped up to lie down on top of him.

She moved into his arms as soon as the door closed. Reached her mouth up for his lips. He obliged and kissed her gently. Holding her tight. Tasting her. He stroked up her back and down to her waist. Reached under her shirt to skin that was smooth as silk. His heart missed a beat. So long. It had been so long.

"I want to make love to you so bad. You are my life. I need to touch you more than I need to breathe. It's been so long." He said as he kissed her again, this time with more need.

She took his need, sucking his tongue in, moaning. Her hands were under his shirt. As he was reaching for her breasts, she was reaching for his zipper.

"I want you. I never thought I would have the chance to love you again," she breathed. "Get your clothes off. I want to feel you on me. In me."

"I want to do this slow. Savor every minute." He let her go long enough to shuck his clothes; she was doing the same. She gasped when she saw the scars. Reached out tentatively to touch first one and then the other. He held his breath, but she was all Cilla. She leaned over and kissed and licked the first.

"I want to make it better," she murmured. "She did this to you. And this." She stopped talking to give the second scar the same treatment and then looked at him with tears in her eyes.

"It's OK," he said. "It's all over. They're healed. You can't let them upset you." And then he saw her notice the brace. He was following Michael's orders and wearing it. "Oh God. I should have told you. Stop. Before we go too far."

She heard the fear in his voice and turned to face him, puzzled.

"My leg isn't better. It might not get better." He spit it out in a rush. "It might not get better. The doctors aren't sure yet that I will keep it. I might not be a whole man." Would it make a difference to her?

She just smiled, but then got a worried expression on her face.

"What?" he asked, his heart leaden.

"Can you love me with it? Or should I get on top?" She saw the relief on his face. "It makes no difference to me which way we do it. It makes no difference how many legs you have. In case you don't know, it's what's inside you that makes you a man. And you are my man. Love me. Now."

He cupped her face in his palms and kissed her deeply. "Slow and easy, honey. Slow, gentle, and long," he promised, laying her back on the bed.

"I won't last long," she said.

He entered her slowly, a fraction of an inch at a time. Savoring the feel of her warm, tight embrace. Slowly. Exquisite torture. All the way in. He paused, fighting for control. He wanted this to last. Wanted, needed, the long, gentle lovemaking.

She found it extremely erotic. She knew she wouldn't last; it had been too long.

He started to pull out with the same excruciating slowness, and she came apart. He stopped and held her tightly, feeling the spasms from the inside and outside. Kissing her to swallow her cries with his mouth.

Held her till the trembling stopped and she lay back against the pillow, a soft satisfied smile on her face.

"Oh God, you make me feel like a man. To be able to do that to you. To be able to put that expression on your face, that glaze in your eyes," he murmured to her with a self-assured grin and started all over again.

Friday

They all stopped what they doing when Ryan's phone buzzed, watching anxiously. The warriors, again, had been making contingency plans and telling tall stories and lies. The gang was working on the sequel.

"OK, where? When was that?" Ryan demanded, disgusted. "Where is she now? How many hurt? We'll be here."

Jake could read disgust and anger on Ryan's face, in equal amounts.

Ryan put his cell away. "That was Jim Waters, the agent running the IA investigation. Sheri shot Collins. She opened up on him as soon as she got near him. Shot him point-blank. Emptied the clip into him. He's probably not going to make it. And then she reloaded and shot two agents when they tried to jump her. They're going to be alright—superficial wounds. They were wearing vests. The other agents returned fire, and she took three bullets in the chest. They are both in surgery, not expected to live. IA apparently misjudged this meet today. They screwed up." He shook his head and then continued.

"They'll let us know as soon as they find out Sheri's condition. Collins' condition too. They have guards on the hospital. They have video and Waters will bring it over for us to watch."

He looked at Jake. "If you want to talk to her or see her, you can go with me when I head over later. No one can get in to see her now. Not till she's out of surgery."

"OK," Ryan said to Jake. "You need to know for yourself that she's finished. When it's time, Macho Man goes with you. No arguments. All the guards stay on until you get back. We are not standing down."

Jim Waters arrived at the gate, followed by Cavanaugh and Jones. Waters shook hands with Ryan, who introduced Jake.

"Jake brought down Sheri and her brother in the first place," Ryan said. "I told you that Sheri has threatened his wife and her family."

Jake looked at him in surprise when he called the gang Cilla's family, but that's what they were. Ryan knew it, so why had it taken him so long? *Forget it*, he told himself. He was on track now, which was what was important.

"How are your men?" Ryan asked.

"Sore and bruised. The vests saved them. There are two-dozen cars with flashing lights outside the hospital, and inside is bedlam. Before you ask, Collins is still in surgery."

He looked at Jake. "That stuff you folks fed us will go a long way toward putting a lot of people behind bars. They did some pretty impressive research on their own. I'd like to meet everyone. We were already looking at Collins, but couldn't get a handle on the problem. Your people did a good job."

Jake was a little surprised at the compliment, especially coming from the guy who wouldn't share where and when he was taking down Sheri. Waters seemed to know what he was thinking and added, "IA. We're IA. Naturally suspicious of everyone. After all, we are investigating our own. Can't take a chance something will leak. Never expected Sheri to come in with guns blazing. She had demanded a meet and money. We were sure that was all it would be."

"So what actually happened? Can you tell us? And how is she?"

"She probably won't make it. They expect to have her in surgery for a few hours, and they'll let us know if her condition changes. Can I get coffee? And I'll explain." He was nodding at Ryan's cup.

Ryan brought him coffee. Waters wiped his face. "She called Collins three times, threatening to do to him what she did to Sanforth if he didn't meet with her and bring half a million dollars. One good thing, Collins was working alone. No other agents were involved.

"Collins couldn't get Sanforth or Hudson; they were already dead. He made an electronic transfer himself.

"Everyone thought this was a meet to transfer the funds to Sheri." He shook his head. "We didn't know the routine of the restaurant and didn't dare keep civilians out. Sheri was dressed as a stooped, old lady, gray hair in a bun, pushing a walker. Walked up to where Collins was sitting, said something to him, pulled out her gun, and shot him, point blank three times. He is only still alive because he was moving backward when the bullets hit him. My men rushed her, and she shot two of them, but they had on vests. The others returned fire. General panic. But none of the civilians were hurt.

"We got the whole screwup on video," he added. "What a mess.

"FBI and FinCEN." He looked at Jake. "That's Department of the Treasury, Financial Crimes Enforcement Network, are working together on that information you got us. We'll want to talk to your people and track exactly what they did and when they did it in relationship to the warrant."

"Nothing before the warrant that wasn't readily available online," Ryan said immediately. "We want the meet here. No one talks to these folks unless I'm present." He looked around at each of them until he got an agreement. "John is an attorney, but I want to be here too."

"OK," Waters agreed. "Anyhow, we need to unscramble the whole mess. See if we can nail some of the mob bosses. We can confiscate the money at least. Your group may be able to help some more there. We'll use that information you got from Vittors yesterday and interview him ourselves. We'll add whatever they find to the charges against Collins."

Jake thought to himself that the agents were going to see exactly what Penney wanted them to see of her research. But he was fairly sure everything she had done was legal. Knowing Penney, it was all by the book. John might have slipped across the line on Black Markit, but he didn't think so. It was John who had said he needed a warrant. He might have peeked first, though, and that would be Munson's problem.

"You locals can keep Sheri, if she survives," Waters said to Cav. "Now I need to review what you all did and when you did it. Let's take it from the top." He stopped. "Is that food?"

Cilla was smiling when she said, "Yes, help yourself, more coffee there too." Cav and Jones followed him. Jake just knew that Cilla was surprised they waited so long. Maybe shooting took priority over food.

When everyone was back at the table John said, "You should know that the computer records everything in this room."

"Yeah, I saw that sign, but assumed it was a joke." They were talking about the sign over the door, which advised that everything in the room would be recorded and saved. "Start at the beginning."

"With Collins?" someone asked.

"Yes, with Collins. What else do you have going on?"

Jake was sure Waters meant that as a rhetorical question, but if he caught them looking at one another, he didn't say anything. U.S. Immigration and Customs Enforcement's Homeland Security Investigations— (ICE—HSI—), would want in soon.

Jake started. "Someone went after my wife three times. The third time, one of the crooks ended up shot, dead. The shooter got away. Cav, Sheriff Cavanaugh"—he nodded at Cav—"was suspicious after the second attempt and called Munson, my FBI contact agent, who didn't know anything either. He checked and discovered that Sheri had escaped from prison. We think she was the shooter. She shouldn't have been out; we should have been notified. There are no coincidences. We started backtracking. Asked Munson for the investigation records associated with Sheri. The next day my wife's friend, Penney, was almost grabbed. He took a breath.

"Munson was also suspicious and made copies of both Sheri's hard drive and Collins's working disc. John and Sarah compared the two disks and found three names missing from Collins's disc. Hudson, Sanforth, and Vittors. The gang Googled all three and found Vital Forth.

"Penney, who is a financial accountant, didn't recognize Vital Forth, and she suggested a Ponzi scheme or money laundering. That's when we decided we needed warrants and the gang needed legal status. We called Ryan."

Ryan took up his part of the story. "I called in some favors and found out you guys, IA, were investigating Collins."

"How did you do that?" Waters interrupted angrily. "Did my team leak? That's not possible."

Ryan let him stay mad a minute and then said, "No one leaked. But when IA does an investigation, they leave tracks. Cops can spot the tracks."

Then he continued, "If Collins was dirty, then he could be connected to Sheri. I brought warrants and legitimacy for the gang. Everything they had done previous to my arrival was public information and readily available, or covered under Cavanaugh's warrants. They dug deeper when they got my warrants." He explained Penney's theory on the money laundering and added that FinCEN would probably be here soon. And Homeland Security too.

"OK, Sheri and her threats explain the hired muscle." Waters nodded toward the guards. "But not all these civilians."

"My wife's family," Jake explained.

Waters looked at each of them and said, "No, I'm not buying family," and waited.

"Not blood relatives. More like very close friends. Blood brothers." He introduced them one by one. "And Michael, Sarah's fiancé, and Peter Conrad, John's fiancé." Jake wasn't sure fiancé was the proper term. Was there a proper term? He watched for Waters's reaction. That would say a lot about the man. But Waters surprised him with his next question.

"Conrad. Not the Peter Conrad who just bought the new game?" Waters asked.

"Bought it from these five geeks," Peter said. "They wrote it. Yup. And I bought the rights to the sequel too." Now they all waited for the reaction.

When Waters got his mouth closed, he looked around the room at the posters. "Well, that explains the posters. That was going to be one of my later questions."

Ryan put his arm around Cilla and bragged, "That's my Cilla in those posters over there."

Jake wasn't sure how he felt about that. If it hadn't been for last night, he knew he'd be angry. Now he decided to be smug and proud.

They watched Waters do a comparison and Cilla rescued him. "Yeah, I get that a lot. But this is the real me. That is the game me."

"Why Homeland?" Waters asked after he digested that. "I could see SEC, but not Homeland."

"Jake's company was working on a security breach for me," Munson said. "That brings in Homeland. We have the problem locked down, and Homeland will be coming by for details."

"I probably don't need to know about that right now. If I need to later, I can get in touch. Show me your hard copies and let me see the digital version also. For now. My people should be able to backtrack everything you did."

But then Homeland was announced. They were checked thoroughly at the gate. No one knew these guys. The guards scanned in the IDs, and John ran them through his system. "They're Homeland," he announced.

"I've heard good things about Ricky Hall," Ryan added. "Smart, plays well in the sandbox. Not out for glory, but to protect the country. We should be able to work with him."

Cilla made a bet with herself and won, when after introductions, the agents headed for the food. Ricky Hall was a quiet, nondescript-looking man. He would blend in anywhere. Except that he was always watching. *That would give him away*, she thought.

He opened the discussion with, "Let's see if I got everyone straight here." He worked his way around the room, naming each person, including something personal that he knew about each one. Showing off? Demonstrating how good Homeland was? A pretty impressive performance, since the bodyguards had been introduced as a group, not by name. He looked at Jones and said, "Some people call me Sherlock too. It's a name that's tough to live up to."

Daffy laughed. "What, you have a bug in the room?"

"No, just thorough. And I think we have a mutual friend. Ask him about me."

Daffy rubbed his mouth, puzzeled. His cell shook. He gave it a quick glance. And looked at Hall with some kind of awe.

"Yeah, I do magic too. Our friend?" he asked, indicating the cell. And got a nod back.

Munson and Jake looked at each other meaningfully.

Cilla figured it must be Heathertons. That name again, even unspoken, earned Hall respect. Of course, the way he seemed to know a little bit about each of them was a little creepy.

Hall looked at them all. "You folks have done some really good work. All we want is to keep the country safe. I would like for each of you to walk my team through what you did, step by step. It will be a long, tedious, repetitious process, and boring. But bear with us. The more thorough we are now, the safer everyone will be later." He looked at Waters and said, "We can work alongside you. Won't slow you down. Let's get started."

Partway through, Annie brought in lunch, but interviews proceeded right through it. The agents were using tablets, which automatically transcribed the vocal interviews and allowed for signatures. These were printed and a copy given to each one. Annie was interviewed too. Even Waters was interviewed. He laughed at that. "I wondered what they were talking about when they said Homeland would be here. Hadn't got around to asking about it before you showed up and explained.

Cilla found the whole thing exhausting. Even watching the interactions had become old. She kept thinking about the wedding and her scrapbook. Funny, she hadn't thought about her book for months, but now she had to have it. Now. She really wanted it. Wanted to go through the pictures with Penney and Daffy. Wanted to show Jake her family. Finally, she asked Ron if it would be safe for her to go to the house, to get the scrapbook. He checked with Jake, and they both decided it would be OK as long as Jen went with her.

Ron pointed at Jen and said, "Go with her." They checked with Waters and Hall, who were both finished with Cilla and Jen.

Jake got up to go with them, but Hall said he still needed him. Daffy was sticking with Penney. Jones jumped up and said he could go. Wanted to.

"OK," Ron said. "Jones, borrow a civilian shirt. I don't want you in uniform. Put on a vest. I know Sheri is in surgery. I don't care." He looked at Cav for agreement.

"The three of you, listen up," Ron continued. "I know Sheri is not out there, but we don't know if there are others." He looked at Jen. "Don't look at me that way. I know I don't have to remind you. I'm reminding Cilla and Jones. This is not just a walk downtown. Be careful and stay aware of your surroundings. Keep your cells handy. Jen, keep your jawbone on."

Jen didn't take the instruction well. She touched her jawbone and shook her head at him. Walked over and standing an arm's distance apart, leaned forward and planted a loud kiss on his mouth. Stood back and patted her butt. No one laughed, but there was some choking in the background.

"I love you," she said. "We'll be careful. I'll remind you that I know there has been no official identification of Sheri yet."

He smiled. This was her job and she was good at her job. "Be safe," he told her.

Jen turned and rounded them up. "Come on, guys. Let's go for a walk. Leave my right side free. And be ready to follow instructions immediately."

Now Cilla wasn't so sure this was a good idea. She looked at Jake. He nodded reluctantly. "Jen is good. And Jones appears to be on the ball. And it has to be Sheri in that surgical room."

It was a short walk. "How does he know about the Sherlock stuff?" Jones asked. "How did Homeland get all that information?"

"Well, a lot of that information could be found on the web," Jen said, slowly thinking. "Some of the more personal stuff could be gleaned from another security firm or guardian. Security is a small world. And I think he was talking about Heathertons when he said Daffy and he had a mutual friend. Did you see the way Munson and Jake looked at each other? That was pretty telling. It's interesting. Four people in one room who seem to know Heathertons. I never met any-one before who admitted to that. Not that they were claiming they knew them. But it was obvious. Daffy never said anything. Neither has Jake. I don't think Ron knew that either Jake or Daffy were part of Heathertons. Jake didn't know Daffy before he stepped in the gate-house, so they didn't meet in a Heatherton operation. I think that's part of Heathertons strength. They don't all know one another. I don't think Ron is a member. Would you call them members? Followers? Supporters? Part time independent contractors? Yes, independent sub-contractors."

"But what about that Sherlock stuff? How could he know that?" Jones asked.

"Spooky," Jen said. "I don't know."

Cilla looked at Jones and said, "You told someone about the Sherlock thing. You did. That's the only way. Who was it? Your sister?"

"My sister," he admitted reluctantly. "And I might have told some of the guys."

"There," Cilla said, satisfied. "That's all it would take. Someone mentioning Jones and a buddy telling that story. No mystery. Nothing spooky. It can all be explained. Thank goodness. Because that really was too spooky." But it really was spooky.

"Let's go in the back door," Cilla said. "You can look around while I get the book. It's a pretty little house. Three bedrooms, two and a half baths."

"Is there a wine cellar? Is there a safe room? And a wall safe? A wall safe with cash and plans?" Jones asked kidding.

"No, none of that. Look around. I'll just be a minute."

She turned to run upstairs and bumped into someone. *Sheri.*

"Oh!" She froze. Terrified. Sheri here. Not in the hospital. Not shot. Here in her house. *Don't show fear. Don't show fear*, she told herself. Those words were all she had to hang onto. Her mind was filled with images. Images of battered children. Jake bleeding out. The man Sheri had shot in her condo. Cilla couldn't speak. Couldn't seem to catch her breath.

"Sheri," she breathed. She felt more than heard Jen and Jones behind her. What was his first name anyhow? Jones's? Why did she still call him Jones? Sheri. Here. In the house. She found her voice. Loudly she said, "Sheri."

Jen had heard the first whisper of the name and pressed the On switch for her jawbone. Turning, she affected a puzzled look. And then said, frowning, "Mrs. Jayden, you didn't tell us you had someone else looking at the house today. I thought we were the only buyers. This isn't really fair, you know." Jen hoped Cilla would be able to get her wits about her. And looked quickly to Jones. He was nodding.

"That's right," he said. "You promised us we could have a viewing today. You didn't mention it would be an open house." He sounded whiny and aggrieved.

Cilla looked between the two of them and stammered, "I didn't. I'm not sure. Um." She pulled herself together and tried again. "I didn't know anyone else would be here. My husband must have brought them."

She couldn't talk to Sheri yet; she had an inspiration. Cilla said to Jen, "I'm sorry this had to happen. This is my husband's girlfriend, and I think things are about to get ugly."

She looked at Jones and said, "I'm sorry, Mr. Jacaby. I imagine there is not anything much worse than being between two people in the middle of an ugly divorce. Maybe you two should go wait outside. Yes, would you please wait outside? Go out the back door, it's unlocked. Wait out there, please, while I talk to my husband about this." She was all but herding them back through the door.

"Where is Jake, Sheri?" she said over her shoulder and then raised her voice as if to reach upstairs. "You can come out now, Jake," she called and saw the confusion on Sheri's face. Cilla looked directly at Sheri and said, "I know he's here with you, Sheri. That's the only way you could get in."

She could only hope Jones would understand what she was planning to do. That he had gotten to the scene she had written for the game. The scene that had the heroine attack the monster. A scene based on her real-life childhood. Dirty fighting she developed to protect herself. She hadn't been in a street fight for years, but she had practiced the movements when she wrote the scene. To perfect the action and get all the steps right. It could work now if she could get close enough to Sheri. Jones might be able to back her up, if he understood what she was planning. She saw his eyes narrow.

At first the sounds had come through as crackles on the loudspeaker, but then Jake heard the words. His heart stopped. He closed his eyes and stopped breathing. But he still heard the word *Sheri* and opened his eyes. Found himself looking right at Ron. Saw the despair move quickly across his face and then blankness replace it. Ron. He was thinking of Jen. Jen was there too. With Cilla. With Sheri! Jen had turned on her jawbone. Everyone else was looking at the speakers. Jake's kneejerk reaction was to jump up and run over to the house and kill the bitch. Instead, he took deep breaths.

"Jen's with her, Jake," Ron said. "Jen is good." He said it calmly. Was that to convince Jake or himself? "She's bought them some time. A story. She had a story for Sheri. An excuse for them to be there."

And then they heard Sheri yell, "Stop. No one is leaving."

"No," Cilla said. "You should go outside too, Sheri. Have the decency to leave Jake and me alone for a few minutes." It sounded as if she was trying to distract Sheri, so Jen and Jones could get out.

For a moment Cilla thought it would work.

"I said no," Sheri screamed. And showed them her gun.

"What? What are you doing with a gun?" Cilla gasped.

"Wow," Jones said. "Look, Jen, she has a gun. This must be a reality TV show. Where are the cameras?" Looking around.

"Shut up. Just shut up." Sheri waved the gun in his face and he backed off.

"Jake's not here, geek wife. Just me. I'm checking out your little house. It's boring. Just like you. Now let's all go into the living room and sit down," Sheri ordered.

When they hesitated, she screamed at them again, "Move."

"All right, we're going into the living room," Jen said.

"The stupid geek first," Sheri ordered. Sheri didn't understand that Cilla had always been proud to be a geek. Didn't consider geek to be an insult, but a compliment. An indication of her computer skills. Sheri thought it was a derogatory term, an insult. It actually gave Cilla more power because it meant Sheri was apt to underestimate her. Cilla was thinking it was good Jones had on a plain shirt. Sheri probably would have shot him on sight if he'd been in uniform.

"How did you get in, Sheri?" she asked calmly. "If Jake isn't here?"

"I broke the slider and walked in," Sheri said smugly and then continued, "What happened? Selling the family home? Jakey decide to divorce his little frumpy geek wife? He said you wanted kids. Maybe you realize there won't be any kids since Jakey can't get it up?"

She laughed hysterically and then continued, "Huh, I'm right aren't I? You should have test-driven him before the wedding, huh, geek wife?" She laughed again and then offered some advice. "Don't you know, honey, that when they can't get it up, you just lick them all over? That's all it takes."

Sheri watched as her comment hit the mark, and then she turned toward the den and said, "Come on out, guys. Come see what I have here. Julio here can't get it up either without encouragement." Sheri leered at him.

Three men came out. Tough looking. Mean. They looked just like what Cilla thought lowlife criminal thugs would look like. And they each had a gun. One of them, the guy Sheri called Julio, was holding his sideways like the gangbangers on TV.

Except this was real. *This is scary*, Cilla thought.

"You know, I think you need to call Jakey and have him come over and join the party," Sheri said.

Jen started to move and said, "I think we should leave," but one of the men shoved her back and waved a gun at both her and Jones.

"I thought he was with you, Sheri," Cilla said. "I thought Jake left me for you, that he wanted to be with you."

"You really are a stupid geek wife," Sheri said, "Now call him."

Cilla reached for her phone and Sheri grabbed it away. "Oh no. Let me. I think he'll get this text from you telling him to come on home."

Sheri typed in the message. "I made him a promise last time I saw him. It's time for him to come collect it." She pressed Send and said, "Now we'll just all sit down and wait."

Jake gulped air as he listened. Her promise. Thought he would be sick.

"What, Jake? What did she promise you?" Ron asked.

He'd never told anyone the whole story.

"When she staked me to the ground in the barn. On top of Juanita. After she shot me. Staked me with the pitchfork through my leg. She watched me bleed and then she said she was going to go get Cilla and bring her to the barn. Shoot her too. We could bleed together. And I could watch while Sheri set her men on Cilla," he hissed tonelessly. "I could watch. She promised to let me watch. She was hysterical with laughter. And I prayed. I prayed I would bleed out before they got back."

"Easy, Jake," Ron advised. "Easy. We have time. We're not going to let that happen. We need a plan. Jen gave us a scene. We need a little time. Wait a few minutes before texting back. And text just the one word: later. Buy us some more time. Sheri knows you're in the middle of a divorce. She shouldn't be surprised if you don't jump when Cilla texts. Let's see if we can get some dialogue going, get us some time to make a plan and set something up. It has to be good. We'll only get one chance."

Jake fought to get himself together; his hands were shaking. He wouldn't be any good to anyone this way. He had to set aside his fears and start thinking like a professional. Ron was doing it. Both their wives were in the same room. If Ron could do it, he could. He put his head down and took some more deep breaths. He could hear Penney crying softly, Daffy mumbling comforting words. He was aware of all the men around him. Ready to do battle. But it was clear that Ron was waiting and Ron was still in charge.

"You have Jen there," Cav said. "And my man might be new, but he's smart and sharp. And your wife is too, Jake. We have a lot going for us here."

"We need a team to go to the house," Ron said, looking around. His men all stood, started gathering the tools of their trade. Vest, weapons, jawbones, earbuds. Cav took off his shirt. He didn't even argue for an official team. One, there wasn't time, and two, these men wouldn't go for it.

"And I have a plan," said Ryan. They all looked at him. "Jen set it up. She and Jones are looking at the house. I go in as a Realtor." He looked around. "And Hall goes with me as a buyer."

"Me?" Hall said in surprise. "You don't even know me."

"Did some research after you showed up. Already knew some stuff. I want you with me. Besides, we're probably the only two Sheri won't recognize. That will put four armed men on the inside. You, me, Jen, and Jones. Ron's team can be ready to move in. And Jake comes in as a last resort, because it's all going south as soon as Jake walks in the door."

"That could work," Ron agreed. He looked at Jake.

"Yeah. OK. Here's the layout of the house." He was finally thinking and quickly drew a diagram. "In the front door, stairs directly ahead, living room where they all are, is to the left. Hall, you make a quick left into the living room. Act as if you're looking the room over. You want to see the den and kitchen, beyond the living room. Cilla said the kitchen back door is open, so one team can go in that way. Another through the den. Hall, see if Sheri will let you walk into the den. Sheri said she broke in that way. It should be open for our team. Hall, you're asking questions as you walk in.

"Meanwhile, Ryan's in the living room talking like a Realtor. Doesn't even notice the guns at first. Our guys can be ready to go in the back through the kitchen and the slider in the den as soon as we know for sure that it's open."

Ryan and Hall both nodded. Jake looked at Ron, who agreed. "Sounds good, Jake. It's a good plan. It should work. Give Ryan your key."

Jake handed him the key. "Leave the front door open or unlocked when you go in, so I can get in later."

"You should send that text now, Jake," Ron instructed.

The men prepared as Jake sent the message. Waiting to hear Sheri's reaction over the speakers.

Sheri screamed. She was swearing as she texted back, "Get over here now, asshole." They could hear her breaking things in the background.

"Tell her twenty minutes, Jake," Ron instructed. "That should give us time to get the men in place. Then go get your vest. Go with Ryan and Hall and be ready to go in when I give you the word."

Ron looked around at his men, waiting for his signal. "Go. Windows, doors. Get inside if you can. Daffy? You're on-site lead. Jason? Find a spot for a good sight and set up. We might need a sniper there."

"I'll go with him," Cav said. "There should be some sort of official presence if he has to shoot."

Jake saw Penney almost hold Daffy back, torn between her sister and her lover. Heard Ron continue, "Ryan, you and Hall need to distract Sheri until everyone is in place. Jake goes in as the last resort if you need him. Like you said, it will all go downhill as soon as he steps in."

Jake went for his borrowed vest.

John went over to Ryan. "Here, I made you an ID." He gave the card to Ryan, who held it in his hand. "Ryan Gibbs, Realtor," it stated. With a phone number and an address. You could almost see the thoughts going through Ryan's head. *An ID? A Realtor ID? In what? Two minutes? Who were these people?* But he clipped it on his pocket.

Ron handed over earbuds and jawbones. Attached a mini camera to Ryan's shirt.

Ryan nodded to Hall and Jake. Ron had a hand on Jake's wrist, stopping him.

"Not yet. Remember, they'll be safe until you walk in there. You'll be the catalyst for Sheri. Wait. Delay as long as you can. You need to be objective about that. Can you be?"

"Yes, I'm OK. I understand. I only go in when you say, when it looks like it's going downhill already."

"We need everyone in place. And you need a jawbone and earbuds." Ron looked at John, who nodded and went to get them for Jake.

And like that, they were gone.

"Twenty minutes," Sheri said. "He'll be here. To see his geek wife. For the last time."

Cilla swallowed. Stared at Sheri. It wasn't hard to act terrified. She was so scared. For herself, her friends. And Jake. Jake was going to walk into this madness, unaware. Because Sheri was crazy. Cilla looked over at Jones and Jen, who were standing across from her. They seemed calm enough. Jen surreptitiously stroked her jaw just below her ear. Cilla froze. Jen was pointing. To her jawbone. Jen looked right at her for a second to make sure Cilla understood and then looked away. She had it on? The guys were listening? That's why Jen was calm? Because everyone at the gatehouse could hear what was going on? Because they would be planning a rescue? She didn't want that. Didn't want people to die for her. Didn't want Jake to die for her. To die because she had wanted to get a scrapbook.

Jen had her version of terrified perfected.

"Who are you?" she asked weakly. "What are you doing here?" *To keep Sheri occupied*, Cilla thought, and turned to see what Sheri would say.

"Me? Her husband murdered my brother. And I'm going to make him pay for it."

"We don't even know her," Jones said. "Or him. We're just looking at the house. You should let us go."

"Yes, you should let Mr. Jacaby and his sister go," Cilla said. Stressing *Jacaby*. The gang would understand what she planned.

Sheri just laughed at them. "In your dreams. And the boring little house is a fire hazard," she sniggered evilly, pointing at the gas cans lined up along the wall.

Oh my God, Cilla thought. She hadn't even noticed them.

Sheri walked back and forth. The men held their guns on them.

Penney was yelling at Ron, "Jacaby! She's saying Jacaby!"

Ron covered his mouthpiece, looking at her like she was crazy.

"It's a scene Cilla wrote for the game sequel. The heroine attacks the monster Jacaby when she gets close enough. Takes him down. Uses tricks she learned, Cilla learned, when she was little."

Ron just closed his eyes for a second.

"Guys," he said into his mike, "Cilla is getting ready to try to take Sheri down. That will be your signal. When she moves. If she moves before I give the signal, you have to go on her action."

Sheri was talking again. "Yup, Jakey is going to pay for what he did to me. And killing Lenny. And geeky wife is going to pay too. All of you."

"But we don't know anything about that," Jones whined. "It's their problem."

"Shut up," Sheri screamed at him, waving the gun. "I could kill you now. But I want Jakey here to watch. Sit down, both of you," she ordered.

Jones cringed back onto the couch.

It was all an act, Cilla realized. Jones and Jen were goading Sheri. Keeping her occupied.

Sheri started waving her gun around again. Cilla tried to distract her. "They said you were dead. You killed that FBI agent. I heard that on the radio."

"Ha. Idiots. They're all idiots. That was Garcia's girlfriend. She dressed up like an old lady to meet Collins. The disguise was her idea.

It really worked to get her close. I was watching. She was only supposed to drop him a note telling him where to meet me. But she blamed Collins for Garcia's death. Maybe because I told her it was his fault Garcia was dead. I guess she couldn't wait for the games we were going to play with him later. I promised to let her hurt him. That disguise fooled everyone. They thought it was me. Fools. Thought they could kill me. Lay a trap for me, and I would just walk into it. Morons."

She was bragging now, convinced she was smarter than the cops. If Cilla could just keep her talking, she knew she could get close enough to fight Sheri. Before Jake came. She knew Jake would come. Sheri was still ranting.

"Stupid bitch. When she shot Collins, she killed my last chance to get my money. Garcia helped me with Sanforth after Hudson died. I did him, Hudson, by myself. He just kept begging for a deal and wouldn't talk. Wouldn't get me my money.

"That weakling, Sanforth, didn't believe we would kill him. Tried to scare us with talk about the mob. Like we would be afraid of the mob. Ha. And then those idiots showed up when we went to get Vittors. Garcia, stupid jerk, missed the turn and ran the car off the road. Idiot had his seat belt on and couldn't get out. Left him there for those idiots. His fault the bitch shot Collins."

She paused and started to point her gun at Jen and then Jones. "Who should die first?" she asked.

The doorbell rang.

Everyone stared at it. They heard the key in the lock. Cilla stopped breathing. Jake? Jake was here already? It was too soon, wasn't it?

Ryan walked in, Hall behind him. Ryan was talking to him, his back to the room.

"You'll like this house. It's a starter home. Perfect for newlyweds. I know you want to see the kitchen first. It's right through there. The den is across from it." Motioning Hall toward the kitchen, he kept his back to the group in the living room.

Ryan turned around and saw them and stopped, but Hall continued on without noticing.

"Oh," Ryan said as he spotted Cilla, "Mrs. Jayden. I didn't know you were here. No one told me there was an open house," he complained, looking around. The guns were all hidden. Sheri was standing right beside Cilla. She had walked over and grabbed her arm, with her gun pressed against Cilla's back.

Ryan tried to walk over to Cilla, but was blocked by one of the goons. Ryan continued talking.

"My client wanted to see the house before he makes an offer. I was just going to walk him through. He'll start in the kitchen, and he wanted to see the den too. We'll be right back to make an offer," he said, already moving in that direction. "We'll stay out of your way."

And again the thugs blocked them.

"Wait a minute." Jones jumped up angrily. "He can't do that. We were here first. We should get to make the first offer." He stopped when Jen jabbed him in the side. She had stood up beside him. He looked ready to say something to her when he appeared to see Sheri and remember the gun. "Oh," is all he said. But the distraction gave Hall time to move toward the kitchen and den.

Ryan considered Jones and then said to Cilla, "Well, my client is ready to make an offer. I'm sure Mrs. Jayden would certainly listen to both of us." By this time Hall was edging around to get a look into the den.

Cilla kept up her end of the conversation. "Um, yes. Mr. Jones, I would have to consider all the offers. It's not a problem who makes the first one." *Is this what they wanted her to do?*

Mollified and sheepish, Jones looked around.

"I liked the kitchen; it looks modernized. I'll just sneak a peek into the den." Hall looked over Sheri's head, through the entrance, where he could see the slider, nodding his head at Ryan and the camera.

So the whole scene was to let Hall get a look in the den? Cilla wondered.

Hall was still talking. "I probably don't even need to go upstairs. What about the roof, how old is it?"

"Um, last year. We modernized the kitchen and put on a new roof. Um, this year, not last." Cilla wasn't sure if what she said made a difference, or even if it made sense, but she realized they wanted to just keep the dialogue going.

"Fifteen year?" Hall asked.

"Um, I'm not sure. I don't remember." Well, that was the truth. She had almost said Jake would know when she realized she probably shouldn't remind Sheri about Jake.

"Well, it will show up in the inspection, I imagine," Hall grumbled, moving back toward the front of the living room.

"Why don't I call you later with the offer, since you're busy now," Ryan said as both he and Hall moved nearer to the crooks in the front of the room. The team would be coming in the back.

But Sheri had had enough. She waved her gun at them all. The three goons showed theirs, aiming at the two new arrivals.

"Wait a minute," Sheri yelled, moving a step away from Cilla.

Cilla saw that Ryan and Hall were now near the two thugs at the front of the room. That was good, wasn't it? Sheri and the third guard were near Cilla and facing Ryan. Sheri was standing almost the perfect distance away from her. Cilla caught movement from the corner of her eye in the kitchen. She stepped closer to Sheri, away from Ryan, and Sheri pointed her gun, yelling, "Stay where you are.

"Do what I say, or someone gets shot," Sheri shrieked, spitting. There was a moment of silence as everyone recalculated. And then Sheri looked at Jones and said, "Starting with you, maybe."

"OK, Jake, go in now," Ron instructed through Jake's ear bud. "Your entrance will distract Sheri and the goons. Keep her distracted. Here's the setup. You'll walk in the door. Hall's to your left near goon one. Ryan is the other side of Hall, to your far left near goon two. Sheri will be right in front of you near the foot of the stairs. And Cilla is to her right. Jen is behind and to Cilla's right near goon three. Jen, nod if you hear me; you get the goon by Sheri." He saw her nod and then look at the man, judging distance. "Daffy or you, whoever is closer, will get Sheri."

Jake nodded to himself and walked in, complaining loudly.

"For God's sake, Cilla, can't you be reasonable? What do you mean insisting I come over now?" That worked to distract everyone long enough for Daffy to edge closer to the room. Close, but not close enough.

Sheri turned and pointed the gun at Jake. The three goons were watching her and Jake, not paying any attention to the other men in the room.

"Hi, Jakey," she said. "Too bad about your leg the other day. Did I get the right spot? Looked like it, the way you went down." Another hysterical laugh. "Almost too easy to take you out. Kind of like the last time we met, when I got to stake you. Before you killed Lenny. Hope you're feeling better."

She was laughing wildly. "Want you to feel healthy for what I have planned. Sorry, but no one is going to buy your boring house. Too bad. We're going to burn it down with you guys inside after we have some fun." She laughed again.

Jake was pretty sure this woman was the other side of sane. Which made her even more dangerous. He didn't dare to look at Cilla. Or behind her to check on Daffy. He kept his eyes on Sheri. Gave her his full attention. He needed everyone's attention on himself for the plan to work.

Jake managed to look surprised. Rubbing his leg, he said, "Sheri? Sheri? What do you mean? That was you who kicked me? Tried to shoot me?" He sounded shocked and disbelieving. He took a step closer toward her.

"Idiot. Yeah, that was me. Too bad about your condo. Kind of got damaged, didn't it? I was going to burn that too."

Jake took a chance. "That was you? You shot your buddy two times and then put a bullet through his brain before you ran away."

Sheri was no longer listening. She was still talking, shrill and on the edge.

"You first. I shoot you first. Then you'll get to watch me shoot her. And then the boys are planning on a little fun. You can watch that too."

The three goons were looking at her too now. He felt Hall move, edge closer to his man. Could see Sheri's finger tighten on the trigger. He might have pushed her too far.

Cilla grabbed Sheri's ear with her left hand, twisting it and pulling Sheri's head toward her cocked fist, doubling the power of the blow. At the same time, she kicked Sheri in the knee. Those moves had saved

Cilla many times when she was younger. She could feel the kick all the way to her hip. Sheri's hand came up with the gun.

Even without hearing Ron's *"Now! Now! Go! Go!"* the men had moved as soon as Cilla reached to grab Sheri.

Cilla was grabbing Sheri's gun hand and grappling for the gun when they spun around; swapping places. She heard a shot at the same time she felt Sheri go limp. Cilla looked up, startled, and saw a fourth man on the stairs, getting ready to shoot again. At her. He'd shot Sheri when they'd spun around. She thought she would freeze, but she was still dragging Sheri's gun hand when Jones pushed in front of her and then knocked her back as she heard another gunshot. Jones fell on top of her, a dead weight. Had he been shot?

It all happened at once. As Cilla grabbed Sheri, Jen ploughed into the third guy, behind her, taking him down. As they tumbled to the floor. Jen landed on top of the guy, knocking the breath out of him. She punched the guy hard in the face.

Jake grabbed Sheri's gun arm, trying to twist the gun out of her hand as she fell down to the floor. Just collapsed. He kicked Sheri's gun away. Ryan and Hall were fighting behind him. Daffy reached up and grabbed the fourth guy by his gun hand and dragged him head first over the rail, twisting his gun hand behind his back. Daffy's knee come up and clipped the guy's jaw. The wrist broke with a loud crack. The guy was done. Daffy kicked the gun away and stepped over to pick it up. Then knelt on his back while slapping on the cuffs.

Ryan punched his thug in the throat, seized his arm as he went down, and twisted the gun loose. He hit the thug hard again. Pounded the guy's head into the floor, twice. When he went limp, Ryan reached over and cuffed him.

At the same time, Hall hit the last guy with a quick double-left hook to the jaw. The guy yelped "Oomph," and fell over. Hall was cuffing him as the teams were spilling out of the kitchen and den to help.

Jake looked for Cilla. Cilla? What was happening with Cilla? Jake picked up Sheri's weapon, didn't pause to check her pulse. It was obvious Sheri was dead.

He reached Cilla just as Daffy pulled Jones off of her and turned him over.

"Where are you hit, boy?" Daffy asked gruffly.

"Shit. He got shot?" Jake asked. "I heard two shots. He caught the second?" His hands searched for a wound. Found a hole in Jones's shirt where the bullet had hit him high in the shoulder. No blood?

Ryan hurried over. "Vest, he's wearing a vest."

"Speak to me, someone," Ron was saying. "Someone tell me what just happened. We can't see, Ryan."

Jen was standing now, reaching down to help Cilla up. She spoke into her jawbone.

"It's OK, sweetie." She got Cilla onto her feet. "We're checking. Sheri's dead, killed by a guy on the stairs. I never even saw him till too late. Sorry. He was aiming for Cilla, got Sheri by accident."

The thugs were all stretched out on the floor, cuffed. The team finished checking them for weapons.

"Jones," Jen said. "The thug on the stairs, he shot Jones. In his vest. Jones stepped between the shooter and Cilla. Wait." Jen was still holding Cilla. "He's sitting up, a little glassy-eyed. Gonna be one sore puppy tomorrow." She finished looking around. "Everyone else is OK, sweetie. We did a good job. Everything looks to be under control."

Jake was reaching for Cilla, who was reaching for him.

Cav come in fast and went to Jones and breathed a sigh of relief. He told them he had an ambulance coming. Ryan had Jones's vest open and off, and Cav could see the impression of the bullet poking out of it. Jones's chest was bruised. Cav didn't want to take any chances.

"Just stay where you are, boy. Let the EMTs check you out."

"I'm OK," Jones said, struggling to sit up and look around.

"Yes, you are. Now just stay where you are and wait. I'm going to call your sister and have her meet you at the hospital."

"You'll scare her. I'm fine. Just a little bruised. I don't have to go to the hospital."

"Gonna do it my way, boy. That's the final word. You did a good job in here today."

"He jumped in front of Cilla," Jen said in awe. "Took a bullet meant for her. My job. He did my job."

They could hear the sirens now. They each took stock. One of the deputies stockpiled and labeled the weapons. The fourth guy was the only one to fire. No one was hurt bad. Except Sheri.

Jake was holding Cilla as close as he could get her. She had her head buried in his chest.

"I was so scared," she said. "So scared someone else was going to die." She took a deep breath and got herself under control. "You're OK?" she asked him. "Tell me you're not hurt."

"I'm fine. Other than losing eight of my nine lives when I heard Sheri over Jen's jawbone and knew she had you, I'm fine. I'm going to spend all of that last life holding you." And he pulled her even closer as she looked around at Jones.

"Check Jones, make sure he's OK. He fell right into me when that guy shot him. He saved me. I don't even know his first name."

"He's OK. I almost lost another life when I saw that guy aim for you and knew I was too far away. And Daffy was too far away. I owe Jones for saving you. That kid is a hero. Stepping in front of a bullet like that. Even with a vest, that takes guts." He held her even tighter.

They made a good team, he thought, these men. Took out four armed men without firing a shot. Jones was really lucky. He was a brave man. Protecting the women. Jake shook his head. He was going to keep an eye on Jones. He could use him if he ever decided to leave the sheriff's department. And Daffy? He was going to kiss Daffy. Another amazing man. Grabbing that guy's gun hand had probably saved Cilla and himself. He'd been too far away to help. That was the hardest thing Jake ever did, let someone else go after Sheri. Someone else protect Cilla.

He let out a long sigh. And Ron? He always knew Ron could run a perfect op. Even with his wife in the middle of the danger. That took a different kind of guts.

And Cilla attacking Sheri? He was going to talk to her about that. Later. He wasn't sure he would be able to watch the video from Ryan's camera. Or even the attack scene in the Midnight +1 sequel.

"Check with the hospital. Get Waters on that. Is that Garcia's girl-friend?" Jake ordered Ron.

It took hours to get clear of the sheriff's department and the house. Even though the locals knew about Sheri, the team still had to tell the story over and over. It helped to have Ryan there, but Hall kept a low profile. Everyone just assumed he was FBI. Finally, they were told they could leave.

"We're coming back in," Daffy said. "The locals are taking the thugs into custody, and Sheri is heading straight to the morgue. She's already in hell."

Then Daffy called Penney on her cell and told her to pack. "We're going to a motel." He added, "Jake may be able to make love in the gatehouse, but we're not going to."

"What? Jake and Cilla?" Penney screamed. "And I didn't know? How could I not know?"

Daffy smiled at the phone. "Only you could get sidetracked like that when I'm telling you to get ready for the best lovemaking you ever had. Twenty minutes, max, and we are out of there."

"We could stay here," she said.

"No, I want to hear you scream. And I'm going to be the only one to hear you screaming." Penney knew she should make a comeback, but she was having trouble swallowing. Thinking what would make her scream. And he was gone.

Cav went to pick up Jones's sister and take her to the hospital. He had promised Jones he would do it himself so she wouldn't worry. He'd tried to tell Jones that, personally, he thought she'd worry more with the sheriff coming to get her.

Daffy went right to Penney and gave her a hot, quick kiss. "You ready? You don't have a bag. Have you changed your mind?" he asked nervously.

"Don't need a bag; we're going to my place. I have a huge bed. And food in the freezer. And delivery on speed dial."

He smiled. Then he handed Jake his jawbone and earbuds. Still smiling, he said, "My turn."

Jake laughed and replied, "I didn't think you were asleep."

"Hold it," Hall said. "Don't forget you are still under a gag order."

"Same here," Waters added. "None of this leaks."

Daffy just nodded.

Penney grabbed his hand and led him toward the door. Everyone but Ron and Jen were watching. They weren't watching, because Ron had his arms wrapped tight around her, his face buried in her hair. They were just holding each other, rocking back and forth.

"Bye, you all," Penney said, laughing. "See you tonight."

"Not tonight," Daffy corrected, giving her a smoldering look.

"Oh. Um, tomorrow," she muttered.

Still looking at her, he said, "Maybe." And led Penney out.

When he got her outside, he stopped her and turned her around and settled in for a long deep kiss. A prelude?

"Scream?" she said hesitantly when he took a breath. "Good scream?"

"Oh yeah." A promise. "We'll take your car." And he led her to the red convertible.

"How do you know that one is mine?"

"Red?" he said. "You drive."

Ron broke off with Jen and turned to the crew. "OK, guys, listen up. Debriefing begins now. Finish with Homeland and FinCEN. After that, you're on your own. Everyone will be paid at least through the weekend."

"And there will be a one-week bonus for a job well done," Jake added.

The men nodded silently. Fair. Jake had always been fair.

Waters got a call, nodded once, and put his phone away.

"The woman in the hospital was Garcia's girlfriend. She died on the operating table. They fingerprinted her in the morgue. We can probably get her story from one of the thugs in jail."

They went back to debriefing and finishing statements with Waters, Hall, and Ron.

Cilla was still shaking. Jake took her hand, rubbing it gently.

"It's OK," he said. "It's over."

"I know, but I keep seeing that gun pointing at me. I felt that bullet plow into Jones just after Sheri got shot. I shouldn't have gone back there. To get a stupid scrapbook. I almost got Jones killed. I put everyone's life in danger."

"No, you didn't. Sheri did that. Not you. There was nothing wrong with you walking into your own home to get your own scrapbook. Believe me. We would not have let you go if we thought you were in danger."

"Part of me knows that. Part of me feels responsible."

"I've been there and done that. Remember? Doesn't work. If anyone is responsible, then it's me. I brought Sheri into our lives. If you're going to place blame, place it on me, where it belongs."

"No. No, it's not your fault that Sheri was a homicidal maniac." She stopped and processed that. "So by your reasoning, it's not my fault either. Sheri did it." Cilla could always fall back on logic. It would help ease her conscience.

Jake pulled her close, wrapping his arms around her. "I'm sorry," he said.

She let his warmth spread through her for a few minutes and then pushed away. Searched his face. "Sorry for what, Jake?" she asked, hoping for the right answer.

He looked inside himself for the right answer. But he understood now what he was sorry for. Where he had gone wrong.

"I'm sorry I didn't tell you the truth about my line of work in the beginning. I thought I was protecting you. Keeping you safe. Instead, I almost destroyed us. I lacked the trust and faith I should have had in our marriage. I lacked trust and faith in you."

She breathed a sigh of relief. He got it. She moved back into his arms, raised her face, and kissed him gently on the lips. "I love you. Let's go home."

"We can't yet," he grumbled, nodding toward Homeland.

"Oh, I forgot. Of course. But soon you, me, and Tiff are going home." They walked over to take their turn to give statements.

Two weeks later

It was a simple ceremony in the garden. A short ceremony, an exchange of vows, in front of family and friends. A small group. Family and friends. The gang, Annie, Peter's brother and sister. Michael's mother. Becca had made it. Just for the afternoon, but it was good to see her. Cilla hadn't talked with her for a while; she would make time before Becca left. Only one of The Boys could get leave. A few friends, Ron and Jen, Cav and Jones, and Jones's sister, Lori. Lori was the best physical therapist in the state. She had Jake walking without pain or a limp. They were still working on strengthening that leg, though.

Annie stood up for Penney.

Ryan was best man. Cilla wasn't sure how that worked. She knew Daffy had no family, but hadn't realized he knew Ryan well enough for him to be best man. Two other men were there for Daffy, with their wives. He introduced them as Tom Jones and Bill Smith. Cilla didn't think those were their real names, but let it go. She didn't have to know everything. No one else seemed concerned, and Ryan seemed to know Tom Jones and his wife. Penney was happy; that was the important thing.

And Cilla was happy. These two weeks with Jake had convinced her it was going to be OK. They were going to be OK. They had gone together to Bob's Resale Shop and bought the ring Cilla hadn't needed when she purchased the necklace. One step at a time. Cilla smiled to herself, remembering the snit Jake threw when Penney told him he couldn't donate his share of the money to Sarah's Child. Big man like him, in a snit. That was the only word for it. She had laughed so hard. And somehow the snit confirmed what she already knew, that he was healing. Penney suggested he contribute those funds to the trusts.

He'd cheered up at that. Said he would put the money in trust for the other rescues. And buy the beach house. They were still living in her condo, but talking about a home on the beach. Jake kept reminding her they would have to take the dining room table. It looked like they would end up right next door to Daffy and Penney. She had to laugh. Sisters, living side by side with two of the bravest men in the world. She looked around at all the brave men. And women. These were all strong, resilient people, her family. Maybe she did want to know a little more about Tom and Bill. She bet they would fit right in with the gang.

They were going to party all weekend. Not the bridal couple. They were leaving soon. But the rest of them would party. Again she laughed at herself. She bet that within two hours, the gang would be working on the game sequel, and the men, the cops, the guardians, would be telling stories. And wasn't it interesting to see Cav holding Lori's hand? Cilla was going to watch them. See what developed.